Strip

A Bargain with the Boss Romance

Elisabeth Caldwell

This book is a work of fiction. Names, characters, places, and incidents either are products of the author's imagination or are used fictitiously. Any resemblance to actual events or locales or persons, living or dead, is entirely coincidental and not intended by the author.

STRIP: A Bargain with the Boss Romance
Spice Up the Night, Book 1

CITY OWL PRESS
www.cityowlpress.com

Cover Design by MiblArt. All stock photos licensed appropriately.

Edited by Mary Cain.

For information on subsidiary rights, please contact the publisher at info@cityowlpress.com.

Print Edition ISBN: 978-1-64898-234-7

Digital Edition ISBN: 9978-1-64898-233-0

Printed in the United States of America

To my favorite cardiologist.
My heart still flutters every time I see you.

Chapter One

Sage Cashman wasn't afraid to perform. She'd been dancing for nineteen years. Granted, most of that time she hadn't been wearing a G-string and five-inch heels, but those things weren't responsible for the nausea swirling in her gut. She'd accepted them months ago. It was what was riding on this one shot, do-or-die audition at the Black Cat that was testing her nerves.

How was this the most important audition of her life?

Sage shoved the thought away. She was being melodramatic, and she despised drama. Her sister, Rosemary, might not even be sick. Her test results hadn't come back yet, so the job at the Black Cat would be insurance. An emergency backup plan. Just in case. Sage needed to work anyway, and the Black Cat was a step up from the Horny Toad. She would make better money here. Plus, bad luck or not, she'd rather have a black cat than a horny toad.

The booming sound system rattled her molars. The club was packed. She'd been lucky to find a seat at the shiny, lacquered walnut bar. She shifted, crossing and uncrossing her legs to relieve the numbing press of the wooden barstool. It was almost her time to dance, and she didn't want her legs falling asleep.

Sage signaled the bartender for a refill of her seltzer water. What she really wanted was a glass of Torrontés or a splash of Tito's in her club soda. Her limbs were stiff, like she'd been playing too long in the snow. Rigid and jerky wasn't sexy. She needed to loosen up. Pronto.

Unfortunately, alcohol wasn't an option. She couldn't afford to be off-balance, mentally or physically. Princes didn't come riding up on white horses to save the day. If you wanted something done right, it was always best to do it yourself.

The busty, strawberry-blonde, heavily freckled bartender topped off her seltzer water. "Are you here for auditions?"

"Yep. I think I'm up next."

The bartender braced her hands on the bar, pushing herself up and forward, peeking over the edge. "No purse, no alcohol, and good solid shoes. It's not your first time, is it?"

Sage slid a hand into the top of her black, strapless, skin-hugging, snakeskin-patterned dress and flashed her cash and fake ID at the bartender. "Nope. Not my first rodeo. I've been dancing at the Horny Toad the past few months. Working there, I learned quickly to keep anything valuable either on my body or locked in my locker."

"The Horny Toad?" The bartender chuckled. "Where do they come up with these names? I heard that place can be a little rough. It's actually pretty good here. Especially with the new owner." She angled her head toward the stage. "I hope they call you soon. That poor girl is struggling up there."

Sage glanced at the twentysomething teetering around the stage. Her lilac thong was the wrong shade for her pale skin, and that was all she was wearing. She'd taken off too much too fast and didn't know how to use her hands to cover herself, allowing only teasing sneak peeks of her breasts. Her shoes were an accident waiting to happen. Literally.

"Those heels are way too narrow for dancing," Sage said.

There was a reason character shoes had thick heels. Even the best performer could stumble dancing on toothpicks. Noreen, her first and only friend at the Horny Toad, had clued her in on the tricks of the trade, and "solid, stable shoes are worth their weight in gold" had been the first bit of advice she'd offered.

The girl attempted to swing around the pole but ended up tripping over her own feet. Sage winced. Pole dancing looked easy when someone else did it, but there were physics and a heck of a lot of strength involved—and not every pole was the same. Some were stationary. Some spun. Some fast. Some slow.

Noreen said stripper poles were like people. Each had its own peculiarities. The Horny Toad had three poles. One was slim, smooth, and fast; another was thick, strong, and steady; and the third was sticky, stubborn, and creaky. That's why she'd snuck into the Black Cat a few hours before opening and tipped the janitor fifty bucks to let her check out the club's poles. She hated variables.

The girl onstage turned her ankle on her spiked heel, sending her into a graceless spin. Luckily, she didn't fall.

Sage's gaze traveled down to her own open-toed, black, patent leather stilettos. The two-inch-diameter heels and platform soles provided the stability she needed to twist, turn, and slither across the stage, and men loved the royal-blue double straps at the ankle. Still, quality shoes couldn't prevent every mishap. Even seasoned dancers took a tumble from time to time.

Her teeth dug into her bottom lip. Falling flat on her face was not an option. Not tonight.

Sage took as deep a breath as she could muster. The Lycra dress shouldn't feel confining, but the urge to gulp air overwhelmed her. Her fingers itched to lower the front zipper that ran the length of the dress for some extra breathing room, but she didn't touch it. It might be amateur night onstage, but club employees were still working the floor. She'd come dressed to impress, and every stripper's eyes were already boring holes in her back. Exposing extra skin when she wasn't onstage or working the floor could make the other dancers think she was trying to steal their regulars. No need to make enemies the first night.

A few patrons close to the stage yelled "Next!" and "Time's up!" The shouts increased in number and volume as purple-thong girl continued to flounder. It sucked to figure out when you were onstage and nearly naked that you weren't as coordinated or sexy as you thought. The poor girl was probably desperate to get back to her table.

Mercifully, the song slowed and faded. Sage laid a twenty on the bar—Rule Number One: Never piss off the bartender—and scrunched her hands into her thick, almost-waist-length waves.

Showtime.

The spotlight circled a few times before settling on her back. The DJ's rich, baritone voice cut through the laughter and conversation. "Who wants sugar when you can have spice? Our next dancer is sure to be a savory treat! Please welcome Savory Sage!"

Slipping the DJ a C-note was definitely money well spent, even it if meant she'd be eating pasta for two weeks. This was the attention-grabbing intro she'd been hoping for.

Sage spun on the barstool, uncrossing and straightening her legs simultaneously, making a quick V in the air. She pushed up from the seat, thrusting her breasts forward and hanging her head back in a catlike arch, then straightened, shimmied her shoulders, and flashed a saucy smile.

The DJ started playing her song, and Sage strutted toward the stage, working the room. She tugged on ties, tickled necks with her hair, and leaned her cleavage toward lust-filled eyes, teasing patrons as she sashayed across the club floor.

She'd scoped out the expensive watches, designer jeans, and custom-made suits while she'd waited. She focused her attention on those wealthy customers, sending a message to management that she knew how the business worked and how money was made. The stage was just a prop in the game. The real cash came from lap dances, private booths, and private rooms. A successful dancer identified who had cash to spend and convinced those men to open their wallets.

The hallway she needed to pass through to access the stage was a few feet away. A tall man stood in the shadows. The reflection of the stage lights against his polished shoes caught her attention, and his sheer size and magnetism kept it. The cut of his suit was expensive, and his posture had the quiet alertness of a lion waiting for prey. She spun toward him.

The man lazed against the wall, arms crossed. His fitted suit was not nearly as slim as the ones her friend Justin wore. Justin was thin, elegant, and dapper, and his clothing accentuated those natural traits. This man's suit was more like a disguise. The material strained slightly at his shoulders and across the thickest part of his thighs. His stance screamed confidence and power. He was a broad-shouldered, thick-legged Viking warrior, hiding his true nature in business attire.

The stage could wait a few more seconds.

Sage shimmied closer to get a better look. His strong-boned face was partially obscured by the dim light, but she could make out black, wavy hair, a straight forehead, high cheekbones, and a square chin. A three-day shadow broke through his warm, bronze skin, like he'd just returned from a beach vacation. That stubble would probably feel incredible against her skin.

Heat rushed to her thighs.

She froze.

Physical attraction to customers was not part of the game. Physical attraction to men was not a part of her life. She was here for a purpose, not to be distracted by some dark, dangerous stranger, but the spotlight still shone on her back, and at this point, retreat would look awkward.

Play the part.

Sage leaned forward and ran long fingernails down the lapel of the Viking's suit jacket. She lifted her gaze and met two expressionless circles of glacial ice.

The Viking slid strong fingers around the back of her neck, calluses electrifying her skin. Warm breath touched her ear.

"Don't waste your time on me, sweetheart. You're not my type, and I'm not a pushover like the rest of the chumps in this place."

Her cheeks blazed. Humiliation she thought she'd put behind her in her first few weeks at the Horny Toad rushed back, mixing with rage.

Who was he to judge her?

Men were all the same. They spent wads of cash to leer at naked women, then condemned them for stripping. It was a ridiculous double standard. Her knee itched to slam up. Hard. That would knock that condescending look off his face—and get her kicked out of the club faster than she could say "You're an arrogant ass."

She needed this job. For Rosemary's sake. So she flicked her long, thick, bouncy hair, spun, then strutted toward the stage, taking deep breaths to calm her pounding heart.

Sage mounted the stage just as the music changed from the slow, sexy blues tune she'd used for her approach to AC/DC's "You Shook Me All Night Long." It was a fantastic song for stripping, fast-paced hard rock, dripping with innuendo. She took a few quick, graceful steps, then launched herself at the pole, spinning sinuously around it. She slid down, landing firmly on her wide heels, spread her legs and arched her back, gripping the pole with one hand and sliding along it suggestively.

She threw herself into the familiar, crowd-pleasing routine, letting it soothe her. Dancing always calmed her, so she let the music take over. She slid her hands over her body as she shimmied toward the front of the stage. She teased the crowd by rubbing the cool zipper of her dress in her warm fingers, tugging it down just an inch. The audience cheered. A few boisterous voices yelled "Take it off!"

This was the worst part. Baring her skin was too much like baring her soul, but she'd do what had to be done, just as she had for the past several months. Rosemary needed her. That was all that mattered.

Sage eased the zipper down until her dress loosened and slid past her hips, pooling around her feet. A step and kick sent the dress flying toward the back of the stage. The overhead vent poured cool air over her body. Dancing was hot, sweaty work, so the stage area was always air-conditioned no matter the time of year. Goosebumps formed, and her nipples instantly hardened from the cold, rubbing against the red silk bows that barely covered them.

More cheers exploded, and patrons pressed close to the stage, hanging over the raised edges. This particular collection of red strings and bows was always a crowd-pleaser. There must be something about red. It was probably good she couldn't afford red shoes. They might cause a riot.

She tugged teasingly at the edges of the bows as she shook her full breasts. Years of dieting hadn't put a dent in them. Thank God her mother had talked her out of having them reduced. Sage would probably only be pulling in a third of the cash if she'd had that surgery.

Despite her teasing tugs, the bows didn't budge. Nor would they. She'd sewn them shut with her own two hands. She never removed her thong or fully exposed her nipples. Those tiny pieces of string protected a piece of herself, a small measure of independence and pride, that she refused to give up.

Initially, management at the Horny Toad had balked at her refusal to dance fully nude, but after a week, she was the most sought-after stripper in the club. There was no challenge in the blatant nudity of her coworkers, and men loved a challenge. Every guy thought he'd be the one to whom she'd show her secret flesh. That was the game. Making each man think he was special, even though none of them would ever win the prize.

The DJ turned the volume louder, and the booming base flowed into her body, demanding motion. She threw her head back, jogged three long, graceful steps, and leaped back onto the pole, gripping the unyielding metal with her thighs.

Madame Gursky was right. Ballet gave a body the strength to do almost anything, although she likely hadn't imagined Sage hanging upside down, mostly naked, as the end goal of her years of training. And Madame had been dead wrong about Sage's body. Her full breasts and curvy hips may have been "très horrible" for ballet, but at a strip club they left the audience with glassy eyes, open mouths, and most importantly, open wallets. Her body had kept a roof over their heads and food on the table and would get her this job and the introduction she needed to the club owner. There was nothing "très horrible" about that!

A professorial-looking, gray-haired gentleman held out a twenty-dollar bill, and Sage abandoned the pole for the green, leaning backward, sliding her hands to the ground, and executing a sharp back walkover. Another cheer erupted. Acrobatics in heels was another big crowd-pleaser. She glided to the edge of the stage and shimmied down to her hands and knees, pointing to the top edge of her garter belt. The professor tucked the bill in with a polite smile. When a floppy-haired, shy-faced boy who barely looked legal waved another twenty, Sage crawled toward him and gave the same nonverbal cues.

Clear instructions avoided hands going where they shouldn't.

A group of rowdy frat boys tossed some bills onto the stage to get her attention. Sage flipped, using her left arm to arch her body into a standing position. Two quick spins brought her face to face with the group. They were young, drunk, and cocky, just like some of the guys she'd been at school with last year.

Forcing herself to retain her saucy smile, Sage pushed the bills back toward the young men with the toe of her shoe while shaking her finger in a "no, no, no, you naughty boy" fashion. Throwing cash on the stage violated club rules.

She pointed a long, painted fingernail toward the rolled cash in her red-bowed garter belt. The men got the message, picked up their bills, and slid them into her garter while she shook her shoulders and breasts to the beat of the song. The bouncer who'd been battling his way through the patrons shot her a quick, grateful smile. The bouncers always appreciated a woman who could manage the crowd.

When the song ended, Sage scooped up her dress, gave a quick wave, and pranced off the stage. Her heart hammered, and it wasn't just from the exertion of the dance. Despite the deafening applause, her nerves wouldn't settle until she was sure she had the job.

Bryce, the club manager, was waiting for her at the bottom of the stairs. He was a tank of a man, tall and wide and all hard muscle. He was so large she could barely squeeze past him. He probably started as a bouncer, and a damn good one at that. Earlier that evening, she'd seen an obnoxious customer turn tail and retreat with only a cross-armed glare from Bryce. If she hadn't experienced his warm, friendly demeanor when she'd signed up to audition, he would've seemed imposing as hell.

She traded her fake smile for a real one and pointed a playful finger toward him. "I told you they'd love me!"

Bryce rubbed a massive hand over his bald head and chuckled, his bright white teeth flashing. "You were right. Can you start right away?"

"Sure. I can start tonight."

Bryce shook his head. "Not tonight. The owner has to approve your paperwork. I'll give you a schedule for the rest of the week tonight, then call you tomorrow after he signs off so you know you're good to go. Do you have any questions?"

She was accepting the job regardless of the terms, but each club had its own financial quirks, and she needed to understand the Black Cat's.

"Do you have a price list I can see?"

Bryce pulled a folded sheet of paper from the front pocket of his black dress pants and handed it to her.

Where did he shop? His clothes fit too well for a run-of-the-mill big and tall shop, but a strip club manager likely didn't make enough to pay for custom-made. She studied the price sheet, noting the charge for lap dances by song and by time, private booths, and private rooms.

"What's the stage fee?" she asked.

"No stage fee. At least, not now. The new owner got rid of it. House gets forty-five percent of the dances. You get the rest."

"The house only takes forty-five percent? That's a pretty good deal. What about tip-out?"

"Bouncers and DJ get a dollar a dance. The new guy wanted to get rid of that too, but I told him not to shake it up too much. Folks don't like too much change at once. Do you have ID? We do everything by the book now, so you'll have to fill out a W-4."

The rumor mill was right on this one. No working under the table at the Black Cat.

Sage felt around for the little pocket sewn into the top of the dress she now held in her hand, pulled out her friend Olivia Dupree's ID, and handed it over. "Sounds like this new owner runs a tight ship. When do I get to meet him?"

"I can't say. He keeps to himself." Bryce squinted at the driver's license. "Olivia Dupree? Why did the DJ call you Sage?"

Because I'm a moron and blurted out my real name when the DJ asked me.

"That's my stage name. Sage sounds a lot sexier than Olivia."

Bryce shined a flashlight on the hard, white card, and the hologram sparkled.

Sage held her breath. She and Olivia both had brown hair, blue eyes, and a petite nose, but the similarities ended there. Olivia's face was square while hers was oval, and Olivia's straight, shoulder-length hair was light brown, nothing like the long, thick, dark, unruly waves currently sticking to her perspiration-soaked back. Plus, Olivia had a good three inches on her.

Bryce handed her back the card and thrust out his right hand. "Welcome to the Black Cat."

Relief jellied her legs and shoulders. It was a good thing everybody looks like crap in their driver's license picture.

Sage accepted the handshake. Bryce's skin was warm and dry against her sweaty palm.

"Thanks for giving me a chance."

He flashed his teeth again. "You're a natural, kid."

Being a natural at stripping wasn't the compliment Bryce thought it was, but Sage chose not to comment. She had long since resigned herself to do whatever was necessary to help Rosemary.

Once the paperwork was complete and Sage was rattling down Columbus Boulevard in her ten-year-old, dinged-up Mazda 6, she fumbled open the glove compartment and traded Olivia's license for her own. Her taillight was out. Getting pulled over with a fake ID would be a crappy end to a pretty good night.

She stopped her car on the narrow South Philly street in front of the cozy rowhouse she and Rosemary rented. It was a steal at $1,200 a month. The kitchen was dated, but the paint was fresh and the carpets were clean. A year ago, she'd never have put up with the owner's refusal to provide a written lease and demand for cash-only payments. What would have once made her suspicious was now a blessing. Anything that helped them fly under the radar was a plus.

Sage hopped out of her car, threw the two neon-orange safety cones that had been reserving her parking spot into her trunk, then parallel parked. She rubbed her goose-bumped arms as she dashed up the cement stairs to her front door. The icy door handle numbed her already frozen fingers as she jiggled her key in the finicky lock. You never knew what you'd get in January in Philly. It could be fifty degrees one day and ten degrees the next. Tonight, the temperature was hovering in the twenties.

The heavy door creaked with her hard shove, and Sage rushed inside, grateful for the dry radiator heat that rushed over her. Rosemary sat on the couch, huddled in a blanket, watching TV.

"It's nearly midnight. Why aren't you in bed?" Sage asked.

"Why aren't you wearing a coat?" Rosemary snapped back.

Because I didn't want it to get stolen.

At the Horny Toad, she locked her coat in her locker. A locker wasn't an option during amateur night at the Black Cat.

"I forgot it. I was late for work."

Sage grabbed sweatpants, a sweatshirt, and white cotton panties from the basket of folded laundry on the floor and changed her clothes in the middle of the living room. The warm, soft cotton was heaven.

Rosemary lifted an eyebrow. "It's a good thing the blinds are closed. And you're a bad liar."

"Am not." Sage flopped onto the oversized, slip-covered couch next to her sister and tugged half the knit afghan over her legs.

Rosemary clicked off the TV. "Stop before you really make me mad. I know you're lying. You didn't go to work tonight. Justin told me you were auditioning at the Black Cat club. Why didn't you tell me? Why are you leaving the Horny Toad? You said you liked it there."

"Justin needs to learn to keep his mouth shut."

"No, Sage. You need to learn to open yours. I shouldn't have to rely on whisper down the lane from Justin to get information about my own sister. You should've told me about the audition yourself. You don't have to keep protecting me. If changing jobs is about money, I can go back to work." Rosemary's face turned wistful. "I liked working."

Sage's stomach twisted. She'd rather run a marathon through a briar patch than do any kind of math, but her sister had loved her job at the accounting firm.

"I know you miss your job. I hate that we have to live like this. I know it makes you unhappy. I'm not happy. I feel horrible about it. It's all my fault."

Rosemary huffed. "Explain to me how this is your fault."

"I should've said something to Mom about Davis. She was too sweet to see him for what he really is, but I knew he was a liar and a cheat. If I'd told her he was having an affair, maybe things would be different. Maybe she would have left him." Sage hesitated. "Maybe she'd still be alive."

"That's crazy talk! The earth calls us home when it's our time. It was Mom's time. There was nothing any of us could have done to stop it. And it's not your fault we're living like this. Davis is the one who kicked us out. He's the one who threatened and attacked you. He's the one who cut us off from what's rightfully ours. That is definitely not your fault!"

"Of course it is." Sage twisted the blanket with white-knuckled hands. "I should never have confronted him. I should have pretended everything was fine. I could have said it was too traumatizing to stay in the house. We could have moved out quietly, and he never would have known I went to the police."

"That's bull crap. The police would've questioned me at some point anyway. I'm the one who can't remember seeing him at the club. I'm the one who couldn't give him an alibi. Davis is just as angry with me as he is with you, probably more."

"I'm not so sure about that. It was my accusations that set him off."

Rosemary shivered and hugged herself. "Let's not talk about him. I don't even want to think about him. It's not worth our energy, and it's bad karma. We need to concentrate on what lies ahead. Now, tell me why you're leaving the Horny Toad."

Sage didn't buy the whole fate and karma thing, but Rosemary, despite her affinity for numbers, lived by it. In Sage's mind, thinking and talking about Davis wasn't going to make things any worse. They couldn't get much worse. Well, unless he found thembut that wouldn't happen. She'd made sure of it. They'd cut all ties, except Justin. Sage only had a few close friends, and since she'd lost her mom last year and her dad and brother, Thyme, when she was eight, there hadn't been that many ties to cut.

Snap. Snap.

Rosemary's snapping fingers filled her vision.

"Yoo-hoo! Earth to Sage."

"What?"

"I asked you to tell me why you're leaving the Horny Toad. Like I said, if we need more money, I can get a job."

Sage fought for patience. "We discussed this. You're not going back to work right now. We need to lay low until Davis gets arrested or we have enough money to move and start over."

"We could save money faster if I was working," Rosemary said. "I could find something local and under the table. I could waitress. There are tons of restaurants nearby."

"That's not an option. I'm not letting you work, not with your fevers coming back." Sage pressed her palm to her sister's face and forehead. "You have a fever now."

"It's just a virus."

"When you have *Doctor* in front of your name, you can self-diagnose. Until then, you'll stay home and rest until your test results come back."

"I'm sure they'll be negative. I feel fine. You worry too much."

Sage prayed her sister was right, because if Rosemary was sick again, in order to get her well, she might have to do more than strip.

Chapter Two

Ryker Madsen was at the club. Again. He'd walked up the red carpet and through the decorative bronze door every night this week. The entrance fused Hollywood with church or a library or maybe even the Supreme Court, which seemed ridiculous for a gentlemen's club, but it worked. Men slowed their pace as they strolled the velvet-rope-lined path, usually hesitating at the heavy metal door, studying the intricately engraved images from the Kama Sutra before tugging on the glistening handle. The entrance created the impression of stepping into another world, a special one.

Too bad the prior owner's money had run out at the door.

From his seat at the bar, Ryker studied the club he'd purchased on a very uncharacteristic whim. He'd had the walls covered with sweeps of sumptuous midnight-navy velvet and installed a new walnut bar, leather booths, and a sleek bottom-lit stage with three gleaming poles and hanging ropes that would make a Cirque du Soleil performer proud. White canopies sparkling with warm-white fairy lights hung over head, mixing with soft, blue lighting to create the impression of an intimate, magical evening. The interior of the club now matched the promise of the approach.

Unfortunately, the improvements didn't extend to the dancers.

The current performer was too bored, too thin, and too obviously disinterested. To succeed in transforming the club from a mid-level strip joint to an upscale gentleman's club, the talent needed a serious step up. He needed more women like their newest dancer, Olivia aka Savory Sage, and Ryker doubted there were more women like her.

Olivia's perfectly curved body, elegant style, and superior dancing were a definite upgrade. Customers waited in line, paid to get in the door, then panted after her like obedient puppies. Money flowed through their fingers like water. All to see a woman take off her clothes to music.

Who was he to judge? He wasn't any better. Olivia was the real reason his car was wearing grooves in the street from his office to the Black Cat. Since that first night, images of her bombarded his brain without warning, and his body reacted every time she crossed his mind. Like it was doing right now.

It was irritating as hell.

Ryker shifted on the cushioned barstool, willing his body to settle.

She was a stripper, for God's sake. Selling sex was her job. She worked the patrons with focused precision, giving them just enough to keep coming back and making them both good money. She fit in perfectly with his vision for the club. He should be pleased, but not horned up like a middle schooler with a *Playboy*. Given his experience with shrewd, deceitful women, he shouldn't find her cool, calculating extortion sexy.

His brain just needed to convince his dick of that.

"Refill?"

Ryker nodded to the friendly, freckled blonde.

"You keep coming back. You must like it here," she said as she filled his ginger ale.

The bartender noticing him hanging around probably meant he'd been doing it too much.

"I guess you could say that," Ryker said.

She opened two Coronas, flicking the lids deftly into the trash, then prepared multiple mixed drinks with clean efficiency. As she worked, a tall, porcelain-skinned redhead and short, fine-boned brunette sauntered by. The redhead nudged her friend and said something to her. They both glared at him, and the short one scratched the side of her face with her middle finger.

"Don't mind those two. They're nasty to anyone who doesn't line their pockets."

"Everyone wants to make money."

"Well, I'm not a fan of the way they go about it."

"What do you mean?" he asked, the anger in her tone raising his curiosity.

The bartender hesitated, then shook her head. "Ignore me."

What had she wanted to say?

"Well, at least tell me why they're giving me the evil eye."

"They're bitter because you don't buy lap dances."

Would she be so candid if she knew she was talking to her new boss? Probably not, but this was why only Bryce knew he was now the club owner. There was only so much information he could glean from pouring over business records. Visiting the club anonymously was the best way to get a real sense of the business and its employees.

He always tipped the bartender and left another sizable tip with the bouncer to share among the dancers, but the bartender was right. He didn't buy lap dances. The ladies flipping him off apparently didn't appreciate sharing tips and were nasty to customers who didn't drop enough cash for their liking. Ryker filed that piece of information away.

"So, if you don't like those two, who do you like?"

"Katrina and Faith are fantastic. They're both reliable, funny, and street-smart. Anise is quiet but super sweet, and I really like the new girl, Olivia. She's friendly to everyone, and she's a crazy talented dancer. She also understands the business, which is rare."

The bartender's assessment was dead-on. Olivia definitely had an eye for the business. She arrived an hour early for every shift and walked the entire room, greeting each customer individually. Just a quick hello and a siren's smile. She didn't try to sell dances or booths or private rooms, and if customers asked, she politely declined because she wasn't officially on the clock, but she *was* working. She worked the room with such practiced cunning, it would have chilled Ryker's bones if the sight of her didn't make his blood so goddamn hot.

She ran a beautiful con. Patrons couldn't get enough of her. They thought they were special. They thought she came early because she wanted to see them, talk to them. They wanted her from the instant they saw her, and the waiting fed that desire. She stoked their need like an expert forgeman.

When she entered, men with one foot out the door settled in for another drink. Dinner plans were canceled. Conversation turned to when she would dance, what she would wear, how she would perform. She'd been at the club for only two weeks, and attendance was up every day she was advertised to perform. It wasn't a coincidence. He knew because he was one of the idiots who couldn't stay away. He couldn't get enough of those endless curves, pouty lips, and come-hither eyes packaged with signature dance moves and five-inch heels.

His lack of self-control was sandpaper on his already thinning patience.

Movement in Ryker's peripheral vision wiped away the minimally dressed and maximally sinful image of Olivia swirling in his mind. Too many years surviving the streets of West Philly had sharpened his senses, and a business suit and boardroom hadn't dulled them.

Something was up. He scanned the club as if checking out the dancers, making his gaze appear to travel casually around the room. His attention lasered in on four figures huddled in a dark area between the back of a plush booth and the fabric-covered wall. Cash slipped from the hand of the redhead who'd given him the nasty look into the front pocket of a stocky meathead in his little brother's T-shirt. The meathead's friend passed two small bags to the redhead, who passed one on to her partner in crime.

He'd seen enough drug deals in his time to know exactly what was happening. They weren't even trying to hide the transaction with a lap dance. It was a slap in the face in his own damn club.

Not going to happen.

Ryker texted Bryce, then hung back. Bryce had been the manager of the club when Ryker took over. Bryce had impressed him so far, but now it was the manager versus another employee. How Bryce handled this situation would be telling.

Bryce edged up on the group, keeping to the shadows. He was a big man but moved like a cat tracking a mouse. Not one of the group even lifted a head until Bryce was on top of them. He was too far away and the music too loud for Ryker to hear what was said, but Bryce lifted a hand and two other bouncers swooped in as if they'd been waiting for his cue. Within minutes, the dancers headed to the dressing room with Bryce, and the bouncers escorted the customers to the door.

Ryker rose, pointed to his stool, mouthed "Save my seat" to the bartender, then strode across the club to the corridor that accessed backstage and the dressing room. He'd hoped to stay anonymous a while longer, but it was time to lay down the law.

A bouncer stepped in front of the hallway to block his path.

Ryker raised both hands in the air to appear non-threatening and took a few steps closer to the bouncer. "I need to speak with Bryce. Tell him Ryker Madsen is looking for him."

The bouncer remained still, empty-faced and wide-shouldered, sizing up Ryker with suspicion. Ryker was fine with that approach. He'd rather have overly cautious security than a guy who'd let someone bully their way backstage.

Ryker texted Bryce.

After a few seconds, the bouncer pulled his phone out of his pocket and glanced at the screen. His eyebrows winged up, and he stepped to the side.

"Sorry, Mr. Madsen. Go on back. Bryce says you know the way to the office."

As Ryker walked down the narrow corridor, the noise of the crowd and music grew muffled, replaced by the thump of his shoes on laminate. Two dancers waiting to take the stage and the backstage security guard gaped at him.

Cover blown.

Ryker opened the office door without knocking. Bryce sat behind the slightly battered oak desk. The drug-dealing strippers were seated in the guest chairs.

Bryce stood, appearing even bulkier in the small room.

Ryker waved him back down, leaned against the cool, painted concrete wall, and crossed his arms over his chest.

"Keep the seat. I prefer to stand."

The redhead glared at Bryce. "Who the hell is that?"

Ryker nodded to Bryce.

"You've always had a bad attitude, Patrice." Bryce's tone was that of a disappointed schoolteacher. "That's the new owner, so I suggest you watch what you say."

Patrice's face vacillated between fury and panic. Her dark-haired friend burst into tears.

"I told you ladies before, we have a zero-tolerance policy for drugs. Zero tolerance. Right?" There was a touch of hesitancy in Bryce's voice, as if he thought Ryker might waver in the face of beautiful girls with tears in their eyes.

There was no way Bryce could know that, to him, these girls weren't pretty. In the bright fluorescent light of the office, Patrice's heavy makeup couldn't mask the bags under her eyes, and her friend had the same tired appearance. They were both over-enhanced at the top and stick-thin everywhere else. Unnaturally thin. Drug thin.

Ryker's mother had always looked like that. Minus the implants. It turned his stomach.

"Bryce is right. I have zero tolerance for drugs in my club." Ryker stared down at the women. "You'll both need to leave immediately. One of the bouncers will escort you to the dressing room and wait while you pack your things. Your final paychecks will be mailed to the addresses we have on file."

Patrice rose from her chair and kicked the desk. "My paycheck? My paycheck is shit. You know all the money in this job is tips. You have no right to come in here and change the rules. You have to give us a warning or something!"

Ryker shrugged. Patrice had been warned. Along with every other employee. Bryce had held a mandatory, all-hands meeting to make sure everyone was one hundred percent clear on the drug-free policy. Plus, even high, there was no way anyone could miss the large signs with three-inch letters plastered all over the dressing room that read:

NO DRUGS ALLOWED!
IF YOU BRING DRUGS TO WORK,
YOU WILL BE FIRED!
NO EXCEPTIONS!

Couldn't get much clearer than that, but he didn't bother pointing it out. Arguing with an irrational, strung-out druggie wasn't worth the effort. He'd tried enough times in his life to know it was futile.

A thick-necked bouncer appeared in the doorway and took each woman by the arm. "Come on, girls, let's get packed up."

Patrice tugged and pulled against the fingers gripping her arm. She spat toward Ryker's shoes as the bouncer pulled her into the hallway, yelling back at him, "You're going to regret this, you asshole!"

She couldn't be more wrong. There would be no regrets. He'd rather close the club than have drugs on-site. Drugs would never touch any part of his life.

Not ever again.

Ryker rubbed his temples as he and Bryce returned to the club floor. His head ached from too many long days and too many late nights. Layering the strip club on top of the luxury condos in Maryland, the student housing deal in Texas, and the historic hotel rehab he was working on in Center City was probably a bad idea.

His initial plan for the Black Cat had been a quick remodel and sale since the adult entertainment industry was outside his expertise. Way outside. But something made him drag his feet. His already full plate was now overflowing. The result was tired bones, gritty eyes, and a burgeoning headache. After Olivia danced, he was going home to get a decent night's sleep.

Ryker glanced at his heavy, silver Jaeger-LeCoultre watch. "When's the new girl going on?"

Bryce's mouth curved up, showing big, white teeth. "You won't be seeing her tonight. She switched her shift. Sage covered for Anise last night because her kid had a fever, so Anise is working tonight instead."

Ryker's shoulders stiffened. He could have been home hours ago. Instead, he'd wasted the night waiting around to see a stripper, which was stupid on so many levels. Still, he couldn't stop from asking, "When is she scheduled to work again?"

"I need to check the notes in my office. I have the schedule pretty well worked out, but I haven't had a chance to finalize it." Bryce's smile faded as he glanced toward the door. "Now who's that? She looks like a debutante at a NASCAR race."

Ryker's gaze shifted to the club entrance, and his headache went from muted throb to pounding jackhammer.

What the hell is Veronica doing here?

"I know her. I'll talk to her. Go check the schedule."

Veronica waved and sauntered over. Her charcoal-gray fitted dress, matching suit jacket with small ruffles on the lapels, and nude, round-toed heels accentuated her tall, paper-thin body. With her sleek, blonde bob and Louis Vuitton bag, she looked like she should be walking into a conference room, not a gentleman's club.

Cool, dry lips brushed Ryker's cheek and even cooler fingers gripped his hand. "I know you told me not to come, but I couldn't resist seeing the place. Ryker Madsen, real estate mogul, now the proud owner of a B-grade strip joint. How the mighty have fallen."

Ryker knew she was joking, but he didn't smile. "You're right. I am a real estate mogul, and my analysis of the numbers says the Black Cat is a damn good investment. Why are you here? I wouldn't have thought this was your scene."

Veronica pulled a manila folder from her bag. "Someone's in a grumpy mood today. I was just teasing, and I'm only staying a few minutes. I called your office, but you'd already left. I tried your cell, but you didn't answer. Your assistant told me you might be here. I need to talk to you about a few things and figured if I came here in person, I could get a glimpse of your newly acquired den of sin. This is so out of the norm for you that I had to see it in person."

Veronica was right. The strip club was an oddity. His roots were hands-on, dirty residential remodels and flips, and all his current investments were commercial real estate or pharma startups. the Black Cat didn't fit in either bucket, but something about it called to him, and having Veronica here pissed him off. Her curiosity shouldn't bother him, but her presence in his club offended him, almost as if she'd violated his inner sanctum.

Which was batshit crazy.

Exhaustion and hunger must be wearing his patience thin.

"What did you need to talk to me about?" he asked, trying to adopt a more friendly tone.

"I had a long call with Davis Anderson's lawyer today. I think we're finally on the same page on the ownership structure and waterfall, so I was able to complete a draft of the partnership agreement. There are still a few blank business points, but we're short on time, so this should get the ball rolling. I figured I'd drop the draft agreement off in person."

He accepted the papers with one hand and squeezed the bridge of his nose with the other. Veronica's cultured, New England accent was like sand in a sneaker.

"The lawyer said that Davis is getting impatient," she continued. "If we don't get moving, he might try to get the deal done with someone else."

Ryker grunted. "You know that's not going to happen. I own the purchase option, and he doesn't have the expertise to do a historic rehab. He couldn't get a deal like this done without me, at least not in this city."

"Yes, but he has the contacts at the hotel franchise, and you told me it was important that you work with him on this."

It was important. Money only got a man so far. Davis could provide something money couldn't buy: elite, blue-blood connections. The Philadelphia aristocracy still looked at Ryker as an upstart from the wrong side of the tracks. Sure, they respected his business acumen and would gladly ride his coattails for a profit, but he knew they'd much rather walk over him than with him if they could.

Ryker didn't give a shit what anyone thought of him, but he did care what people thought of Christian. His brother would come home when he finished his MBA, and Ryker was hell-bent on making sure that when that happened, no one ever told Christian he wasn't good enough. Ryker had handpicked Davis Anderson because his family was old Philadelphia money. His grandmother had lunched with Grace Kelly, for God's sake. It just stunk that the guy was such an asshole, but he'd suck it up and work with a man he didn't like or respect if it helped his baby brother.

He'd do anything for Christian.

"Agreed. But be clear with his attorney that I'm the one driving the ship and Davis is lucky to be along for the ride. From a financial perspective, he needs this deal more than I do. I'm not going to have some overpriced attorney using bullshit threats for bargaining power. Remind him that Davis doesn't know shit about rehabbing an historic hotel."

"I already did, and I will again, but I do think Davis is really trying. He's put a lot of time and effort into this deal."

"I'll keep that in mind," Ryker said. "Did the Part 1 approval come in? I thought we expected that today."

"No, but it's a condition precedent to your initial capital contribution."

"That's not good enough. I'm not signing the partnership agreement without the Part 1. We need that ASAP."

Veronica's thin fingers grazed his arm. "Settle down. I'll follow up on the Part 1. Just give it a few days. Now let's talk about something fun. What's the plan for your friend's wedding? Are we going for the whole weekend? Do I need to leave work early the Friday before? If so, I can block my calendar."

He never should have mentioned the wedding to Veronica. Going stag wasn't ideal, but he'd rather have Alex throwing every eligible bachelorette in the tri-state area at him than go with Veronica.

"Like I said before, I think going to the wedding together is a bad idea. You're my lawyer. It's not good to mix business and pleasure."

She lifted her right hand, fluffed her blonde hair, and laughed. "You're ridiculous. We already mixed business and pleasure, remember?"

Ryker remembered. Taking Veronica on a date was a mistake he wasn't going to repeat. She'd found a reason to stop by his office every day for a week since they'd gone to dinner.

"Our relationship has to be business only from now on. I'm not looking for romance."

Veronica rolled her eyes, stepped toward him, and rubbed his shirt collar between her thumb and forefinger. Her heavy floral perfume assaulted his nostrils.

"I'm not looking for romance either, but I'd love to have sex with you. I know you want it too. Let's just go to the wedding and see what happens."

Never going to happen.

He gently peeled Veronica's hand from his chest. "Thanks for the offer, but I've already found another date. I appreciate you dropping off the partnership agreement. I'll call you after I've had a chance to look it over."

"Ryker..." Veronica started, but then stopped as Bryce approached.

"This is Olivia's schedule for the week. Now you don't have to sit around waiting for her." Bryce pressed a folded piece of paper into Ryker's hand.

Veronica lifted one perfectly plucked eyebrow. "Oh my. Usurped by a stripper. I'm not sure whether to be flattered or offended. Call me after you've read the partnership agreement."

She gave a quick wave and headed toward the door.

"Sorry about that," Bryce said. "I didn't mean to cause a problem with your girlfriend."

"She's not my girlfriend. She's my lawyer."

"Hmph. Looks like she wants to be your girlfriend."

"Well, she's out of luck. I don't do the girlfriend thing. Relationships are for fools and men who enjoy being stabbed in the back. I'm neither." Ryker clapped a hand on Bryce's muscled shoulder. "I'm headed home. Keep an eye on the security cameras and talk to the bouncers. Make sure Patrice doesn't get back in here. I don't trust her."

Bryce nodded. Ryker knew the man would take care of his club while he was gone, so he exited through the grand entrance back onto the red carpet, unfolding the paper Bryce had given him while he walked. Olivia was off tomorrow. Her next shift started at eight p.m. on Saturday. He'd be here, waiting. He didn't bother telling himself he wouldn't come. He'd tried that the past couple weeks, but if Olivia was working, he couldn't seem to make himself stay away.

She was a weakness, and he a was man who wouldn't tolerate having one. Something had to be done.

Fighting his desire clearly wasn't working. His daily visits to the club were proof of that. It was time to change tactics. If he couldn't stop himself from wanting her, he'd have to find a way to have her, get her out of his system, and move on. Having her shouldn't be too difficult.

Everybody had a price.

Chapter Three

Doctors were never on time. Never. After years of accompanying Rosemary to her appointments, Sage should have been prepared to wait...and wait...and wait, but it still annoyed the heck out of her. The unspoken condescension was unbearable. Just because someone had an M.D. after his name didn't mean his time was more valuable than everybody else's. Unfortunately, it appeared they taught the opposite lesson in med school.

Sage huffed and turned the page of the six-month out-of-date *People* magazine she wasn't reading. She looked for a wall clock. Of course, there was none. They didn't want patients knowing how long they'd been waiting.

Sage pulled her phone out of her purse despite the "No Cell Phone Use in Waiting Room" sign hanging right over her head.

10:54.

Rosemary's appointment was for ten o'clock. They'd been waiting almost an hour. Sage stood and dropped the magazine on the muted blue, generic, could-have-been-in-any-office-anywhere chair.

"Don't you dare throw a fit with the receptionist," Rosemary hissed.

"I'm not going to throw a fit. I'm simply going to request that Dr. Gerard see you. Immediately."

"You can't do that! I'm sure he's busy with another patient."

Sage scrunched her nose. "You're too nice. Didn't anyone tell you nice girls finish last? You're exhausted and sitting here with a fever. The sooner he sees you, the sooner I can get you home."

"We're not going home." Rosemary pushed her words through tight lips. "We're going for pedicures and out to lunch like we always do. Changing our routine is bad luck."

Sage sucked in a not-so-calming breath and flopped back down in the chair. "You feel like crap. I know you do."

"And I know I want to spend time with my sister."

Sage considered the gazillion germs they'd encounter at the nail salon and again in whatever corner pizzeria they found for lunch. Gone were the days of spa treatments at Toppers and lunch at either the timeless Friday Saturday Sunday or the trendy restaurant of the hour. Rosemary always wanted to try something new, while Sage, thinking life had already handed them too many surprises, preferred the tried-and-true.

Their mother was the one who came up with the idea of alternating restaurants. She was also the one who started the tradition of pairing Rosemary's doctor visits with outings. She wanted Rosemary to link her illness and treatments to positivity. She said it would help her heal, mentally and physically. She'd been right.

Caroline Cashman had been right about most things.

Just not Davis.

Rosemary's warm fingers pressed against Sage's hand. "Are you thinking about Mom?"

Sage nodded. She couldn't speak. Her chest was too tight.

There'd been too many doctor visits. Too many treatments. Too many waiting rooms. Now Rosemary was sick again, and this time there'd be no beautifully sweet, amazingly strong mom holding Rosemary's head while she puked, laying cool towels on her neck, and making fruit and veggie protein shakes that somehow tasted like heaven.

"Rosemary..." The nurse clad in her scrubs looked up from the iPad she was holding and smiled a picture-perfect smile without a touch of warmth.

Rosemary rose from her seat. "You don't have to come in with me."

Sage grabbed her sister's clammy hand. There was no way Rosemary would be hearing her test results alone.

"Your fever must be spiking. You're delusional if you think I'm waiting out here."

Sage didn't practice any religion, but she sent up a quick prayer as they entered the exam room. Gray walls. Linoleum floor. Antiseptic air. She hated everything about it, especially the nurse's bored weight, temperature, blood pressure, dumb question drill.

Would it kill the witch to smile?

After the nurse left, the waiting started all over again. Tension sat like a grain sack around Sage's shoulders. Nerves pushed her feet back and forth, pacing across the small office, while Rosemary sat statue still on the exam table holding her Pepto-Bismol-colored paper gown closed with one hand.

The oppressive silence forced inane words from Sage's mouth. "Why do they cover the table with that horrible paper?"

Rosemary smirked. "To keep it clean, dummy. I don't want to be sitting in someone else's dirt, especially since it feels like this gown is going to rip every time I move."

Sage's shoulders dropped a touch. Rosemary always knew how to make her smile.

"No shit, Sherlock. What I meant is why does it have to be that horrible, over-white, slippery, crinkly paper. It sounds like an earthquake every time you shift a millimeter. It's scratchy, and it makes you afraid to move."

Rosemary laughed. "They probably make it this way on purpose, so patients don't want to stay too long."

Sage turned her head toward the quick tap on the door.

Dr. Gerard breezed in.

"Rosemary, Sage. It's nice to see you both again."

Sage hated doctors as a general rule, but Dr. Gerard wasn't so bad. He was a dark-haired, reasonably handsome man with the build of a long-distance runner and a kind smile. She still had to fight her irritation, slowly taking a seat and gripping the armrests, forcing herself to wait patiently while he applied hand sanitizer, listened to Rosemary's heart and lungs, felt her lymph nodes, and went through the rest of the pointless standard protocol.

The exam meant nothing. All that mattered were Rosemary's lab results and, if they were positive, whether Dr. Gerard had gotten her into the Remiza drug trial. Rosemary had been diagnosed with a rare form of bone cancer when she was fifteen, and it had come back again five years ago when she was twenty. Those two bouts of cancer had plowed through all the FDA-approved treatments. If the cancer was back, the drug trial was her only hope.

Dr. Gerard settled back onto his rolling stool, tapping his iPad with his stylus and talking at the same time. "I'm sorry to tell you this..."

Sage's heart was pounding so hard the rush of blood in her ears muted the doctor's words. It didn't matter. She didn't need to hear every word. She knew it. She knew it from the look on his face and the cadence of his voice. She'd known it before they'd stepped foot in the office. The exhaustion. The low-grade fevers. The pallor in the day replaced by a too rosy flush at night. Rosemary was sick again. Yet again, her sweet, kind, loving, ever-hopeful sister was going to suffer.

Panic surged, but she forced herself to focus. To listen.

"Since this is the third recurrence, our options are limited. A combination of some of the earlier treatments is our only choice."

Rosemary shifted on the table. The crackle of safety paper was like a firecracker.

"You said before that repeat treatments probably wouldn't work and that my insurance wouldn't cover them."

"That's right. Unfortunately, your insurance likely won't cover repeat treatments due to their greatly reduced efficacy."

Greatly reduced efficacy. Such horrible words.

"How much is the treatment without insurance?" Rosemary asked.

"I can't say for sure, but you're probably talking tens if not hundreds of thousands." Sympathy softened the sharp lines of his face. "I can give you the names of some nonprofits you could contact that have programs to help cancer patients with these types of expenses. I don't want to get your hopes up, because their resources are limited. But it's worth a try."

They didn't need a goddamn charity to pay for treatment that wasn't going to work. Rosemary needed something that would heal her.

"What about the Remiza drug trial you told us about? You said it was her best chance of going into full remission."

"I'm sorry, Sage. Rosemary wasn't accepted into the study."

"That's bullshit! You said she met all the requirements! Tell them to put her in the goddamn study!"

She was screaming, but she didn't care. He hadn't tried hard enough. She had to convince him to try again. He had to try again. He had to.

"The trial just closed. They already placed their final test group. They're going to market after this last trial. We missed the window to add her in."

"Ask them again. Make them add her. One more person can't make a difference"

"It's not that easy. I wish it were. Once a study is in process, adding a patient could impact the data. The drug company can't risk that. Sometimes, in rare cases, the company will provide a non-FDA-approved drug to a patient who has no other treatment options under the Right to Try program, so I even asked about it, but the company said no. There's nothing else I can do." His eyes darkened with emotion. "I'm truly sorry."

"How long until Remiza is available to the public?" Rosemary asked.

Her voice was calm and gentle, as usual.

How could Rosemary be so gracious when all Sage wanted to do was rip the iPad out of Dr. Gerard's hand and smash it on the floor?

"At least eighteen months. Remiza works only in the early stages of the disease. Even with repeating the existing treatments, your disease process will likely be too advanced at that point."

Rosemary smiled hesitantly. "So repeat treatments it is. I'll take that information regarding the nonprofits. Sage and I will try to figure out our finances and get back to you."

Dr. Gerard rose and pulled the door open. "Let me get you the information."

A faint, familiar voice carried down the hallway. "Thanks for letting me know they're here. I really need to talk to my daughters."

Sage's blood froze. They did not need this. Not here. Not now.

"Shut the door!" she ordered.

Dr. Gerard grimaced. "Goddamn Sherilynn. I thought she was acting oddly. She must have called your stepfather. He was here a few weeks ago asking about Rosemary."

"He probably bribed her."

Dr. Gerard met her gaze. "I know it's bad between you, but maybe he could help you pay for the treatments or help you get the company to give Rosemary Remiza under the Right to Try program. It's a long shot, but it might be worth a try."

The idea of talking to Davis made her nauseous, but he'd always had a soft spot for Rosemary. She might have to ask him for help, but now was not the time or place. Sage grabbed their jackets and purses while Rosemary ripped off the pink paper gown and tugged on her jeans, sweater, and shoes.

Dr. Gerard cracked the door and peered out. "I don't see him. There's a back exit. It's near the bathroom. You might be able to avoid him if you leave through there."

Sage gave her sister's slightly larger hand a fast squeeze, then pulled Rosemary out the door and down the corridor in the opposite direction of the main waiting room.

"Sage! Rosemary!" Davis's voice filled the hallway, but they didn't turn back.

Sage gripped Rosemary's damp hand tighter, pushed the exit door open, ran down the hall, and darted down a staircase, dragging her sister behind her. Her chest ached from panic and running, but as soon as they hit the street, she hurried around the block and kept running until Rosemary pulled her to a hard stop. Sage flagged a cab as her sister stood on the sidewalk, bent over, hands on her knees, breathing heavily.

Once they were in the taxi, Sage apologized. "I'm so sorry. I shouldn't have made you run like that. I know you're not feeling well."

"It's OK. I'm OK. I can't believe we ran out on him. He's going to be royally pissed." A sunshine smile brightened her face, and she cackled. "I love it."

Sometimes, Rosemary was just plain crazy. Sage turned to stare out the window, watching rowhouses, shops, and cafes as they passed. Rosemary's hand was hot in hers. Too hot.

"Maybe we should have stayed and tried to talk to him. You need to get better. I can't lose you. I need you."

"I'm not going anywhere, and we are not asking Davis for help. It's not safe. That's like jumping from the frying pan into the fire. If I go back to work and the nonprofits come through, maybe we can come up with enough money to pay for the chemo and maybe even another bone marrow transplant."

Sage whirled to face her sister. "Have you lost your ever-loving mind? You are *not* going back to work. You have cancer! You need to rest and heal."

Sage pressed her head back against the hard pleather of the cab headrest. She couldn't lose Rosemary. Not after losing Mom and Dad and her sweet baby brother. It was unthinkable.

Nausea clenched her stomach. The heat blasted the faux evergreen aroma of the tree-shaped air freshener hanging from the rearview mirror into her nose and lungs. She hit the automatic window button to let in some cool air, praying she wouldn't puke.

The cabbie twisted in his seat, eyeing them as if he was debating throwing them out of the cab. "You alright back there?"

Sage sucked in a deep breath of icy air, trying to slow her rolling stomach. "Yes. Fine. Just needed a little air." She lowered her voice to continue her conversation with her sister. "Sorry I yelled at you."

Rosemary waved a dismissive hand at her. "We're both under a lot of stress."

"How can you be so calm? You know we can't afford the treatments, and they might not even work. We either need lots of money and better doctors or we have to get you one of those exceptions Dr. Gerard talked about."

"We'll figure it out. We always do."

Sage recognized the fake cheer in Rosemary's voice. They were running out of options.

"You heard Dr. Gerard. Maybe we should ask Davis to help."

Rosemary's fever-flushed face turned even redder. "You listen to me, little sister. We are not giving in to him. I won't have it. I'd feel like we were betraying Mom."

"I'm not going to give in to him. I'm just going to talk to him."

"It's not safe!"

"I'll be fine," Sage reassured her sister. "Tonight's the Let's Keep Celebrating party. I'll go with Justin. They'll be tons of people there. Davis won't have the nerve to do anything in front of a crowd. As much as I hate him, if talking to him gets you the treatment you need, it's worth it. I have to try."

"What if he refuses to help?"

"Then I'll move on to Plan B."

"Plan B? What's Plan B?"

"Going straight to the source. After your last visit when Dr. Gerard talked about Remiza, I did some research on it. I found an article about the guy who owns the company running the Remiza trial. He lives here in Philly. I had Justin look into him, and I figured out a way to meet him." Sage flashed her sister a smile. "Maybe I can talk him into giving you Remiza under the Right to Try program. You know how persuasive I can be."

Rosemary shook her head, blonde hair bobbing around her shoulders. "You're absolutely crazy, Sage, you know that?"

"That's one of the many reasons you love me, sis."

Chapter Four

Hours later, Sage decided Rosemary was right. She was crazy—crazy to think she could talk to Davis without punching him in the face. She whacked the dashboard of the passenger seat of Justin's Porsche 911 with her silver-sparkled clutch. Purse glitter sprinkled down over her legs and onto the black carpet.

What else should she expect from a ten-dollar bag? Hopefully, the dress would hold up a little better. The silver, spaghetti-strapped sheath was cheap but looked good enough. She couldn't waste money on clothes. She needed every penny to pay their bills and save for Rosemary's medical care.

"What did my car do to deserve that?" Justin asked, angling his head toward the now- sparkling floor.

"I can't believe he has the audacity to have this party." Sage punctuated her sentence with a second whack on the dashboard. "My mom started the Let's Keep Celebrating tradition. It gave her an excuse to keep all her trees up until the end of January. She's been gone only a few months. He should still be in mourning, not throwing a goddamn party. He's such a bastard."

"It's been more than six months, Sage."

"Six months? Six months? It feels like yesterday. In most cultures, the mourning period is at least a year. He's not mourning because he killed her!"

Justin released a slow breath. "I know you're upset. I loved your mom too. She was one the kindest people I've ever met, but maybe it's time to let this go. Your mom fell in the bathtub. The autopsy you demanded said so. It was an accidental death."

"Accidental! How can you say that? You know the autopsy was inconclusive, and you know he tried to choke me when I told him Rosemary wouldn't lie for him. He literally wrapped his hands around my throat! Who does that? And why the hell did he want Rosemary to give him a fake alibi? I'll tell you why. Because he has none. Because he's a murderer!"

"Calm down, Sage. I agree that Davis is acting like an asshole. Attacking you was inexcusable. Kicking you and Rosemary out of the house was dead wrong, but he was so drunk that night. I think he went into a blind panic after you told the police he was cheating on your mom, and things just snowballed."

"He was cheating. You even saw him with that woman."

Justin blew out another exaggerated breath. "I saw him with more than one woman, but that's not the point. The point is Rosemary's cancer is back. If you want Davis to help pay for her treatment or help you talk the drug company into giving her that Remiza drug, going in there raging at him and calling him a murderer is *not* the way to convince him."

Davis *had* murdered her mother. The desire to scream the truth she knew in her heart consumed her common sense like a forest fire, but Justin was right. She sounded like a nutball. Rosemary wasn't even completely convinced Davis had killed their mother, and she was the one who he'd pressured for an alibi. Plus, Justin was an incredible friend. Losing her temper on him wasn't fair.

Sage stared at the sprawling stone mansion and manicured bushes, all still twinkling with white Christmas lights. Nostalgia lumped in her throat, straining her voice. "I was so happy when we first moved here. We were desperate to build a new life, away from all the pain and loss in Cherry Hill. Even when Rosemary got sick, this house was our comfort. How did it change so fast?"

Justin laid his long, thin, warm fingers on her bare leg. "I wish I had answers, but I don't. Even with the infidelity, I thought Davis really loved your mom...and you and your sister. He's so angry now. Especially at you. It's like he wants to ruin you. He's been telling everybody he had to ask you to leave because you have a drug problem. He says he's giving you tough love."

Sage's ebbing anger flashed hot again. "I'll give that bastard some tough love. No one in their right mind would believe I have a drug problem. How could I dance?"

Justin didn't speak.

"No one believes him, do they?"

He shrugged. "You know how it is. Davis has a lot of friends. He puts on a good front. People respect him. Take my dad, for instance. I told my dad it wasn't true. I told him what Davis was doing to you and your sister, but he and Davis have been friends forever. He doesn't believe me. It really pisses me off."

"Don't be mad at your dad," Sage said. "I don't blame him for trusting Davis. I don't think I'd believe what he's done if I weren't living it."

Justin lifted his hand, cupping her chin. "I hate that you have to ask him for help. I wish I could do more for you and Rosemary. You know I would if I could."

Sage did know it. They weren't just neighbors. Justin was like a brother to her and Rosemary. He'd give her the shirt off his back, and his coat and pants and shoes too. The problem was his clothes, his car, his apartment, and just about everything else was owned in trust, and Justin's dad was the executor.

Mr. Hartmann gladly funded custom-made suits, extravagant dinners, overpriced college courses, and trips to Capri, but when Justin pleaded for money to help Sage and Rosemary, he'd received a firm denial. Jonathan Hartmann would not involve himself in Anderson family matters, no matter how much Justin begged. Blue-blood loyalty and all that.

Sage tugged Justin's hand from her face and gave it a quick squeeze. "You are helping me. You sit with Rosemary when she's sick, you're our constant chauffeur, you make us laugh when we want to cry, and now you're my official bodyguard. What else could I possibly ask for?"

Justin smiled. "You could ask me to marry you. You know the rules of the trust. If I get married any time after I turn twenty-five, I get half the trust money right away. That's only a couple months away. If we got married, I could support you and Rosemary. I could buy her way into getting Remiza. There's always someone to bribe."

Which was exactly what Sage was hoping Davis would do. Bribe someone at the Remiza drug company into giving Rosemary the drug under the Right to Try program.

"I could never do that, Justin. You know that. I'd feel like I was taking advantage of you." Sage lowered her voice to a whisper. "Plus, I don't think Rosemary can wait that long to start treatment."

If marrying Justin would help Rosemary, she'd do it. She'd do anything for her sister, but some deep, selfish part of her was glad it wasn't an option. Despite the disappointment she felt in her father and stepfather, marriage was still something sacred and special to her, and she didn't have many fanciful notions left. Reality had smashed most of her romantic dreams to bits.

An engine raced as a car sped past them and stopped hard at the front door. Sage watched the standard valet exchange through a haze of reminiscence. Images of snowball fights, baking, art projects, and pool basketball flooded her mind. She'd spent so many amazing moments in this house with her mother and sister. Now her mother was gone. What if she lost Rosemary?

That wasn't an option. She would *not* lose her sister, and she was wasting time sitting in the car. Davis had the money and connections to help Rosemary. The house might be full of loss and pain, but it was time to woman up and get her ass in there.

"Come on, let's get this over with."

Justin opened her car door, and Sage dashed up the drive as fast as her stripper heels allowed. Her budget hadn't included new party shoes.

Despite her trepidation about talking to Davis, cozy warmth, like hot chocolate, curled through her as she and Justin stepped into the large foyer. Fresh evergreen garland trimmed with warm-white lights encircled both banisters on the grand spiral staircase, and a Christmas tree sparkled in the alcove created by the curve of the stairs. Instrumental holiday music played softly while cocktail-dress-attired guests mingled, laughed, and chatted.

Justin pointed toward the stairs. "Remember when we tried to slide down those on our plastic sleds?"

Sage laughed out loud. "I sprained my ankle so badly I couldn't dance for a month."

"Caroline never got mad." Justin's voice was wistful. "She used it as an excuse to give us a lesson in physics and anatomy."

"And the healing power of herbs and crystals," Sage added.

Joy and aching loneliness mixed in her stomach. She kept expecting her exquisitely beautiful, graceful, kind as Mother Teresa mother to round the corner with a tray of home-baked Russian tea cookies.

She pushed down the tears. This was not the time for emotion. She needed her A game to get through her conversation with Davis.

"I'm going to look for Davis. He's probably holding court in the kitchen."

"Or giving a tour of the greenhouse," Justin suggested. "You know how he loves to show off those flowers."

She stepped toward the kitchen, but Justin's fingers circled her arm.

"I should come with you," he said. "Davis is still really angry with you. I don't think you should be alone with him."

"We won't be alone. The house is packed. It's better if I go by myself. He'll be less defensive."

Justin gestured toward the dining room. The heavy custom-made table had been cleared of chairs. A runner down the middle served as half-decoration, half-heat protection and was covered by gleaming, round, sterling silver chafing dishes. Cold shrimp, caviar, imported meats and cheeses, sushi, and other cold hors d'oeuvres filled the rest of the table. A portable mahogany bar was set up in the corner of the room.

"Fine. I'll get a drink and something to eat while I wait, but if you're not back in ten minutes, I'm coming looking for you."

Sage grabbed a champagne glass from a passing waiter. The cool, sweet liquid tickled her tongue. She downed the glass and grabbed a second one, ignoring the waiter's quirked eyebrow. Bubbles danced down her throat, taking the edge off her knife-sharp nerves. Normally, she preferred the slow, relaxing burn of wine, but tonight the champagne rush would give her that calm, distant sensation she needed to face the man who'd murdered her mother.

Wasn't there a saying about needing nerves of steel to dance with the devil? If not, there should be.

The house was more crowded than she'd ever seen it. Her mother would never have invited so many people, but excess had always been one of Davis's many vices. The thick crowd pressed and jostled her as she made her way to the kitchen. The smell of fresh pine mixed with perfume, sweat, and the mouthwatering blend of garlic, spice, and roasting red meat. Her stomach growled. She hadn't eaten since breakfast.

She recognized faces as she battled her way through the sea of humanity, but it was as if she'd shown up in ratty, unwashed gym clothes. No one smiled or greeted her, and most people avoided eye contact. Last year, she wouldn't have made it six inches without being embroiled in some boring conversation. It seemed like Justin was right. People were believing Davis's lies.

When she made it to the kitchen, what she found was akin to the New York subway during rush hour. Her five-inch heels pushed her height up to five foot eight, but it was still hard to see through the mass of bodies. She set her champagne glass on the counter and pressed her hands on the cold granite, pushing up on tiptoes to scan the room. Hard, human warmth pressed against her back, and strong hands encircled her waist. The scent of crisp winter air and evergreen filled her nostrils. Soft breath tickled her shoulder and neck.

"Looking for someone?"

The voice was pure sin, casting a hypnotic spell. She recognized the familiar deep timbre instantly.

It was the Viking. From the Black Cat.

Her champagne-buzzed mind relished the sexual promise contained in those three short words. Her eyelids dropped as electricity curled from her stomach to the juncture of her thighs. Strong, muscled legs pushed between her own, forcing her feet slightly apart. The desire to press back into firm male heat welled up from a place long buried. It would be so nice to let go, give in, escape, forget. Forget about paying the rent. Forget about finding money for Rosemary's treatment. Forget about having to strip to make ends meet—and escape into a hard body, strong arms, and ice-blue eyes.

But escape wasn't an option, and her body was a traitor.

Escape into a man?

That was pure insanity. Look where it had gotten her mom.

Champagne brain.

That was the only possible explanation for her wayward body's reaction. She never acted like this. Men couldn't be trusted, and sex wasn't really her thing. The reality never lived up to her fantasies.

Sage tried to turn, but pure steel pinned her against the granite countertop.

She twisted her head. "Let go of me!"

As the pressure eased, she whirled around.

Shit. Turning around had been a crap idea. They were pressed breast to chest and thigh to thigh. Her nipples instantly hardened. The back was too low on the dress for a bra, so she wore none. Each shift of his ridiculously expensive suit against her body created a scorching friction.

She lifted her gaze. The unyielding angles of his face appeared slightly softer. The glacial blue of his eyes now shimmered with need. His nostrils flared slightly. His lips were...far too close to her own.

Sage pushed at the Viking's chest. He moved only a couple of inches, but it gave her the bit of breathing room she needed. She shook the heavy weight of her hair into a protective cape around her shoulders.

"What do you want?"

He leaned close, his lips grazing her ear. "I asked if you were looking for someone."

That featherlight touch sent lightning to her core. Muscles clenched, and her thong dampened. Her body was more aroused than it had ever been.

It had to be the champagne.

She fought for a sensible sentence.

"I'm...I'm...I'm looking for the host, Davis Anderson."

She sounded like a blithering idiot, but at least she'd managed to speak.

He lunged back, withdrawing his addictive heat. The shimmer in his eyes shifted to glass. A muscle ticked in his jaw.

"Of course, you are. Davis is a rich, successful man. I imagine he's exactly the type of man a woman with your talents would be looking for. I believe he's in the greenhouse."

The Viking dipped his head toward her in a mocking Old World bow before cutting easily through the throng in the kitchen.

She should call the bastard back. He didn't deserve the last word.

What had he meant by a woman with her talents? What talents did he think she had, and why had his toned implied they weren't talents to be admired? Why did she care what one more spoiled, rich man thought of her?

She was here for Rosemary. There was no time for distractions, especially not wealthy, condescending, judgmental ones. No matter how handsome.

Sage fought her way through the bodies in the kitchen, annoyed at the way the Viking had seemed to glide through the crowd. She escaped through the side door and shivered down the familiar flagstone path to the greenhouse.

If Davis was here, there was no doubt he'd be holding court, showing off his prize orchids. Humid warmth surrounded her as she entered the building. She tried to ease the glass door closed behind her, but the condensation made the handle slick, and it slipped from her fingers, thudding shut with a loud bang.

Eight male eyes fixated on her. One pair belong to Davis. His mouth opened and closed like a hooked fish.

After sucking air for a few long seconds, he said something in a low voice, and the other gentlemen trailed off in the opposite direction, deeper into the building. Unease pricked Sage's spine. She hadn't planned to be alone with Davis, but it was too late to turn back.

She squared her shoulders as Davis strode forward.

"Sage, what a wonderful surprise. I've wanted to speak to you. You've been a bit hard to track down, but I'm sure you know that. I'm glad you decided to come to the party. It's always been one of your favorite events. Where's Rosemary? I've been missing her."

She was sure his overpolite greeting was for the benefit of the retreating guests who might still be within earshot.

"Rosemary's not here. She hasn't been feeling well, but I'm sure you know that." She intentionally echoed his words back to him.

"I'm sorry to hear that. Perhaps she'd fare better living at home. She's always been delicate."

Sage couldn't quell her flash of irritation. "Delicate? She's been fighting cancer nearly half her life. Rosemary's one of the strongest people I know."

Davis moved closer, encircling both her upper arms with his sweaty hands. "Strong and stubborn. Both of you."

His grip was tight but not hurtful. Sage shivered but didn't push his hands away. She recognized the glazed look in his eyes. He was drunk. The question was how many drinks had he had? If he was only a few drinks in, he'd be emotional and kind. If it was more than that, he'd be angry and argumentative and probably wouldn't remember enough of the conversation to follow through and help Rosemary. She should have thought of this before she'd come tonight. Of course, he'd be drinking. It was a party.

Too late to retreat. She had to tread carefully. "Well, it's a good thing Rosemary's strong, because she's sick again. That's why I'm here. I'd like you to consider helping her."

"Help her? Why should I help her when she betrayed me?"

Be calm. Be persuasive.

"I don't think refusing to lie to the police is a betrayal. You're her stepfather. You love her. You should want to help her."

Davis moved fast, pulling her closer. Spicy whiskey breath filled her nostrils. His voice was an iron whisper.

"You and your sister are ruining my life with your lies and accusations. You want help? Move back into this house and get the goddamn police off my back. If you don't, you'll both regret it!"

Davis's manicured hands were now squeezing her arms as if he was strangling them.

Just like he'd strangled her mother.

Bile rose in her throat. Davis's fingers felt like they were boring holes through her skin. She craned her neck from side to side. The guests were gone. She and Davis were alone in the greenhouse. Panic froze her limbs for an instant that felt like an eternity. Then, instinct kicked panic in the ass, and Sage's knee connected with soft flesh.

Davis's thick grunt of pain was pure satisfaction. He doubled over, and she kicked her platform shoe into his ribs, hopefully hard enough to break a few.

"You're a monster!" she yelled, not caring who could hear.

She fled, heels clicking on the concrete floor. Her fingers fumbled with the wet handle of the greenhouse door, but she managed to pull it open and escape. Outside, the icy night air nipped at her skin as she dashed down the dimly lit flagstone path, staring hard at the uneven stones, willing herself not to trip.

Whoompf.

Her body struck something big and hard, pushing her backward.

Her heel hit the edge of a flagstone. Her arms flailed. She braced for impact, but deft, strong fingers grasped her arms before she hit the ground. When she opened her eyes, she found herself staring into a pool of blue ice.

The Viking pulled her upright, steadying her. "Leaving so soon? I thought you'd spend more time with Davis."

She didn't want to speak. She might laugh like a lunatic—or cry. Both were crap options.

She managed a rough "I have to go."

Dark eyebrows winged up. "That was quick, but I guess if the customer's satisfied, there's no reason to hang around...unless you're looking for more company."

What was he talking about?

He wasn't making any sense, and she didn't have time to figure it out. She glanced over her shoulder. The path was still empty. She needed to get going before Davis recovered and came after her.

The Viking brushed a rough-skinned thumb across her lips. "If I hired you, it'd be for the whole night, not a rushed ten minutes in a greenhouse."

Sage had fallen in a pond once when she was little. It was winter, and she'd walked on ice that was too thin. Her realization felt like the shock of that freezing water.

He thinks I'm a hooker.

She glanced down at her skintight dress and stripper shoes. Why wouldn't he? She was frustrated, scared, exhausted, and pissed off all at the same time. She just wanted to be home.

She twisted her arm, but powerful fingers held fast.

"Come home with me." His face was stone, but his once-cold eyes now burned like the flame of a torch, and his voice was deep and entreating. "Let me take you away from here. Escape with me."

He was propositioning her. She should be insulted. Escaping with this intense, angry, rude, incredibly strong man was insane.

So why did she feel insanely tempted?

"I...

"Sage! Sage!" Justin's voice cut the cold night air, and footsteps pounded on the flagstone walkway.

The Viking released her arm and ran a gentle finger down her cheek. "Maybe another time."

He strode past Justin, nodded politely, and disappeared into the house.

"I didn't mean to interrupt your conversation with Ryker. I was just worried about you." Justin gave her a quick hug, then rubbed her arms with his hands. "It's freezing out here. You need to get inside."

"Ryker?"

"Yes. Ryker Madsen." Justin gestured toward the Viking's retreating back. "The man you were talking to."

The cold must be slowing her brain. "Who's Ryker Madsen?"

"I told you before. He's the owner of Origin Pharmaceuticals. You know, the company producing Remiza."

Her heart stopped. "That can't be right. You told me the owner of Origin Pharmaceuticals and the owner of the Black Cat were the same person. That man's not the owner of the Black Cat. He's a customer."

Justin scrunched his nose. "No, Sage. That was definitely Ryker Madsen, and I'm absolutely certain he's the owner of both the Black Cat and Origin. I thought that was why you were talking to him."

The truth hit her like a hammer. Sage didn't know whether to laugh or cry.

If she wanted to get Remiza for Rosemary, she might just have to take the Viking up on his offer.

Chapter Five

"Just email me the project summary and the financials," Ryker ordered into the phone.

He wasn't giving the conference call the attention it needed. Better to just end it and look at the information later when he could concentrate.

For what seemed like the hundredth time that morning, his eyes flicked to the electronic calendar that always occupied one of the three computer monitors sitting on his hand-carved hickory desk. Despite being made by Amish woodcrafters, his desk and working table were sleek, almost modern. The deep-brown leather couch, Oriental rug, art deco lamps, and local artwork made the space warm and personal. Usually, his office inspired efficient productivity.

Not today.

All Ryker could think about today was the 11:15 appointment he'd allowed his assistant to squeeze into his schedule.

Olivia Dupree.

After their exchange at Davis Anderson's party, he'd forced himself to avoid the Black Cat for the rest of the weekend. To prevent himself from giving in to temptation, he'd taken his private jet to Austin to check out a few possible student housing investments. He toured properties, met with a local attorney, played golf, and dined with a potential investment partner. He'd done everything he could to keep his mind occupied with work.

It hadn't worked.

Images of Olivia in that tight, black strapless dress she'd worn the first night at the Black Cat kept invading his brain. He'd see a woman with dark hair, and a picture of Olivia flipping her waist-length, nearly black waves would skip through his mind. At night, he'd lay in the anonymous hotel room and imagine her full lips grazing his stomach and thighs and her huge, blue, heavily lined cat eyes looking up at him while those sensual lips closed over him. He'd touch himself, envisioning her hot mouth around him.

He was obsessed.

And he hated himself for it.

She was a stripper. A prostitute. A woman who used her body to control and manipulate men.

She was an exquisitely packaged con artist. Like Bethany, his ex-fiancée. But Olivia was far more beautiful and far more dangerous. Olivia was a threat because she managed to appear bright, innocent, and sweet yet wantonly sensual at the same time, and for some reason, that combination robbed him of his normal cool rationality.

He'd tipped his hand at the party.

Now she knew how desperately he wanted her, but that was probably a good thing. A woman like Olivia would have done her research. To her, he'd be a walking, talking dollar sign. The cards were on the table. He wanted her body. She wanted his money. They could move forward. Strictly business. No bullshit. No feelings. No lies.

That's how he liked all his interactions, especially in his private life. Women couldn't be trusted, so it was best to keep them at arm's length.

Bethany had been the forge for the iron walls that surrounded his heart. He'd been a fool, but she taught him a lesson he needed to learn. Even after years of his mother betraying him for the bliss of a needle in her vein, his soul had still hoped for love, so he hadn't given up. Not until Bethany. Bethany's betrayal had been the nail in the coffin of his capacity for emotion.

Women were simply a means to an end. Sometimes, he needed a plus-one for an event. Other times, he just needed to relieve the demands of his body. In exchange, he provided wealth, status, jewelry, and maybe a trip to Paris or Costa Rica. He was always kind, polite, and respectful but also crystal clear that the relationship was one of mutual benefit, not romance.

All the women he'd "dated" over the years were sophisticated, educated socialites. Olivia was not. Questions swirled in his mind.

Could he have sex with a hooker? And pay for it? Was there really any difference between cash and a diamond necklace? Hadn't all his relationships just been a different form of prostitution? Did it even matter?

Unfortunately, it did. The idea of paying for sex offended him. He couldn't bring himself to do it, but he needed to do something to get that wild-haired siren out of his mind. She'd become a distraction. No. An obsession. He needed to find a way to have her. Maybe once he'd taken her to bed, he'd get her the hell out of his system.

Ryker snapped his head up at the sound of a light tap on his office door. He glanced at the time on his computer screen. He'd been ruminating longer than he thought. Much longer. Which, again, was why he needed to start thinking with the head on his shoulders, not the one in his pants.

He fought for normalcy as his assistant announced Olivia's arrival. He shuffled papers on his desk, feigning disinterest. When he finally allowed himself to lift his gaze, he found Olivia standing less than six feet away, waiting calmly.

Gone was the Olivia in the sheer, silver mini-dress and barely-there thong who had been using his brain stem as a stripper pole. She wore a trim, black pantsuit, a pale blue blouse, black flats, and a strand of what looked like high-quality pearls. Her thick hair was pulled back in a long, low ponytail, and her face was free of makeup except a bit of lip gloss and mascara.

He stood and walked her body with his eyes. "You do know how to surprise a man."

Olivia rolled her eyes as she shook his hand. "Did you expect me to come to your office dressed for the Black Cat?"

He remained silent, and she arched one eyebrow. "You know what? Don't answer that. I'll be offended if you say yes, and that isn't the way I'd like to start this conversation."

Ryker settled back in his seat, unsure how to respond. The truth was always the best first choice, or at least that was what his old dojo master, Senpai Joe, always said.

"I wasn't trying to be insulting. I was just expecting more sex appeal and less schoolteacher, but you look fantastic. Please have a seat. I'm curious to know why you requested this meeting."

Olivia rubbed her palms along her upper thighs, then lifted her hand and twirled one of the pearls between her thumb and forefinger. Her gaze was directed at the floor, but he could see her worrying her bottom lip with her teeth. She was biting so hard she might cut it.

The thought was unbearable.

He rose, circled the desk, and touched her lip. "Don't do that. You're going to hurt yourself."

She looked up, her eyes so round and big, he could see straight into her soul.

But it wasn't her soul, he reminded himself. She was playing a part. He was seeing only what she wanted him to see. He couldn't let her think he'd fall for her nervous, innocent act. It was time to set the tone for their relationship. Time to take control.

Ryker leaned against the edge of his desk directly in front of Olivia, intentionally standing over her, crowding her. After spending too many years of his childhood subject to other people's whims, he knew how to adopt an imposing posture.

But she didn't seem intimidated.

They stared at each other, neither willing to show weakness by looking away. Olivia finally broke the silence, but his body's instant reaction to the husky sensuality of her voice made him wonder whether he'd really won the stand-off.

"I came to discuss a business proposition with you."

"This isn't something we could have handled at the club?"

Olivia licked her lips, and his dick throbbed. He felt like a fool. Like a high school kid with no self-control.

She slid one long fingernail from the top of his thigh to his kneecap. "It's more of a personal proposition, so I thought we might want to avoid the prying eyes and ears at the Black Cat."

Ryker retreated to his desk chair. That one touch had brought him far too close to teenage embarrassment. If he stayed close to her, he'd give her the advantage of knowing how easily she affected him.

"I'm listening."

Olivia slipped her jacket down her shoulders and unbuttoned her blouse to her waistband. Ryker could see her sweet pink nipples though the lace of her flesh-toned bra. She lifted her hands to her own breasts.

Not even his fantasies were this good. There was nothing like a woman's hands on her own breasts, and Olivia's were exquisite. The building could've exploded, and he wouldn't have been able to tear his eyes away.

She pulled down the lace of her bra cups, allowing her lush, golden breasts to spill out. "I see how you watch me. I know you want me."

Ryker's tongue was thick in his mouth, but he managed to keep his voice even. "I do want you. I think every man who lays eyes on you dreams of taking you to bed, but I'm sure there's something you want from me too. So as much as I'm enjoying the view, why don't you button your blouse and tuck your gorgeous breasts away so I'm not distracted while you tell me why you're here. And just so we're on the same page here, I'm not paying you for sex."

Something flashed in the depths of Olivia's wide blue eyes. Shock? Hurt? Anger? Fear? Ryker wasn't sure what it was, and it was gone by the time she lifted her head from straightening her clothes.

Her voice was all business as she spoke. "I don't want money from you. I want a favor."

Interesting.

"I won't do anything illegal, and I'm not going to hurt anybody."

"No. No. No," she said quickly. "It's not illegal, and I'd never want anyone hurt. It's actually helping somebody."

"And what do I get in exchange for this help?"

"I'm willing to sleep with you." Olivia's voice was a whisper, and her fingers fluttered near her breasts, twisting a button on her blouse.

She was back to her shy, nervous schoolgirl act. Probably thinking he'd jump at the chance to be her hero. Ten years ago, he might have. Now he recognized her as the professional manipulator she was.

Still, maybe they could work something out, but first he wanted to make one thing clear.

"I'm not convinced that's the best idea. I don't want a woman having sex with me out of a sense of obligation. That won't work for me."

"Are you good in bed?" Olivia's question was a sensual purr.

"I've been told I'm not too bad."

"I'm attracted to you. You're attracted to me. We can both get something out of this. Why are you being so stodgy and old-fashioned?"

Was he being old-fashioned? Why was he hesitating when the perfect solution to his Olivia obsession had landed squarely in his lap?

"You're being ridiculous," she said.

He brushed his reservations aside.

"Fine. A mutually beneficial agreement it is. I have three events coming up over the next month. A wedding, an awards dinner, and a charity event. I'd like you to be my companion for those events and spend some additional time with me in-between. After the last event, our arrangement will terminate. If you agree to that, I'll grant you your favor."

"Sounds reasonable."

"I have a few conditions."

"Conditions. Of course. Do tell."

Ryker pressed his lips together. His dick was so hard he could barely create a cogent thought, and she just sat languidly, now back to playing with her pearls. Pearls some other man had probably given her as a gift.

His temper raced. Sexual frustration was making him edgy. Once their deal was set and he knew he'd get his chance with her, he'd feel better.

"First, I require monogamy. We'll have an exclusive relationship until all three events have passed. I don't like being part of a crowd and won't tolerate being the subject of public gossip. Alright?"

Olivia nodded.

"Second, I require honesty. I won't do business with anyone who lies to me. Understood?"

She nodded again.

"Third, this is a business deal, a contract. If you hold up your end of the bargain, I'll hold up mine. If you don't, no favor. It's as simple as that."

"Anything else?" she asked, again with that light, almost mocking tone in her voice.

He hated it. Both her tone and her iron-clad control. He wanted her as desperate and unnerved as he was.

"I need to kiss you."

"Please do."

Ryker stood and walked slowly toward her, retaking his prior position leaning on the edge of the desk, facing her. He pushed her suit jacket open and slid his fingers down the cool, silky material of her blouse. When he reached the buttons, he unbuttoned a few, filling his hands with her lush, heavy breasts.

He circled the dark pink nipples with his thumbs before taking each one between his thumb and forefinger and tugging gently on the hardened peaks.

Her head dropped back, her eyes slipped shut, and her nostrils flared. Her breath quickened as he continued to twirl the hard buds between his fingers. His cock twitched in his pants. He wanted to push her breasts together and suck both her rigid nipples at the same time, but first he needed to taste her mouth. He released one breast, wound a hand into her hair, and tugging lightly on her nipple and her ponytail, lifted her from the chair and pulled her face to his.

Her lips were silk, and her tongue was molten lava. As he explored her hot, sweet mouth, he dropped his hand from her hair, filling his palm with her delectable ass. Her curves were luscious. He pushed a knee between her legs and pulled her tight against him, pushing his raging dick against her core, hating the clothes separating them.

Lust erased all thoughts. Nothing mattered. Not that they were in his office. Not that anyone could walk in. Not that she might be a manipulator willing to sell herself to the highest bidder. Not that it was dangerous to want a woman this much.

He needed to be inside her. Now.

An intercom buzz broke through his passion-induced haze. His assistant's voice filled the office. "Veronica Huntly's arrived for your lunch appointment."

Ryker tried to steady his voice, but it was low and rough when he answered. "I'll be out in a minute."

He gently pushed Olivia away.

"Fix your clothes. I don't want my assistant speculating about what's been going on in here."

He'd tried to sound distant, but his breathing was heavy and his voice gravel. His erection was tenting his pants. He'd let things get out of hand. Way out of hand.

Olivia buttoned her blouse and straightened her jacket. She pulled a small mirror from her purse, smoothed her hair, tightened her ponytail, and carefully reapplied her lip gloss. She was the epitome of cool control, while he was on the verge of making spontaneous human combustion a reality.

It was annoying as hell.

He tried to hide his lack of composure by returning to his desk chair and writing his home addresses on the back of his business card. As he finished, his office door opened, and Veronica waltzed in.

"Ryker, what on earth is taking you so long...?" Veronica's words trailed off as her eyes settled on Olivia.

He pointed toward the door. "I'm in a meeting. Wait outside. I'll be with you in a minute."

Once the office door was closed and they were alone again, Ryker pulled Olivia close. He needed one more taste to hold him over until he'd see her again. Adrenaline still had his heart pounding, so he made sure his touch was gentle. He didn't want his passion to make him too rough. He kissed her long and slow, savoring the way her body melted into his. How long would Veronica wait before knocking again?

He instantly pulled away.

He needed distance. The fact that he was making his lawyer wait while he seduced a woman in his office meant he was out of control, and control wasn't something he was willing to give up.

He adopted the voice he used with off-schedule contractors as he pressed the card with his home address into Olivia's hand. "This is my address. I'll expect you tomorrow evening at seven."

* * *

Sage pulled Ryker's business card out of her purse as she shoved the measly $167 she'd made during her shift into it. It was sleeting, so the crowd had been thinner than the normal light attendance on the dayshift, which she'd had to switch to in order to accommodate Ryker's demand she visit him tonight. Which sucked. On so many levels.

She'd worked the eight to two last night, then been up most of the rest of the night with Rosemary, who'd come down with the flu. So she'd made shit for cash, was functioning on no sleep, and now was going to have sex with a stranger to get her sister Remiza, when all she wanted to do was go home and get some sleep.

Sage lined her lips in the mirror at her small vanity station in the dressing room, then filled them in with a neutral lipstick. She was freshening up at the club because she'd be tight on time if she went home before heading to Ryker's, and she wasn't up for the questions she was sure Rosemary would ask if she did. Rosemary would lose her mind if she knew about Sage's business arrangement with Ryker. She'd threatened to pack her bags and move out when she'd learned about the stripping. If her sister knew about her latest scheme, Rosemary would probably tie her to a kitchen chair to keep her away from Ryker.

Sage closed her lipstick with a loud snap. Rosemary didn't understand. She had no choice. Losing her sister was inconceivable. Rosemary was all she had left. If selling her body was the price, she'd gladly pay it ten times over, but now that the sale was only an hour away, panic was setting in.

Dancing was one thing. Years of serious training combined with a reasonable number of theater roles allowed her to feel comfortable playing the part of a stripper. She'd done a great job at convincing Ryker she wanted him. She did want him. He was so tall, strong, rugged, and fierce, she got wet just looking at him. But actually having sex with him was a whole different ballgame. One that, despite her act in front of Ryker, she didn't have much experience playing, and when she had played, it had only been so-so. She didn't know crap about pleasing a man in bed, and the info she'd found in her frantic internet search only increased her anxiety. Looking sexy and being good at sex were two entirely different things.

She was screwed.

Figuratively, and in a couple of hours, probably literally.

Sage twisted back and forth in the mirror. Her wardrobe was limited, so she'd gone with a skintight, asymmetrical, single-strapped, royal blue dress she used for work. The dress showed all her curves and ended just a few short inches past her derriere. Despite the cold, she wore open-toed, black patent leather, ankle-strap pumps with silver heels and silver buckles.

Hopefully, looking the part would be enough.

Sage pushed open the heavy metal door to the back parking lot and hurried toward her car. A niggling thought that something was off tickled the base of her skull, but she was rushing, so it didn't fully register until she'd almost reached the Mazda. The car was too close to the ground.

Her stomach lurched.

She dashed the last few yards and circled the car, crouching down next to each tire. Slashed. Every single one of them.

"Shit. Shit. Shit." She kicked one flat tire with each curse.

She hoofed around to the front of the building, cold whipping up her legs. Her short pleather jacket provided little protection from the icy wind. She scanned the street for a cab. Of course there wasn't one. That was the kind of day she was having.

She hurried back into the club to call a taxi.

Bryce waved at her from the house phone at the bar and covered the receiver with his hand. "Hey, pretty girl, I thought you were headed home."

Sage slammed her purse on the bar. "Me too. Someone slashed my tires. Can you believe it? I am so mad! I can't even deal with it now because I have an appointment at seven I can't miss. I came in to call a cab."

"I'll call you back." Bryce hung up the phone and leaned over the bar. "Someone slashed your tires? Here? In our parking lot? Who would do a thing like that?"

Sage's stomach flipped. Hopefully, Davis hadn't found her.

"I don't know. An angry customer? You know how some of these guys can get."

"Normally, we'd be able to see who did it on the outside cameras. The boss had all new cameras put in when he took over the club, but someone smashed them up last night."

"All of them?"

"Yep. The boss was fit to be tied when I told him."

The mention of Ryker, even as the innocuous "boss," sent butterflies parading through her stomach. Anticipation and dread mixed and bubbled. Neither was any use. What she needed was a functioning automobile.

Sage picked up the bar phone. Her cell had no service in the club.

"I hate having to take a cab. I'm short on time and even shorter on cash."

"I know how that goes," Bryce said. "Why don't you Uber? It's cheaper."

Sage rolled her eyes. "Can't. No credit card."

"Cab'll take forever. I'll get the Uber through my app, and you can give me the cash later."

Thirty minutes later, Sage was thanking God for both Bryce and Uber as she stood in the hallway of Ryker's penthouse apartment on Rittenhouse Square. It was 7:02. There was no way she would've arrived on time without Bryce's help.

When she rang, a stately, gray-haired gentleman opened the door and escorted her to a cozy room lined with bookcases and offered her a drink. She gladly accepted a glass of wine. She needed it. The butterflies in her belly had turned into elephants.

She paced while she waited, studying the artwork surrounding the fireplace. A small, expensively framed, heavy-lined pencil sketch caught her eye. The strokes were beautifully bold, modern, and geometric. She peered closer, her gaze falling to the artist's signature. Her breath left her body. The sketch was an original Klimt.

The elephants stampeded.

She'd known Ryker had money, but to own a picture like this he had to be really rich. Private jet, own your own island kind of rich, which was one more raincloud in an already stormy day. Men, as a general rule, were jerks, and in her experience, the asshole factor increased in direct proportion to a man's wealth.

Can I ever catch a break?

"You're late." Ryker's deep, masculine voice filled the room.

Sage spun to face him, almost spilling her wine. "Me? I'm late? I'm the one who's been standing here for ten minutes waiting for you."

"It was after seven when you rang the bell. I told you seven o'clock."

That condescending tone was the proverbial straw, and she was the camel with the broken back. Nerves, lack of sleep, worry for Rosemary, slashed tires, sore feet, a jacket that did nothing to protect her from the wind. It was all too much.

Selling herself was hard enough. Selling herself to an arrogant, snobbish, controlling jackass was unbearable.

She couldn't do it. She'd find another way to help Rosemary.

Sage grabbed her crap jacket and Walmart handbag from the sofa, muttering as she marched toward the doorway.

"*Va au diable.*"

Ryker's strong fingers circled her wrist firmly but carefully. "What did you say?"

"*Va au diable.* It means go to hell. Now let go of my arm. I'm leaving."

"Why are you so angry?"

Was he actually asking why she was so upset? Was he so out of touch with the real world that he really didn't know?

She shouldn't be surprised. He was a spoiled, rich asshat who had no idea what life was like for normal everyday people.

"Who do you think you are to lecture me about arriving a few minutes late? I can't spend time with someone like you."

"Someone like me? What the hell do you mean by that?"

"Men like you think everyone's beneath you. You buy whatever you need, take whatever you want, and don't care who gets destroyed in the process."

Ryker's face remained impassive, but his normally frozen eyes burned. "How dare you presume to know anything about me?"

Sage's simmering pot of emotions boiled over. "How dare *you* presume to know anything about *me*? You have no right to come in here chiding me like a schoolgirl for being two minutes late. I don't live in your world of chauffeurs and personal chefs"—she waved her hand toward the wall—"and original Klimt sketches. I have a job. I work. For *you*. On a shift that didn't end until six. You don't know anything about needing to work for money and searching in the freezing cold for a cab you can't afford to sell your body to some asshole who doesn't even respect you!"

Sage jerked out of Ryker's grasp. She hated anyone knowing her dire financial situation, and she'd just thrown it out in the open. Her face was boiling. Tears were brimming the edges of her eyes, and she couldn't afford to let Ryker see her cry. Men like him stomped on the weak and kept walking.

She fumbled with the front door lock, blinking so she could see. A strong hand pushed the door shut just as she managed to pull it open. Warm, gentle fingers curved around the top of her shoulder.

"Don't go."

She tugged on the door handle even harder.

"Please don't go. You're right. I was acting like an ass. Come back in. Sit down. Finish your wine. Please."

She sucked a few deep breaths in through her nose and blew them out her mouth.

Think. Breathe. Don't let your anger drive you. Think about Rosemary.

Fury had sent her racing toward the door, but pragmatism made her slide her index fingers under each eye to eliminate any tell-tale runny eye makeup. Her options were Ryker or Davis. Jerk or not, sleeping with Ryker was a hell of a lot better than throwing herself and Rosemary to the mercy of a murderer.

Sage turned around. For Rosemary, she'd give this another shot, but she would not lose her pride in the process. It was one of the only things she had left.

"I'm not going to let you treat me like hired help."

Ryker brushed a long, bronze-skinned finger down her cheek. "I know you won't believe me, but I'm not normally like this. I'm not comfortable if I'm not in control, and you make me feel like I'm racing down a mountain on a bike with no brakes."

The elephants in her gut settled a bit at his effort at kindness. "Your high school English lit teacher would be proud of that imagery."

Ryker laughed. It was a full, warm, deep, rumbling laugh. He took a step back, as if surprised by the sound coming out of his own body.

"Yeah. I guess that sounded pretty dramatic, but it's true. I don't get you, Olivia, and that bothers me."

The sound of her friend's name on Ryker's lips was unsettling.

She'd used Olivia's ID since she'd started at the Horny Toad, so she'd gotten used to being called Olivia at work, but something deep inside her rebelled at the idea of Ryker using a name that wasn't her own.

"What's there to get?" she asked.

"I want to know why you picked me. You've got Davis and the kid in the Porsche. They should have plenty of money between them. Why do you want to add me to the list?"

Wow.

Ryker thought she was sleeping with both Davis and Justin. She shouldn't be surprised after their exchange at the Let's Keep Celebrating party, but his assumption still stung. She shouldn't care what Mr. Lifestyles of the Rich and Famous thought. He was a means to an end. The key to getting Rosemary well. Yet her insides felt like they'd been pierced with shards of ice.

Still, she had to keep her eye on the prize. Doing that meant keeping her identity a secret.

Ryker didn't know she was Davis's stepdaughter. He thought she and Davis were lovers. Gross, but probably for the best. She needed to make sure Ryker didn't learn the truth. Davis had already turned everyone in her social circle against her. She couldn't afford to have him do the same thing with Ryker. Plus, Justin said he thought Ryker and Davis were building a hotel together. Ryker likely wouldn't want to risk his business arrangement with Davis over her.

Time to tread carefully.

"To set the record straight, I've never had sex with Davis Anderson, and I never will. I'm not sleeping with Justin either. He's just a friend."

Ryker quirked an eyebrow, but he didn't push the issue. "Your past is your own. You don't have to explain yourself to me. I'm focused on the present. So again, why me?"

This was some crucial testing point. She could feel it. She knew Ryker wanted her. He'd made that clear, but she also got the sense that if he didn't like her answer, he was going to walk away. Truth was the only option.

"You have something I need, desperately."

"What's that?" he asked.

"My friend, Rosemary, is sick. I need you to help her."

One of Ryker's thick, dark eyebrows winged up. "I'm not a doctor. You know that, right?

"She doesn't need a doctor. She needs medicine. I know you own Origin Pharmaceuticals, and Origin is manufacturing Remiza. Rosemary missed the cutoff for the last drug trial, so the only way for her to get Remiza is through the Right to Try program. I want you to get her that drug." Sage reached out a long fingernail and ran it up Ryker's inner thigh. "If you do, you'll have me for the next month. All of me."

Chapter Six

When you had money, someone always wanted something from you. Especially women. Ryker had given up expecting anything else. It made his relationships easier. Reduced them to the most basic elements. His relationships were a modern version of the barter system. Exchanging the satisfaction of his body's needs for whatever a woman wanted from him. Notoriety, wealth, an introduction. They always wanted something.

That pragmatism usually eliminated surprises, but what had just come out of Olivia's beautiful mouth was a big one.

"You want me to get your friend access to Remiza? That's why you're pursuing me?"

She nodded.

Shit. This is not what he was expecting. So not what he was expecting. He didn't want her to have altruistic motives, and certainly not a motivation like this.

He'd had a stressful day at work, waited impatiently for her to arrive, and been pissed when she was a few minutes late. At work, no one ever dared to make him wait. He thought she'd been pulling a power play. Now that his initial anger had faded, his eyes registered

Olivia's overly pale face and makeup that didn't quite cover the circles under her eyes.

His mother was always stick thin with bags under her eyes. That's what heroin did to a person, but Olivia didn't have the haggard pallor of a druggie. Her face was the kind of tired he used to see in Mrs. Garcia on Sunday nights at the bodega.

"Let's go back to the library. You can sit down by the fire. I'll pour you more wine."

She didn't answer, but she did let him guide her down the hallway to the library, the heels on her jaw-dropping shoes clicking firmly on the Brazilian pecan flooring. Her hand was small and soft, but her grip was strong.

She was a tangle of contradictions. Silky soft skin with a spine of steel. A stripper with excellent grammar and diction. She railed at him for being rich but spoke French and could recognize an original Klimt. She had an altruistic goal but sang to his soul like a siren.

The problem with sirens was that they lured capable men to a saltwater grave.

Just like Bethany had almost done to him.

For a moment, memory made the years-old betrayal fresh and new, crushing his chest. He dropped Olivia's hand as if it were a brand. He poured a bourbon at the bar, needing the cool, hard crystal in his hand combined with the burn of whiskey in his throat to slow his racing heart. He hated thinking about Bethany, but tonight the memories were a good thing, his brain's protection mechanism, forcing a mental step back from the spell Olivia was slowly weaving.

She'd thrown him off-balance with the Remiza request. He couldn't bear the thought of Olivia spending time with him or having sex with him to help a friend. It was one thing to know that a woman was with him because she wanted gifts or trips or to climb the social ladder, but he would not prey on desperation. It violated his basic sense of honor.

"Hello? Ryker?" Olivia waved a hand in front of his face. Even with makeup smeared under her eyes, she was tempting and achingly beautiful.

"What's your friend's full name?" he asked.

Trepidation flashed across her face but disappeared so quickly he wasn't sure it had been there in the first place.

"Rosemary. Rosemary Cashman. She's my roommate."

Cashman. Familiarity tickled his skull, but the connection eluded him.

"Why are you coming to me? Why not have her doctor contact Origin directly?"

"He did. She missed the cutoff date for the last trial, and his request for Right to Try access was rejected. I don't know why. The doctor told me we might have more luck in getting Rosemary's Right to Try request granted if we knew the right people." She shrugged her muscled, slender shoulders. "I guess medicine's no different than anything else in this world. The people with money, power, or influence get what they need. For everyone else, it's a crapshoot."

Ryker's chest tightened. Olivia's words struck too close to home. In the construction business, contracts were bought with envelopes under tables and permits were paid for with box seats. The rich generally got richer, while those with fewer resources struggled to make it. At one time he'd been an exception to that rule, but now he was the one with the money, power, and influence, and he wasn't shy about using it. He excelled in that dog-eat-dog world, but being good at it didn't mean he liked it.

That was one of the reasons he'd started investing in drug research. Science was black-and-white. Pure. The answers were straight, and no agendas were hidden.

Does Olivia have a hidden agenda?

"How long have you been planning this? Did you take the job at the Black Cat just to meet me?"

Olivia worried her bottom lip with her teeth, just like she'd done in his office.

"I go with Rosemary to all her appointments. When we learned her cancer was back, the doctor said Remiza would be the best choice. He said there was risk she wouldn't get into the trial, so I wanted a backup plan. My friend, Justin, did some digging and figured out you owned both Origin and the Black Cat. Once he told me that, I figured getting a job at the Black Cat was the best next step."

Ryker's spine stiffened. Justin again. That man's name on Olivia's tongue put a sour taste in his mouth. "That's the kid from the party, right?"

Olivia bit her lip again. It seemed to be a nervous habit.

"That's right."

"If he's such a good friend, why didn't he try to buy Rosemary's way into the study?" Ryker didn't like it, but he was smart enough to know things like that happened from time to time.

"It's complicated."

"Complicated? What's complicated about helping a friend?" He had no patience for assholes that were all talk and no action.

Olivia frowned. "He's desperate to help, but he can't. Everything he has comes from a trust fund. His car, his apartment, his clothes. Pretty much anything of value is paid for by the trust. He has no real access to cash, and the trustee isn't keen on my friend. So like I said, it's complicated."

There was more to the story, but the firm line of Olivia's lips signaled an end to the subject.

"So your plan was to come to open auditions, get a job, meet me, then seduce me to get Rosemary access to Remiza? What if I were married? Or seventy years old?"

Sage flopped down on the leather sofa. "Seduction. Pleading. Indentured servitude. They were all options. After I met you, seduction seemed like the best route."

Of course seduction seemed like the best route. He'd made his lust for her clear. Renting a skywriter to pen "I want you" in the air would've been less obvious.

"You said you wanted me to be honest." Olivia's husky, hesitant voice filled the heavy silence.

"I do, but now I'm not comfortable with our arrangement. I'm not going to take advantage of a situation like this. I'm not that kind of man."

He wanted Olivia. Desperately. But his sense of honor was stronger than his lust.

She leaped from the couch, crossing her arms over her chest, causing her lush breasts to push up, the golden curves spilling over the upper seam of her dress. They rose and fell with her breaths as she shouted, "Oh no you don't! We made a deal. You are *not* backing out on me! Rosemary needs this drug!"

"Calm down. I'm not backing out. As long as she meets the criteria, I'll have my team give her Right to Try access to Remiza. You don't have to follow through with your end of the bargain."

He would do it. He'd do anything to never again see that horrible, broken look on Olivia's face that appeared when she'd talked about her friend.

"No! No! No! I don't believe in gifts or free rides. Look at what happened to the Trojans." Olivia's index finger pressed into the center of his chest. "Men can't be trusted. They don't do anything out of the goodness of their hearts. They bail when the going gets tough, or worse, they say they'll help and decide later they want something in exchange for their trouble. I can't risk you changing your mind. We do this just like we agreed. A business deal. Tit for tat. If you're getting something you want from me, you won't be tempted to back out."

That one finger Olivia had buried in his chest sent electricity through his entire body. Something deep and visceral flowed between them. Even angry and exhausted, she was strong, fierce, and wholly irresistible.

"What would you do if I said no?"

She pursed her lips and scrunched her nose like she'd sucked on a lemon. "I have a backup plan."

"Based on your expression, I assume this backup plan is less palatable than me?"

Olivia huffed out a sarcastic laugh. "That's an understatement.

You're a bit of an arrogant ass, but at least you seem honest. Plan B's a slimy snake."

Ryker's stomach got that pre-car-crash feeling. Olivia offering the deal she'd given him to someone else was not an option. He knew he'd keep his word, and he wasn't going to make her have sex with him to do it. Once Rosemary got set up with Remiza, there was no way he'd cut that off. He could never be that big of an ass, but from Olivia's tirade, it was clear he wasn't going to be able to convince her of that. If she insisted on a tit-for-tat arrangement, he'd let her think she was getting one.

"Alright, we'll stick to the original plan if that's really what you want."

She eased back down onto the couch, leaned her head back, and closed her eyes.

"That's what I want. You and me, a month of amazing dates, and all the fun stuff that comes along with that." Her tone was light, but she was biting her lip again. "It might be easier if we knew each other a little better."

Funny. In his experience, distance made everything simpler. If two people never really came together, there wasn't anything to break apart. But he wasn't going to say that. If she wanted to share, that worked just fine. She was a mystery to him. If he solved the puzzle that was Olivia, maybe he'd get over his obsession. It didn't mean he had to reciprocate.

"Tell me about yourself," he said.

"What do you want to know?"

There were lots of things Ryker wanted to know, but his newly acquired green-eyed monster forced his most pressing question through his lips. "Are you an escort?"

Olivia's eyes sprung open. "No. I don't know why you keep saying that."

He stared at her.

"OK. I guess, for a lot of people, escort isn't such a big leap from stripper, but I don't have sex for money. I know you probably don't believe me, but I've never done anything like this before."

Her answer shouldn't fill him with content. Women lied. She could be bullshitting him as part of some swindle he hadn't figured out yet, but her response still took the edge off his smoldering jealousy.

Olivia had settled back into the couch cushions. She was far too young to be as bone-weary tired as she looked. There was more to Olivia than met the eye, more than she wanted the world to see. Maybe that's why she was so compelling.

Hopefully, once he figured her out, he could get her huge, lonely eyes out of his head.

Olivia shivered and rubbed her bare arms with her palms. Ryker grabbed the moss-green throw from the back of the reading chair near the fire and sat next to her on the couch, wrapping the blanket around her and rubbing her leanly muscled arms. It gave him an easy reason to touch her.

"*Merci*," she said softly.

"Where did you learn to speak French?"

"In school like everyone else. I started French in fourth grade, then took both French and Spanish since middle school."

"Are you fluent in both?"

"Yes. I love languages."

Public schools didn't double up on foreign languages and didn't start teaching foreign language that early. Private school meant money. Money she clearly didn't have any longer.

"Why do you dislike men so much?"

"I like men just fine."

He chuckled. "Earlier you said men can't be trusted. I think you boiled us down to leavers and liars. Dislike is a generous interpretation of what you said."

She lifted her head, meeting his gaze. The blanket slipped down her arm, revealing the tea with heavy cream color of her shoulders.

"I've never had a woman let me down. My mother was the most amazing, creative, loyal, loving person you could ever meet. My sister's heart is pure gold. Both of them would do anything to help someone in need."

Olivia's wide blue eyes swirled with emotion as she spoke. If he weren't careful, he'd fall into them and never get out.

"I guess the men in your life weren't cut from the same cloth?"

"You could say that."

"Tell me."

For a few minutes, the crackle of the fire and Olivia's soft breaths were the only sounds in the room, and when she finally spoke, her voice was quiet and tinged with sadness.

"It started with my father. My younger brother died in an accident. He was only four. My father ran into the house to get something, and my brother fell into the pool. By the time my dad figured out where he was, it was too late. It was...I don't even know how to describe it. He was this bright light in our lives, and then he was gone."

In that moment, Ryker would have done anything to take away the heartbreak in her voice. He reached under the blanket and squeezed her hand.

"Forget I asked. You don't have to tell me."

"It's OK. It's better to talk about it." Olivia blew out a steadying breath and continued, "My father couldn't forgive himself. He ended up committing suicide. It's horrible to say, but I feel like he took the easy way out. He left us alone in our pain and grief, living without both of them, struggling to make ends meet. My uncle offered to help with our finances and stole all our savings. We lost our house."

Ryker had heard too many sob stories over the years to believe everything he heard, but the pain in Olivia's voice was so intensely raw it was hard to hold on to his normal skepticism.

"That's terrible. How old were you?"

"I was eight when Thyme died. I don't know exactly when we lost the house, but I know it was before my tenth birthday. That was a pretty rough one, so I remember it."

Olivia shivered.

Ryker pulled the blanket tighter around her body and again rubbed her arms through the fluffy, nubby material.

"What happened on your birthday?"

"After we lost the house, we moved in with our neighbors across the street so my mom could save some money and get back on her feet. My mom was a dance teacher but got a secretarial job during the day and was teaching dance at night. She was so grateful to have a place to live and adults to watch us while she worked."

Olivia paused.

Ryker's heart pounded. Sweat beaded on his back. Dread slowed his blood. He knew this story was not going to end well.

"What happened?"

Olivia shook her head quickly. "I don't want to talk about it. They were not good people and are not worth my energy. The shit hit the fan on my tenth birthday, and we had to go to a women's shelter. My mom was so upset, but she still found a way to celebrate. I had cake and ice cream with a room full of women and children I'd never met before, but, somehow, it still felt special. My mom had a gift for making the best of every situation."

His mom hadn't been anything like that. Ryker's first birthday cake and gift had come the day he turned eighteen, and Christian had made them both with his own two hands. The cake from scratch and the ring in woodshop. Ryker rolled the ring around his finger with his thumb. He'd put it on that day and never taken it off.

"Is that a wooden ring?" Olivia asked.

"Yes. It was a gift from my little brother. He made it himself. When he gave it to me, he said he put all his love inside it when he was making it. It probably sounds crazy, but it's worth more to me than anything else I own."

Why am I telling her this? He never shared personal stories. He didn't want anyone really knowing him except Christian.

"It doesn't sound crazy at all."

"How long did you stay at the shelter?" he asked. Time to direct the conversation back to her.

"Not too long. My mom got a new job and met my stepfather. It was a whirlwind romance. In a few months, they got married and we moved in with him. For a while, things were good, but in the end, he was the worst of them all." Her voice lightened and lost its wistful tone. "And that, Ryker Madsen, is why I'm not willing to accept favors from any man, including you."

The pain emanating from Olivia was so strong, it was nearly palpable. His instinct was to do anything to ease it. Anything.

And that was a dangerous thought.

He dropped his hand from her arm. "It sounds like we both have good reasons to distrust the opposite sex."

"What do you mean?"

Ryker shifted on the couch, putting a few inches of distance between their bodies. He couldn't concentrate with her bare leg slowly burning a hole through his pants. "You've had your share of trouble with men, but in my opinion it's women who can't be trusted. I've met too many beguiling gold diggers to accept what any woman says at face value. In my experience, it's women who lie and scheme to get what they want."

"That's ridiculous," Olivia scoffed.

And just how would she explain Bethany and the rich witches who'd viewed him like a prized breeding stud?

"Ridiculous? Think about why you came here tonight. You know I desire you, and you're using that to help your friend. The cause may be noble, but to you I'm just a means to an end. Don't get me wrong, I don't mind it. I like that we've laid our cards on the table. It's when a woman pretends to feel something she doesn't that I hate. I have no tolerance for lies."

God help them both if Olivia was lying.

Chapter Seven

A sassy country singer's voice filled the air as Sage walked along the edge of the dance floor. She glanced in the mirror-covered wall, wondering where the hell she'd gotten the hot pink strapless leather dress she was wearing. It was an odd choice, but no stranger than the rest of the patrons. Everyone else in the club was dressed in jeans, button-up shirts, cowboy boots, and hats, but their clothes were all solid white.

Except Ryker.

Ryker's tall, broad-shouldered frame stood in stark contrast to the crowd. He wore dark jeans and an untucked black-on-black striped shirt with gray triangle buttons. Her thighs weakened at the unfettered lust blazing in his cool-blue eyes.

Sage reached out to stroke his chest but gripped empty space. Her second effort yielded the same result. Even though he stood motionless, each time she extended her arm he seemed farther away. It was so odd. No matter how many steps she took or how far she stretched, she couldn't make contact.

The music slowly shifted from fun to irritating. The intense need to make contact with Ryker was instinctive, almost primal, but the discordant notes interrupted her focus. An annoying twang punctuated every beat.

No. Not a twang.

A beep.

There was some weird, annoying beeping in the music.

Sage opened one eye. Reality hit. The beeping was her cellphone alarm. Her body went on autopilot, trying to grab the phone off her nightstand, except the phone wasn't there and neither was the nightstand.

Sage pushed herself up, blinking. A soft blanket slid down her shoulders, and cool air surrounded her bare arms. She glanced left, then right. Ebbing flames smoldered in the fireplace. Books lined the walls.

She was still in Ryker's library. She must have fallen asleep on the couch.

Shit!

She didn't remember falling asleep. Had she forgotten anything else? Sage pulled the blanket away from her body. She was fully dressed, including her shoes, and two glasses of wine weren't enough to cause blank spots in her memory. Relief and disappointment mixed.

It would've been nice if she'd gotten the sex out of the way in a tipsy haze. Per their arrangement, it was going to happen sometime, and fear of Ryker's disappointment over her lack of experience clung to her groggy mind like soggy clothes.

"Good morning. It's about time you woke up." Ryker strode into the room, looking the quintessential business tycoon in a charcoal suit, crisp white shirt, and dark tie.

The same stately butler who'd answered the door last night followed carrying a silver tray. He set the tray on the coffee table in front of her, gave her a quick wink and warm smile, and glided out of the room.

"Kenneth prepared coffee and breakfast for you. After you eat, we're going shopping," Ryker said.

Sage eyed the calorie-laden tray. The ballerina in her shuddered.

"I think Kenneth is sabotaging my waistline, and I can't go

shopping. I need to get home and check on Rosemary. She was sick yesterday."

Ryker pointed at the tray. "Eat. One scone isn't going to kill you. And you'll be home to your friend soon. We won't be long. If you want to shower, just call Kenneth. He can get you what you need. We'll leave in half an hour."

Sage sucked a long breath in through her nose and blew it out through her lips. She would not lose her temper.

"I told you. I can't go shopping. I need to get home to Rosemary. Plus..." She gestured toward her royal-blue minidress. "I can't go out dressed like this. What's the big rush?"

The muscle in the side of Ryker's jaw twitched, and he slowed his speech as if he were talking to a child. "The charity event is in two weeks. It's an awards banquet honoring a group of us who've helped establish local counseling and care centers for children of drug addicts. Andre DeMarco is one the people being recognized. He's a designer, and he offered to dress all the honorees and their dates. He's already designed my tuxedo. It would be rude not to allow him to provide your gown. We're short on time, so he wants us to come by this morning. Is that enough of an explanation for you?"

Sage bit her lip. She was worried about Rosemary, and the last thing she wanted to do was walk into a boutique looking like a hooker. She'd also been there a few times with her mother. What if Andre recognized her?

"So you're one of the people being honored?"

"I am. I provided the majority of the funding for the centers."

"And DeMarco designing my gown is part of our deal?"

"It is."

With the way she was repeating his words, Ryker was going to think she was a simpleton. There was no way around it. Going to the charity event was part of their business arrangement and so was the dress. As much as she loathed the idea, she'd just have to suck it up and go.

"Do you volunteer or only donate money?" she asked.

Ryker's left eyebrow lifted. "What do you mean?"

"The counseling centers. You said you funded them. I want to know if you volunteer your time or just donate money."

Some part of her needed to understand this man. To know what really motivated him.

"I don't know why it's relevant, but I provide the funding. I don't have time to volunteer. My business takes all my time."

It was dangerous to push him, but as usual, she couldn't keep her mouth shut.

"Hmm. Do you think you're too good to rub elbows with the lower classes?"

Ryker's eyes flashed like diamonds. "I don't have time for this. Eat and get ready to go."

Ohhh. She'd hit a nerve. She lifted her hand in a mock salute.

"Yes, sir."

Sage ignored the food and spent her time texting and showering. Rosemary was feeling better, and Justin was going to deal with getting her tires fixed. She'd have to work an extra shift to cover the cost. Maybe two. It sucked, but moaning about it wouldn't help.

Sage studied her reflection in the bathroom mirror. There was nothing she could do about the too-short dress and too-high heels, but with a fresh face, her wet hair braided, and bare shoulders covered by the blue-checkered dress shirt Kenneth had kindly loaned her, she felt presentable.

She wandered out of the guest bathroom and headed toward the library. The hallway was lined with color sketches of Boathouse Row, Elfreth's Alley, Rittenhouse Square, and other familiar Philadelphia landmarks. One sketch depicted a sunny graveyard. Graveyards shouldn't be welcoming, but this one was. She leaned in closer. It was so familiar, but she just couldn't place it.

Still trying to place the scene, Sage turned and...*thump*! She walked straight into a tall, lean, bob-haired blonde in a sleek black suit. Sage recognized her immediately. It was the lawyer from Ryker's office.

The office where he'd kissed her, touched her in ways she hadn't even known she wanted, and left her wet and wanting.

"I'm sorry," she apologized as she crouched down and gathered the papers she'd knocked from the blonde's hand. "You're Veronica, right?"

Sage resisted the urge to tug down the hem of her dress as she handed over the documents and extended her hand. "I'm Olivia. Olivia Dupree."

Veronica ignored the proffered handshake, crossed her arms, and glowered. Literally glowered.

"I don't know what you're doing here, but you need to leave, and you need to find a back way to exit this building. If you can't, you better not tell anyone whose apartment you're coming from. I don't want anyone associating Ryker with a goddamn street whore." Spit flew from Veronica's mouth as she spoke.

Street whore?

Sage imagined kicking Little Miss Better Than Everybody Else in the shins. Women were supposed to stick together and support each other, not attack each other. As a woman in a businessman's world, Veronica should know that, but it seemed like she'd missed that memo.

Before she could respond, Ryker's voice filled the hallway. "Good morning, Veronica. I see you've met Olivia."

His tall, muscled body leaned lazily against the library doorjamb. His posture appeared relaxed, but his glare could have frozen lava.

The ice in his eyes did nothing to cool Veronica's anger. "Ryker! What are you thinking? How could you bring a prostitute into your house? Anyone could see her coming or going. Have you lost your mind?"

"No, Veronica. I think you're the one who's lost her mind." Ryker pushed away from the door and stalked toward them. "Sage is not a prostitute. She's my date, and, in case you've forgotten, you're my lawyer. For business matters only. I don't need or want your advice on my personal life. Yesterday you barged into my office without knocking, and today you insult a guest in my home. I won't tolerate it. If you can't behave professionally, I'll call the firm and ask that a new partner be assigned to my matters."

Veronica's already pale skin turned ghostly. "You wouldn't."

"I would. Leave the documents on the table by the door and let yourself out. I'll call you later."

The slam of the front door vibrated up Sage's legs into her ribs. Shock left her speechless.

Ryker had defended her.

It was the last thing she expected, and it was the last thing she wanted. She didn't want him to be the good guy, the hero riding to the rescue. The problem with knights in shining armor was the overwhelming disappointment that hit when they fell off their horses.

Been there, done that.

Still, he'd stuck up for her. She should probably say something.

"I appreciate you defending me. Thank you."

Not exactly the speech of the year, but it would do.

Ryker shrugged. "Don't thank me. I put you in a bad position. I had a couple of issues come up on a project and had to push some conference calls to squeeze in getting to Andre's this morning. I was in a hurry. I should have been more sensitive when you said you were uncomfortable going out in your"—he waved a strong, tan hand toward her dress—"evening wear. If you'd like to go home and change, I'm sure Andre could see you later today. I just can't go with you then. I'll give you cab money."

"I don't need cab money. My car should be fixed by this afternoon. I can drive to the boutique."

"What's wrong with your car?"

"Some jerk slashed my tires. All four of them. Right in the club parking lot. Bryce says we'd have it on video, but all the cameras are broken."

Ryker crossed his arms over his chest, tightening the expensive material of his suit coat across his broad shoulders. Instead of hiding his amazing physique, his suit accentuated it. And the way his wide chest narrowed to a trim waist and strong legs made her mouth dry. His strong jaw and cheekbones together with the hard glint in his eye and twitching muscle in his jaw intensified his rugged, Viking look.

He was too handsome. Distractingly handsome. Dangerously handsome. Especially with his face frosted. Even in the suit, he looked ready for a street fight, and for some bizarre reason, that was hot as hell.

He was staring at her. She'd been drifting. Hopefully, her wayward thoughts didn't show on her face. They were certainly impacting other parts of her body.

"Did you say something?" she asked.

Ryker quirked an eyebrow. "I said it's an interesting coincidence."

"What is?"

"That all the cameras were broken, and the very next day your tires were slashed. It could have been the same person. Someone could be targeting you."

What if Davis had found her?

Her stomach flipped, then flopped.

He couldn't have. She and Rosemary had been so careful. Plus, slashing tires didn't seem like his style.

"I don't think so. Kids probably broke the cameras, and the tire slasher was probably a disgruntled patron. You know how those guys get sometimes."

"I do know, and I won't allow that bullshit at my club. I already filed a police report regarding the cameras. I'll do the same with respect to your car, and I'll pay for the repairs."

She didn't want his pity or his charity. Any ties outside the clear, defined lines of their business arrangement were potential complications.

"That's not necessary."

Ryker's eyes narrowed, and the frost level increased a few notches. "Your car was damaged on my property during working hours. I'll compensate you as I would any other employee. And just so we're on the same page, you're going to have to miss work over the next few weeks to keep up your side of our bargain. I intend on paying you what you would have made during those shifts."

Sage rubbed her bottom lip against her teeth. She hated the idea of taking cash from Ryker. She wasn't kidding herself. She knew she was selling herself, but accepting cash made it feel different. It felt off. Wrong. Sleazy.

"I don't want your money."

"I don't care if you want it. You're getting it. Let's just say we're finalizing the fine print of our contract."

Ryker's unyielding tone made it clear he wasn't going to change his mind.

Sometimes you had to lose a battle to win a war.

"Fine, but this is it. No more additions. No more fine print. No gifts, no money, no anything. I know what you're trying to do, and it won't work."

No way was Ryker going to make her dependent on him. It was the same crap Davis had pulled with her mom. A knife wrapped in silk, ribbons, and bows.

"What am I trying to do?"

"Make me feel obligated. Beholden to you. I won't put my livelihood in anyone else's hands. I take care of myself."

Ryker tipped her chin up with his finger and lowered his mouth within a millimeter of hers. His crisp, minty scent enveloped her.

"And I take care of myself. I guess we make a perfect pair."

Chapter Eight

Ryker couldn't wait to get to the Black Cat, but it was only mid-afternoon. The sun was moving across the sky like molasses. He had a heinous amount of work to do and was meeting Veronica to go over an agreement of sale at six. That meant the earliest he'd get to the club was eight—just in time for Olivia to start her shift.

He'd thought about offering her a lift. How someone chose to live spoke volumes about them. He burned to know everything about her. And that was exactly why he didn't extend the offer.

Curiosity had killed the cat. He wasn't about to get knocked off his feet by a curvy, dark-haired kitten no matter how many times she danced through his mind, distracting him from his work.

Just like she was doing right now.

He was thinking about her only because he hadn't seen her in a while. He'd spent the last week in San Francisco dealing with bullshit his construction manager should have handled weeks ago. Now the project was back on track, and he had a new construction manager, but his lust had grown exponentially while he was gone. He wasn't sure if absence made the heart grow fonder, but it sure as hell made his dick more demanding.

In his fantasies, Olivia danced only for him, sheltered from greedy, lascivious eyes. His jealousy was ridiculous. He owned the club, for God's sake. Dancing was her job. The whole point was for her to use her body to entice men to spend money. It was basic capitalism. He should be thrilled she was so popular.

Instead, it was slowly driving him mad.

That sense of ownership was dangerous. His brain knew that, so he tried not to think of Olivia, but some deeper, fundamental instinct kept pushing images of her into his mind. When the fantasies hit, it was better to just let them play themselves out.

Ryker closed his eyes and leaned his head back against the top of the cushioned leather office chair. He'd read the same paragraph three times and hadn't absorbed a word. He gave up trying to focus and let imagination consume him.

Olivia was clad in the same black dress and made-for-sex heels she'd worn at open auditions, but this time it was just the two of them, and the stage was the Oriental carpet in his library. The firelight cast a soft light on her skin. Her glorious hair fell in tousled waves down her back and shoulders. She sauntered over to him and slid onto his lap, hanging her legs over the arms of the chair. Her long fingernails dug into his skin as she gripped his shoulders and arched her back, sliding her core along his throbbing length. He slid his hand up her warm, silky thigh, desperate to feel her slick, wet heat on his fingers.

A quick rap on the door sent him careening back to the present. The fantasy was gone, but it would take his body a few minutes to catch up.

His assistant cracked the door and peeked in.

He managed to keep his voice businesslike despite the distraction in his pants. "Yes, Mary?"

"Veronica Huntly is here. I saw you weren't on the phone, so I told her I'd check to see if you had time to see her."

He didn't want to see Veronica right now, especially since he couldn't stand to greet her. He'd rather let his mind wander back to

Olivia, which was why he told Mary to send Veronica in. Letting some dark-haired siren prevent him from doing his job was weak and stupid. He'd never let his intimate desires interfere with business before. He wasn't about to start now.

Veronica settled gracefully in one of the guest chairs across from his desk, but shifted, crossing and uncrossing her legs and tugging the hem of her dress toward her knees. She was three hours early for their meeting and obviously had something on her mind. She wanted him to talk, to ask her why she'd come.

He waited.

Finally, she broke, her words rushing like rapids. "I couldn't wait anymore. I called you while you were away but didn't hear back from you. I know you were busy, that the job in San Francisco is behind. I'm sure you know I was assigned to review the construction manager's contract to make sure there weren't any issues before you fired him."

"Yes, I know. I got your email. Thank you for the quick and thorough summary."

Veronica lifted a too-slender arm and smoothed her already perfect blonde hair. "That's not why I'm here. I didn't come to talk about the contract. I came to apologize. I feel horrible about what happened the other day at your apartment. I know I was out of line, but you're not just my client, you're my friend."

He cut her off. "I don't need any more friends."

"I know you don't need my help. My point is that I care about you the way I care about a friend, so I feel protective of you. Clearly, I misread the situation. I want you to be happy. I'm sure your girlfriend... what was her name?"

Ryker didn't want to tell Veronica anything about Olivia, not even her name. That spoke volumes about the impact Olivia was having on him. Veronica worked hard for him. She was a great negotiator, and she always pushed hard for what was best for him on every deal she worked on. Olivia was scrambling his thoughts and emotions, making him irritable and illogical.

"Her name's Olivia Dupree, and she's not my girlfriend."

Veronica lifted her gaze but continued to pull at the hem of her dress. "It's not my business whether she's your girlfriend or not. Your personal decisions are private. It was wrong of me to confront her. We went on that one date, and I allowed it to affect our working relationship."

He never should have taken Veronica to that dinner. The woman he'd planned on taking had come down with the flu. He should've gone alone, but Veronica was at his office, so she was a quick and easy fill-in. Now he was paying the price for taking the easy route.

"It's going to be hard to work together if you have feelings for me."

Veronica shook her head. "I don't. Not like that. I know I seem jealous, but I'm not."

He raised an eyebrow, and she laughed in an easy, relaxed, friendly way.

"I'm not jealous. Really. I'm just worried about you. Ever since you bought that club, it's been consuming you. You haven't been yourself, but I haven't been myself either. My behavior's been unprofessional. It came from a place of friendly concern, but I was still out of line. That's why I came here today. To apologize."

Veronica stood and picked up her purse. "I understand if you don't want to work with me any longer. I'll make sure whoever's assigned as my replacement is fully up to speed. It's been an honor working for you."

An odd, hollow feeling squeezed his gut.

It was shame.

Veronica was damn good at her job. He was difficult. Tough, demanding, inpatient. She didn't sugarcoat the truth and wasn't afraid to tell him when he was wrong. She'd been trying to tell him the truth as she saw it, and instead of respecting her for it, he'd damn near fired her.

Her assessment was dead-on. From a profit perspective, he'd been giving the club way more attention than it needed. Profit was always the driving force of his decisions. Flipping the club was the best business decision. He'd make money on a long-term hold, but it wasn't worth the loss of time he could give to other projects or the risk to his reputation and professional contacts.

Veronica had tried to tell him that when he first took over the club, but he hadn't listened. Hadn't wanted to hear it. There was something magnetic about the Black Cat. Something that made him stray from his standard business approach. Something that had him substituting emotion for reason.

Realization hit, hard and unsettling. The real estate, the drug companies, the money, the success. It wasn't enough. He felt empty. Lost. Purposeless.

He'd bought the Black Cat to fill a void.

What the hell was he missing, and did he really expect to find it at a strip club?

The sound of his office door opening interrupted his racing thoughts. Veronica was leaving.

"Wait. Please. Sit back down."

Veronica returned to the guest chair.

He wanted to talk to her about this. He needed a disinterested perspective, and who better to give it than a lawyer?

"You're right. I am wrapped up in the Black Cat. There's something about that club that compels me. I don't know what it is."

"I think it's a who, not a what, and I met her last Thursday morning," Veronica teased.

Ryker relaxed a bit. This easy banter was good. It was how they'd been before the whole date fiasco, colleagues with a hint of friendship. That was the type of relationship he was comfortable with. He didn't want or need anything else.

Not from Veronica or Olivia or anyone else.

Except his brother. His love for Christian was like an eternal tsunami. Fierce, forceful, and never-ending.

Ryker picked up the framed picture of his brother from his desk.

"How's Christian doing at Georgetown?" Veronica asked. "I hear the MBA program there is really challenging. I was a little surprised when you told me he was going. I thought he was into the whole computers, cybersecurity thing."

Ryker's lungs filled with pride and loneliness. "The computers are more of a hobby. He wants to go into real estate, like me. He said he loves Georgetown, but I still wish he'd stayed at Penn. I miss him."

Some people would think D.C. was close to Philly, but two and half hours meant no dinners together, no early morning runs on Kelly Drive, no impromptu trips to the shore. He hadn't even gotten down to visit yet. Christian kept saying he was too busy. He hated the idea of his baby brother so damn far away.

What if something happened?

He didn't give a shit that his brother was twenty-three. To him, Christian was the little kid gripping his hand in fear as they ran from the store after Ryker shoplifted their dinner, the kid he'd taken jujitsu classes for so he could defend him in the streets of West Philly, the kid he'd bought a secondhand gun to protect after they'd gotten mugged walking to school.

No matter how grown-up Christian became, Ryker could only see a dirty-faced, scuffed-kneed, floppy-haired, smiling baby brother. Maybe his obsession with the club was his subconscious trying to fill the yawning gap of Christian's absence.

Relief flowed at the logical explanation.

He just needed to get used to Christian being away. Then his crazy preoccupation with Olivia and the club would disappear, and his life would go back to normal.

In the interim, he couldn't have Veronica or anyone else thinking a woman was impacting his business decisions, particularly when that woman was a stripper.

"You're wrong, Veronica. Olivia isn't the reason I'm so wrapped up in the club. I think I'm just enjoying the challenge of something new. The Black Cat is different than anything I've done before. It's been refreshing, but you're right. It's taking too much time away from my other projects. I'll get the club stabilized in a few weeks and sell it."

"Whatever you think is best. I'm done sticking my nose into your personal business." She pulled a stack of papers from her briefcase. "Since I'm here, do you have time to go over the comments we received on the agreement of sale for the hotel? I'd really like to get a redraft out before the end of the day."

"You only have a couple of hours left," Ryker said.

Veronica lifted her slender wrist and eyed a nonexistent timepiece. "Not by my watch. Nine-to-five is a thing of the past. End of day nowadays is midnight. I've got lots of time to work, old man."

Ryker felt the edges of his mouth turn up. They had an age difference of one month to the day. He relaxed his shoulders and bent over the documents. The tension of craving Olivia and fighting to control his ridiculous, animalistic jealousy faded as they got to work. This was what he knew. This was where he was comfortable.

This was his home, not the Black Cat.

* * *

"For the thousandth time, you are *not* coming in with me!" Sage slammed her hand on the steering wheel, stinging her palm. "I could've been in and out of the house in the fifteen minutes you've been arguing with me!"

"And if you'd just let me come in with you, we wouldn't have spent fifteen minutes arguing," Rosemary shouted.

Sage fought for patience as her silver Mazda idled in the semi-circular driveway in front of Davis's house. She wished she'd never told Rosemary about her clothes retrieval mission. If she hadn't, Rosemary wouldn't have insisted on coming along, and they wouldn't be in this predicament.

"Oh no you don't!" Rosemary huffed. "I know you, Sage Cashman! You're sitting there thinking you should have lied to keep me home. Sisters don't lie to each other!"

Sisters did lie to each other, especially when one of their lives was on the line, but she couldn't tell Rosemary that. If Rosemary knew how Sage had gotten her access to Remiza, she'd quit it faster than Sage could pole-spin, which proved her silent point. Sometimes sisters had no choice but to lie to each other.

But Sage remained quiet, and Rosemary softened just like Sage knew she would. Rosemary hated confrontation. She was a natural peacemaker.

Rosemary twisted her hands in her lap. "I don't like any of this. The whole thing seems fishy. The owner of Origin pushes through my Right to Try request just because you ask him to, and now you're going to a wedding with him just as—" Rosemary made air quotes with her fingers. "—friends? I don't buy it. I'm afraid this guy has ulterior motives."

Rosemary would lose her mind if she found out how close she was to the truth, that Sage was the one forcing Ryker to follow through on his ulterior motives.

"That's my line," Sage said. "I'm usually the one warning you about being too trusting."

"It just seems too good to be true."

"We've had a string of bad luck. Losing Mom. Davis kicking us out. Your cancer coming back. Missing the deadline for the Remiza trial. You put tons of positive energy into the world, Rosemary. I think some of it's finally found its way back to you."

Rosemary visibly relaxed. Sage knew she would. Rosemary and Mom had always put a ton of faith in karma. Sage didn't buy into the whole positive energy nonsense. She was more of a survival of the fittest kind of girl, and there was no way Rosemary wasn't surviving on her watch.

"Maybe you're right, but I still don't like the idea of you going into that house alone."

"I don't like it either, but I have no choice. I need clothes for this wedding. It's a whole weekend shindig, and all I've got is my casual stuff and my work clothes. I don't think sweats and rip-away dresses are going to cut it. Money's too tight to waste it buying new things when I have a whole wardrobe sitting right through that door." Sage pointed toward the house. "I'll be out in five minutes. You can be my lookout. Switch into the driver's seat so we can get out of here fast."

Before Rosemary could argue further, Sage jumped out of the car and dashed away. The front door was always locked, but the side door was usually open. She still had her keys, but, knowing Davis, he'd probably changed the locks, so the side door was the best bet.

She paused at the familiar white door and blew out a long, calming breath. There was nothing to be afraid of. Davis was a creature of habit, and Thursdays were racquetball days, followed by drinks and dinner at the club. He'd be out for hours. There was no chance she'd run into him. Still, her hand shook a bit as she turned the doorknob.

Sage eased the door open and tiptoed through the mudroom into the kitchen. The savory smell of cooking onions and garlic filled her nose. Rosa stood at the stove, stirring a large, gleaming pot. One of the wide-plank floorboards creaked as Sage crept toward the back stairs. Rosa whirled around and yelped, pressing her hand to her chest.

Sage stared into Rosa's warm, brown eyes. She lifted a finger and pressed it to her lips. Rosa frowned, her face a mix of nerves and disapproval.

Sage pointed toward the stairs and whispered, "Two minutes. I need two minutes."

"I'm not saying anything and I'm not seeing anything. Just hurry up." Rosa turned back to the stove, muttering to herself, and continued stirring the pot.

Sage wanted to hug Rosa, chat, catch up, help her bake a cake, but she couldn't do any of those things. It wouldn't be fair. Time was too short, and Rosa was just as afraid as she was. With one last glance at Rosa's strong shoulders and gleaming black hair, she hurried toward the kitchen staircase. The bounce of the narrow hardwood steps was familiar under her feet. After years of hide-and-seek, Sage dodged the creaky steps by habit. At the top of the stairwell, she raced down the hall to her bedroom.

The room looked like it hadn't been touched since the day she'd left. Makeup was strewn on her dressing table. *The God of Small Things* lay facedown on her nightstand, marking her page. Her toe shoes were still on her bed next to her sewing kit. She grabbed the shoes and clutched them to her chest, wanting nothing more than to slip them on and lose herself in her standard practice routine. She hadn't come for her shoes, but there was no way she was leaving them behind.

She grabbed the leather knapsack she used as a dance bag from the closet floor and shoved the shoes inside, then pulled an oversized Vera Bradley tote from the top shelf. She'd done a mental rundown of what she'd need for the weekend and knew exactly what she wanted: her go-to LBD, her nude ankle-strap Louboutins, her Burberry jeans, the white fitted blouse that looked adorable under her caramel-colored, butter-soft leather jacket, her wear-anywhere black dress pants, chocolate knee-high leather boots, black flats, a couple of casual dresses, and a few chunky sweaters. Since her room hadn't been touched, the clothes were easy to find.

Just as she tucked the last sweater into her bag, the familiar cadence of Rosa's voice echoed up the stairs. The words were too muted to understand, but Rosa didn't usually talk to herself. Sage's heart rate spiked when a deep, male voice answered.

Shit.

Sage didn't know who Rosa was talking to, but chances were it was Davis. It was time to get the hell out of here. She just needed to grab her mother's jewelry. Not the expensive jewels Davis had given Mom. He could do whatever the hell he wanted with those. She wanted the family jewelry her mother had brought into the marriage. Things like her grandmother's wedding ring and rosary and the pearls her mom had bought herself with her first real paycheck. The family jewelry might not be worth a lot, but to her it was priceless. If she didn't get it now, there might not be another chance.

Her heart pounded, and despite the chill in the house, her skin felt hot and clammy. The master bedroom was down the long hallway on the other side of the front staircase. She made a run for it. When she pushed the door open, her breath fled her body. She gulped air, but her lungs wouldn't fill.

This wasn't her mother's bedroom.

It was a stranger's room.

The antique, mahogany four-poster bed with pineapple finials and rich purple bedding was gone, replaced with pine-colored, ultra-modern bed and dressers. Cold, hard tile that masqueraded as hardwood covered the floor where the lush, cozy carpet had been. Every bit of warmth and charm, every bit of her mother, had been stripped from the room.

The violation was too much to bear, but she couldn't let herself think about that now. She had to find that jewelry before Davis found her.

She scanned the room. Everything was designer-perfect except the worn, cardboard file box sitting in one corner of the room. "Caroline" was printed neatly on the lid in faded black Sharpie in her mother's own hand. She'd recognize those looping, curling letters anywhere. Maybe the jewelry was in the box.

She hustled over and hefted it up. It was heavier than it looked. As she stood, her gaze flicked toward the master bath, and an image filled her vision, freezing her in place.

It was her mother, naked in the tub, blood flowing from her head, turning the water in the gleaming white bath a sickly pink.

Although she hadn't actually seen her mother in the bathroom, Rosemary's descriptions had been so vivid that she'd developed a clear picture in her mind. They talked about that horrible day late at night when Sage woke Rosemary from her nightmares.

Why did all the terrible things happen to Rosemary?

Her sweet, gentle sister had pulled their mother from the tub. Rosemary had been the one to call 911. She'd been the one pushing warm hands into cold, wet skin, fighting to force life back into a lifeless body. The chest compressions had broken their mother's ribs, but it hadn't been enough.

Sage would never forgive Davis for that.

Her chest ached and her eyes burned. She had to get out of this bedroom. Out of the house. Away from imagination and memory. Yet she forced herself to walk out of the room when her soul was screaming to run.

The voices were getting closer, coming up the back stairs. Rosa's voice was high and fast, and she kept breaking into Spanish, which was her habit when she was nervous or excited.

Sage quickened her pace, wincing at the thud of her sneakers on the grand staircase.

Rosa was a good woman. Whoever was in the house, the cook would try to slow them down.

Sage methodically unlatched the front door chain and turned the lock. She'd waste time fumbling with the locks if she rushed. When she pulled the door open, welcome brisk air filled her aching lungs.

The battered Mazda idled a few hundred feet away. Rosemary was half-hanging out the driver's side window. Her sister's relieved smile was quickly replaced with a look of sheer panic. Rosemary shouted a warning and waved frantically.

Sage started to run, the cobblestone driveway hard and uneven under her already sore feet.

Footsteps pounded behind her.

Just as her fingertips grazed the ice-cold metal of the door handle, a hard hand circled her arm, pulling her away from the car.

Sage lunged to the side, dropping the box and her backpack. Instinct kicked in, and she settled into a defensive side stance. The heavy, brassy scent of Davis's cologne was unmistakable.

"What the hell are you doing in my house?"

His face was ruddy red, and his eyes were blazing. He'd been drinking. His breath had the same sweet liquor smell the night he'd grabbed her by the hair and physically thrown her out of the house. The night he'd told her if she and Rosemary didn't play by his rules, they'd end up like their mother.

That had been months ago, but the memory was still sharp and cutting.

"Davis, you need to calm down."

His face progressed from red to purple, and his hands clenched into tight fists. "Don't tell me what to do. You're trespassing. I should have you arrested."

Her mind raced. Davis was still under investigation for murder. Did he have the balls to call the cops? Was he so drunk he wasn't thinking straight? The last thing she needed was to miss the wedding because she was locked up for breaking and entering.

The temperature was below freezing, but her armpits grew damp.

Adrenaline sweat.

"I'm not trying to tell you what to do. I just needed a few things from the house. My things. Things Mom bought for me or that I bought and paid for myself. I didn't touch anything of yours. Please just let me leave in peace."

She spoke in her most calming voice, but Davis lunged for her, squeezing both her arms this time. His eyes were wild and unfocused. His fingers dug deep into her soft flesh, and he shook her hard, rattling her teeth in her skull.

"You're ruining my life with your stupid accusations. You need to stay here. Stay here and fix this."

How had the kind, gentle man her mother married turn into this?

The change had been gradual over the years. Davis's business ventures were hit-and-miss, and the misses stressed him out, so he'd have a few drinks now and then to help him relax. Now and then turned into a few nights a week, and a few nights a week turned into every day. Her mom thought it was too often and too much. The drinking turned into arguments, the arguments into cheating, and the cheating into more arguments. The more they fought, the more Davis drank. It had been a vicious, slippery slope of a cycle. Her mother's death had sent him careening over the edge.

Maybe because his guilt is driving him mad.

Now wasn't the time to think about her mother. She needed to get Rosemary out of here and home safe, and Davis's fingers were bruising her arms.

"Let go of me. You're drunk," she ordered in her most no-nonsense tone.

"If I let you leave, you'll just hide from me again. If you move back home, the police won't believe your crazy lies. They'll leave me alone."

"Davis, let her go!" Rosemary yelled from the car.

His hands relaxed a bit.

Sage used the distraction to yank one arm free. She stepped back and threw a basic front kick, connecting with his solar plexus. She was a little rusty, but she hadn't completely lost the muscle memory of six years of kickboxing.

While Davis lay on the ground, clutching his abdomen, Sage heaved the box and her bags into the back, then jumped into the Mazda's passenger seat. Rosemary was halfway down the driveway before she even pulled the door shut.

Rosemary hunched over the steering wheel, driving with clenched white fingers.

"I'm so sorry. I didn't see him. I would have called your cell if I'd seen him go into the house." Rosemary's voice shook, and she was breathing too fast.

"It's OK. It's not your fault." Sage tried to slow her own racing heart. "He came in the side door. He must have come up the driveway from the opposite direction and pulled down by the garage."

"Did he hurt you?" Rosemary asked.

"No. No. I'm fine," she lied.

The bruises on her arms would heal soon enough, but her heart never would. In the beginning Davis had been so good to them, playing games with them, splashing in the pool, nudging their fruit-and-veggie-loving mother to give them a second serving of dessert. Davis had been as much of a father as her real dad.

"Why does he have to be like that?" Rosemary asked. "I don't understand. I thought he loved us!"

Sage didn't know how to answer, and even if she did, she didn't know if she could find the strength to. The adrenaline rush had faded, and exhaustion turned her bones to lead. Being in her mom's room, being attacked by her own stepfather, fighting for clothes to wear so she could have sex with a stranger to save her sister's life. It was like Frodo and the ring, fighting like hell to carry something she knew was probably going to destroy her, but doing it because she was the only person who could.

Chapter Nine

"Dead squirrels? What the hell is going on around here?"

Bryce shrugged his wide shoulders. "Beats me, but it's pretty messed up."

Ryker gripped his hair in his hand. Bryce had to be pulling his leg. "This is a joke, right?"

"I wish it was."

Ryker sighed. What else could go wrong today? The new general contractor on the San Fran project had a ruptured appendix and was going to be in the hospital for a week. An inspector in Houston was holding up their occupancy cert on a bullshit technicality. The bank was playing hardball on the subordination agreement on the hotel project with Anderson. They had to leave for the wedding in half an hour, and there were dead squirrels in the Black Cat dressing room.

"Give me the details one more time," Ryker said. "The girls were talking so fast I couldn't follow what they were saying."

Bryce leaned back in the chair across from Ryker's desk in the club office.

"Carla and Anise got here around 10:45 for the dayshift. They came in together like they usually do. When they walked into the dressing room, they saw a bunch of dead animals hanging from the mirrors, dripping blood. You know Bobby, the cook?"

Ryker nodded.

"Well, Bobby was doing prep in the kitchen. He heard them screaming like banshees and went to check it out. He's the one who called me. I got here, left that message for you, took some pictures, and cleaned up the mess. The girls were losing their minds. I couldn't leave it like that." Bryce nodded to a black trash bag in the corner of the office. "The squirrels are in that bag. All except the one in the locker. I thought you might want to see that, so I just shut the locker door."

Ryker cursed under his breath. If he and Bryce had connected earlier, he would've told him to leave everything as is until the police arrived, but he'd been on conference calls.

Bryce frowned. "Did I make the wrong choice? The girls were freaking out. If I left bloody animals hanging around, no one was going to get any work done."

Ryker shook his head. "You did great. I delayed in calling you back, and you had to make a decision. I respect that. How long did the police say it would take for someone to arrive?"

Bryce glanced up at the wall clock in the office. "The cops said forty-five minutes and that was two hours ago."

Of course. Because that was the way his day was going.

"Show me the locker while we wait for them to get here," Ryker said.

A couple of the dayshift dancers were in the dressing room, fixing makeup and changing clothes. The rest were already out in the club.

Ryker gave the ladies a quick nod as he and Bryce approached the bank of lockers. A large-font sign printed on standard letter-size copy paper hung on the outside of the locker door:

LEAVE AND NEVER COME BACK
OR YOU'LL REGRET IT!

Ryker ran a hand down his face, calluses rubbing his ever-present five o'clock shadow. He was too damn tired to deal with this shit. He'd slept fitfully last night while Olivia danced through his dreams. The third time he'd woken up edgy and hard, he'd taken matters into his own hand. Literally. But it hadn't helped. His body was still ready and aching for her.

He glanced at his watch. She'd be here any minute, and they could get on the road to the wedding. She'd be his and his alone for the entire weekend. No work, no distractions, no sharing her with the leering eyes of the Black Cat patrons.

He just needed to get this mess sorted out first.

"That sign was here this morning?" he asked Bryce.

"Yep. I didn't touch the sign. Do you want me to open the locker now?"

Ryker nodded, and Bryce used the bottom of a pen to enter the master combination into the electronic lock. There'd been so many people in and out, preserving prints was probably useless, but Ryker didn't want to risk Bryce further contaminating the scene.

Once the locker popped, Ryker took the pen from Bryce and used it to push open the door. A squirrel hung by its neck on a rope affixed to a hook at the top of the locker. A long cut extended from its neck to the bottom of its stomach. Entrails spilled from slashed fur. Blood pooled on the locker's only contents, a pair of black platform stilettos with royal-blue ankle straps.

The shoes Olivia wore in every single one of his fantasies.

His already simmering anger popped and flashed. His club. His woman. A stranger had violated both.

Ryker leaned in for a closer look, and a fetid smell assaulted his nostrils.

"Pretty rank, isn't it?" Bryce waved a hand in front of his face. "That's why I shut the door."

"So the door was open when Carla and Anise arrived?" Ryker asked.

"That's what they said, but it seems strange to me."

"Why's that?"

"This one's Olivia's locker. I've got a master code, and each girl sets her own combination. No one should be able to get in there except Olivia and me. Sometimes the girls will tell each other their codes, but Olivia is very private. I don't think she'd share her combination with anyone."

"I certainly would not! Why are you two in my locker?" Olivia strode across the dressing room, pushing past Bryce. She gasped and lifted a hand to her mouth. "What...what...what the hell is that?"

Ryker didn't respond. He was too busy watching Olivia. If he'd been a cartoon character, his jaw would have hit the actual floor. She wore crisp, fitted, dark-wash jeans and a cream-colored cashmere sweater. Her leather boots were knee-high and a brand sold only in boutiques. Her light brown leather jacket was the same. She looked like a movie star in one of those candid shots on a magazine cover where the photographer caught the celebrity crossing the street with a coffee in hand.

Where had she gotten the cash for clothes like that?

Several answers filled his mind and too many of them involved other men. His gut clenched. She'd told him she wasn't an escort.

Was she lying? What game was she playing? If no one had her locker combination, how had someone gotten inside? Could she have orchestrated the whole squirrel thing? Was it part of some master plot to play on his sympathies, to make him worry for her? To suck him in just like Bethany had?

Could seemingly sweet Olivia be that sinister and calculating?

His hands were shaking. He couldn't think clearly.

Veronica was right. Emotion was consuming him, and the last time he'd given in to emotion, Bethany had nearly destroyed him.

He needed distance.

He kept his voice neutral as he answered Olivia's questions. "It's a squirrel. A dead one."

She scowled. "The dead part is pretty obvious. How did it get in there?"

"Did you give anyone your combination?"

"Of course not!"

"Did you put it there?"

"Have you lost your goddamn mind?"

His gut twisted again over her shocked, pained expression, but he had to press her. He had to know the truth.

"If you didn't tell anyone your locker combination, how did someone get inside?"

"How on earth am I supposed to know the answer to that?" Her sinful, husky voice was indignant. "And why does it sound like you're accusing me?"

"Maybe you have a guilty conscience."

Olivia stepped toward him, and a mix of lavender and vanilla enveloped him. His blood flowed hot and fast. It was insanity. Even angry and suspicious, standing in front of a mess of blood and gore, his body reacted to her.

She slid slim, firm fingers over his shoulder and rose onto her tiptoes. Warm breath grazed his ear.

"I don't know what bee's flown up your bottom, but you're making a scene. Do you really want to get into an argument in the middle of this dressing room with everyone watching? If you don't want to take me to the wedding, that's fine, but I'm here and ready to go, holding up my side of bargain, so you better damn well hold up yours."

Ryker glanced around the dressing room. Olivia was right. He was making a scene. The other dancers were staring. The smart thing to do would be to tell her to go home. She was already too deep under his skin, impairing his thought processes, making him frustrated and irritable. He'd already told the trial team to push through Rosemary's Right to Try petition as quicky as they could. He should walk away from Olivia, sell the club and never see her again. He'd keep his word and maybe keep his sanity.

But then he'd never get her out of his head.

He stepped back, resisting the urge to slide one of her silky curls through his fingers, and nodded toward the side exit door. Once they'd left the club, Ryker transferred Olivia's bags from her clunky Mazda to his sleek black Audi, then they climbed into the car without speaking. There was construction on 95, so the trip to Lambertville would take about an hour, which was a good thing. It would give him some time to think.

* * *

When they were young, Rosemary always won the quiet game. Sage never wanted to waste time being quiet when there were so many amazing things to talk about. Now she was older and wiser. Loose lips didn't just sink ships. They could cause a hell of lot more damage.

Still, silence wasn't always the best option. They were almost to the hotel, and neither of them had spoken a word. Ryker sat in the driver's seat, eyes forward, as if he were navigating a treacherous, ice-covered mountain road at midnight instead of a generic highway on a clear Friday afternoon.

She was already dying of nerves, and the thought of being intimate when they were barely speaking to each other was unbearable. He was a complete asshat for accusing her of hanging a dead animal in her own locker, but he was the asshat she was going to have sex with. So she'd be the better person. She'd swallow her pride and break the silence.

"Have you been to Lambertville before?" That seemed like a safe enough question.

"Yes."

"When was your last trip?"

"Six months ago."

"I love Karla's in New Hope. It's one of my favorite restaurants. Have you ever eaten there?"

"No."

Were you born this big of a jerk, or is it something you have to work at?

Sage swallowed that question and chose a more appropriate one.

"Have you ever been running on the canal path? After we get settled, I was thinking of taking a jog."

"You're not going running through the woods alone."

The canal path was not really the woods, and apparently, in Ryker's mind, issuing edicts counted as driving conversation. Her patience was fading. Fast.

"Money doesn't give you the right to tell me what to do."

"Actually, it does. I bought you, remember?"

In kickboxing, she'd learned what it felt like to be kicked in the gut. The crack of pain. The loss of breath. Her body instantly hunching to protect itself.

This time, words had done the damage.

Ryker hadn't turned on the radio, so her gasp was audible.

He released a long breath. "I'm sorry. That was uncalled for. Completely uncalled for. I'm not the kind of man who takes cheap shots."

He squeezed his thick, dark hair in his long, tan fingers. "I don't know what the hell's wrong with me."

Sage couldn't speak. If she did, she'd cry, and he wasn't worth it. So *not* worth it. His opinion of her should not matter. *Did* not matter. He was a job. A business arrangement. The path to save her sister.

So why did his words have the power to take her breath away?

"Olivia?"

Now she was the one staring at the road. If he hated her so much, why had he brought her on this trip? Why was he kind one minute and a complete jerk the next?

Strong fingers gently pressed the top of her thigh. "Say something."

She didn't want to say anything. She wanted to be gone. Away. Safe. Back in a world of sunshine and smiles. A world where she had someone to rely on. A world where her mother always had her back.

But her mother was gone, and reality was the man sitting next to her.

She pressed her fist between her breasts to push the tightness down and let the truth flow from her lips. "I feel like a pinball. You kiss me and say you want me, then demand to know if I'm a prostitute. You defend me to Veronica, then accuse me of hanging a dead squirrel in my locker. You tell me you can't stop thinking about me, but I've barely heard from you since Monday. You say you want us to have a business arrangement, but instead of acting like a professional, you're acting like a jerk!"

As she spoke, Ryker turned the Audi into the parking lot of the Lambertville Inn. The nineteenth-century, stone train station-turned-hotel overlooked the Delaware River. The late afternoon sunlight sparkled and danced against the huge wall of windows that faced the river and reflected brightly off the snow-covered ground. The scene was charming, postcard-perfect, and made for romance.

They didn't belong in this beautiful place.

When the car stopped, she didn't turn to look at Ryker. She couldn't. She might fly apart.

His hand still rested on her thigh, warming her skin through her jeans. Clothing rustled, his seat belt snapped, and the leather seat creaked. Hot breath tickled the side of her neck, and the scent of balsam touched her nostrils. He was too close. She squeezed her eyes shut, waiting for what he would say or do.

A sharp rap shattered the silence.

Sage's eyes flashed open, her head turning automatically toward the sound coming from Ryker's window. Jeans and red-and-blue plaid filled her vision, followed by a young, handsome face with eyes squinted, either from laughter or the sun. Even in profile, Sage could see Ryker's tight lips spread instantly into an answering grin. He pushed his door open and leaped out, pulling the man close.

Curiosity pushed Sage out the passenger door. Once she rounded the car, she got a good look at the stranger. He was not quite as tall or wide as Ryker, but he was close. Ryker pulled a flat-billed maroon Phillies hat off the man's head and ruffled his curly blond hair. Deep, warm words and laughter filled the air.

She hung back. Ryker's eyes were bright and welcoming with no trace of the familiar ice. His lips stretched into a full-face smile that softened every harsh Viking angle. His hands were in perpetual motion, moving from hair to shoulders to back to around the man's neck. The stranger accepted the attention good-naturedly, but when Ryker pulled him close for a second full-body hug, the man shot her a quick, friendly wink over Ryker's shoulder.

Finally, Ryker stepped to the side and linked arms with the younger man, pulling him toward the back of the car where Sage was standing. Ryker lifted his gaze, and surprise flashed across his face, almost as if in his joy at seeing the stranger he'd forgotten she was here. She should be offended, but that was impossible. Ryker's happiness was too infectious.

Ryker cleared his throat. "Christian, meet Olivia Dupree. Olivia, this is my brother, Christian. I didn't think he was coming this weekend. He's supposed to be at Georgetown working on a project. He's getting his MBA. They are so lucky to have him. He got a perfect score on his SAT. Can you believe that?"

Christian elbowed his brother. "That was like seven years ago. I think we can let that go now."

Ryker pulled his brother in for another quick hug. "I'm so damn glad you decided to come."

Ryker's voice was light, and his face beamed. There was no trace of the arrogant ass who'd been sitting next to her in the car a few short minutes ago. The transformation was almost unbelievable.

Almost.

She had Rosemary. She knew exactly how powerful and transformative love for a sibling could be.

Christian shook Sage's hand. "Sorry to crash your date. I expected my brother to be alone. He usually is."

Ryker? Alone? Even with his boorish personality, it was hard to believe there was a shortage of women eager for his attention. Handsome, rich men didn't normally struggle finding dates, and Ryker wasn't just handsome. He was walking-on-the-surface-of-the-sun hot.

Christian was staring. She'd been silent too long. She had to say something. Something innocuous and polite.

"Ryker's clearly thrilled to see you, so I'm happy you made the trip."

"I finished the project early." Christian gave Ryker a playful punch to the arm. "I felt bad for the old man thinking he'd be here all alone, so I decided to drive up and surprise him. If I knew he was bringing a date, I wouldn't have come. Especially since I didn't plan things very well. The hotel is completely booked"—Christian shrugged happily—"but I'm sure I'll be able to get a room somewhere nearby."

Chances of Christian getting a room someplace close were slim. There was a wine festival in New Hope that weekend. If he didn't stay with her and Ryker, he'd end up miles away.

Sage's spine relaxed, and the tightness in her chest eased. If Christian was sharing a room with them, there was no way she and Ryker could have sex. Maybe Ryker would just send her home. It would only delay the inevitable, but after the horrible trip in the car, going back home sounded divine.

"I'm not sure you'll be able to find a hotel with vacancy," Sage said. "Festival weekends book up months in advance around here. I've stayed here before, and the standard rooms are actually a good size. There's enough room for all of us. Or, if you and Ryker want a brothers' weekend, I can easily grab an Uber back to the city. Whatever Ryker wants is fine with me."

Christian laughed. "Those words are music to my brother's ears. He loves to be in charge. Of everything and everyone."

She expected Ryker to snarl a nasty retort, but he didn't. His rugged cheeks flushed, and she didn't think it was from the cold. He opened his mouth, closed it, reopened it, and closed it again. He looked like a pufferfish. A smile spread across her cheeks. Now that sex seemed safely off the table for the weekend, she could enjoy the sight of Ryker flustered and unsettled. It leveled the playing field a bit.

"Well? Are we bunking up, or am I headed back to Philly?"

She looked from brother to brother, but neither spoke. Both seemed reticent to commit to a plan, so she took matters into her own hands. "I'm going to give you two some space to figure this out. My friend

Theo owns a dance studio nearby. I told him I'd try to stop by this afternoon. Why don't we get our bags inside, then I'll Uber to the studio. You guys can talk about arrangements for the rest of the weekend and let me know what you decide when I get back."

After unloading the trunk, they crossed the parking lot in a horizontal line, Christian carrying her suitcase, Ryker in the middle pulling his own, and Sage carrying her dance backpack and purse. Christian goofed around, leaning one shoulder toward the ground, making huffing noises, pretending her bag was too heavy to carry.

"The prettier the girl, the heavier the suitcase. Didn't someone famous say that?"

Sage snickered. "Umm, I think you're the one who said it, and I don't think you're quite famous yet."

Before Christian could shoot back a reply, a red Range Rover whizzed past them, hot and fast. Too fast. Fear slammed her eyes shut. In the same instant, a heavy arm crossed her chest, pushing her back.

When she opened her eyes, Ryker stood with his arms splayed protectively in front of both her and Christian. She laid cool fingers to her cheeks, trying to press away the sensation of hot metal passing far too close to her face. The bracing strength of Ryker's arm across her chest helped slow her pounding heart and heaving breath. For the first time in months, she felt safe, protected, cared for, and when he dropped his arms and stepped away, an odd emptiness swirled in her belly.

Ryker's long legs ate up the parking lot as he strode toward the Range Rover idling in the covered, curved driveway in front of the hotel entrance.

Christian nodded his head toward the car. "I almost feel bad for them. Ryker pissed off is scary as hell."

She was glad Ryker was going to give the driver a piece of his mind. Another couple of inches and they would have run over Ryker's foot—or worse.

"He has a right to be mad. They almost ran him over."

Christian lifted an eyebrow. "You don't know him very well, do you?"

Sage eyed the ground. Soon enough she'd probably know every inch of Ryker, but that wasn't what Christian meant.

"What makes you say that?"

"Because you think he's angry for himself. He doesn't care how close that car came to him. It's us he cares about. He's furious because that car could have hit us, because *we* could have been hurt."

Christian stared at Ryker's striding figure with nothing less than hero worship.

"My brother always takes care of his own."

Chapter Ten

It was his childhood neighborhood dropped into a different place and time. Crumbling steps, boarded-up windows, houses with padlocked front doors. Empty beer cans and broken bottles littered the edges of the street.

The heat in the car was set at seventy, but a chill crept up Ryker's spine.

What the hell was Olivia thinking?

Twenty-five minutes was not "nearby," and this was not the kind of place for a woman to come alone. Most of the people who lived here were good people. Ryker knew that from his youth. They were disadvantaged victims of a broken system trying to make ends meet with a shit education from underfunded schools while living in a goddamn food desert. He also knew circumstances like this made people desperate, just like he'd been when he was young.

The neighborhood wasn't safe.

At least it was winter. He'd read that crime rates sank in the cold. No one wanted to be outside. Of course, the three men leaning on the idling car at the next corner put a quick hole in that theory. Ryker rolled through the stop sign, temper rising as he watched the exchange out of the corner of his eye. With drugs, some things would never change. Someone always wanted to buy. Someone was always ready and eager to sell, and kids ended up paying the price.

Was the story about visiting a friend's dance studio a lie? Was Olivia coming here to buy drugs?

Addiction was a terrible thing, but it wasn't something he could tolerate. He couldn't live with that pain again. Not after his mother.

Crack!

A bottle bounced off the hood of his car. His fingers tightened around the heated steering wheel. Annoyance flared, not with the bottle thrower but with himself. When he was a teenager, he'd have thrown something at a fancy car with the nerve to show its shine in his neighborhood.

Shame heated his face.

He'd left his neighborhood and barely looked back. Yes. He'd created a network of support centers for children of drug addicts, but he'd done nothing to really help address the root of the issues behind the poverty cycle. He'd let himself forget his past. Or maybe he was just afraid to face it. That's what Olivia had accused him of when she'd asked if he only donated money or actually volunteered his time—being afraid to look poverty in its face.

What would Senpai Joe say? Joe had taken him under his wing. Taught him to fight but only to protect himself. Taught him pride and discipline and honor. Taught him the difference between right and wrong. What would Joe think of him now doing mixed martial arts at a swanky, private gym every morning before heading to work in a thousand-dollar suit to build a fancy hotel?

He'd been acting like a fool. Putting his priorities in the wrong places. No, not the wrong places. There was nothing wrong with building hotels and multifamily housing. Everyone had to work, and he worked his ass off. There was pride in working and earning money. He should enjoy the fruit of his labors—he'd earned it. But he should be doing more. A lot more. So folks had a better starting point than he'd had. He knew just how hard it was to get ahead when you had nothing. He'd been lucky, but instead of using that luck to really help change the system, he'd thrown some money around to ease his guilt and run as far from his past as he could get—because it hurt to remember.

And that was weakness.

The battered, red minivan turned right at the next block. Ryker accelerated and clicked on his turn signal. It had been touch and go, but he'd managed to follow the van since it left the hotel. He made the decision to follow Olivia the instant he'd seen the burly, tatted-up driver eye her from head to toe.

It wasn't the tats or the size of the man that concerned him. Looks were so often deceiving. He'd seen a clean-cut rich boy slip Molly in a girl's drink and a long-haired, tattoo-covered biker punch his lights out for it. He knew better than to let the shine on a man, or lack thereof, be the measure of his soul, but eyes rarely lied. The cold calculation in the Uber driver's eyes hadn't sat well with him. He'd seen too many men with that look in their eyes to let Olivia just ride off with him, and from the way his phone kept buzzing, Christian was still riding him about his disappearing act.

He ignored the heart and kissing emojis from Christian. He'd deal with them later. He couldn't risk taking his eyes off the road and losing the van.

Over the next several minutes, the surroundings changed. The sidewalks grew progressively cleaner, and occupied homes replaced those with boarded-up doors and windows. Cozy loveseats, wrought iron dining tables, or rocking chairs furnished porches. Steps and sidewalks looked swept and doors and shutters nicely painted. Warm lights glowed behind soft curtains. The knot in Ryker's chest loosened a bit.

The red minivan stopped at the corner. Olivia jumped out of the back, smiling and waving to the driver as if he were Mr. Rogers. She'd changed her clothes before she left the hotel. With her black sweatpants, sneakers, off-the-shoulder sweatshirt, scarf, messy bun, and weathered leather knapsack slung over her shoulder, she looked like an eager, fresh-faced college student, not the seductive stripper who constantly invaded his dreams.

Ryker slid the Audi into a parking spot midway down the block. Olivia noticing his car could stir up a shitstorm. She'd probably be angry that he'd followed her. It might seem kind of stalkerish, and they'd already had a rough morning. Better to stay out of sight.

Olivia paused, studying the building in front of her for a moment, then climbed its wide, long concrete steps bordered by bronze banisters. When she was halfway up the staircase, one of the ornate double-front doors swung open and a man walked out. He was medium height, lean, with defined muscles and long dreads pulled into a ponytail. He wore black tights, a fitted black tank top, and some type of tight, black leather shoe. He rushed down the stairs, pulling Olivia into his arms.

One one-thousand, two one-thousand, three one-thousand, four one-thousand, five one-thousand.

The hug seemed endless. Ryker's fingers flexed with the urge to push them apart. They finally separated, and the guy linked his arm with hers, leading her up the remaining stairs and through the door. Ryker stared at the closed barrier between them.

What had Olivia said her friend's name was? Ryker craned his neck toward the passenger window to see the sign affixed to the front of the building, but he couldn't make it out. He could just look at it when he drove past the building to go back to the hotel, but instead of turning the car back on, he grabbed his phone from the cupholder and climbed out.

Just one peek. One quick peek in the window. Then he'd be on his way.

Ryker shut the door behind him and crossed the street. The sidewalk was hard and cold under the soles of his Berluti loafers. He stopped across from the studio. Spotlights illuminated the sign over the door.

Theodore's Dance Academy.

Theo. She'd said his name was Theo.

The second concrete step of the front stairs to a darkened house across the street afforded a perfect view into the large wall of windows across the front of the building. The studio was a huge, empty space with a high ceiling and a rich caramel-colored wood floor. The side walls were mirrored floor to ceiling, and hip-high, circular wooden bars ran across the length of each. The back wall looked like the employee break room at Denny's. It was a mix of shelves, cubbies, and hooks.

Olivia sat cross-legged in the middle of the floor. She'd shed her sweatpants and sweatshirt and wore only a one-piece swimsuit-type outfit that highlighted her every lush curve. Ryker searched his mind for the word for what she was wearing. *A leotard?*

Theo was tucking her discarded clothing into one of the cubbies in the back of the room. He turned his head and said something. Olivia threw her head back, laughing, then grabbed a pink shoe from her bag and tossed it toward Theo's head.

Emptiness twisted Ryker's gut. He was a voyeur, witnessing an intimate friendship that was nothing like his own cool business arrangement with Olivia. He pressed a closed fist to his chest, trying to rub away the drinking-hot-coffee-too-fast feeling burning his sternum.

Suck it up.

If he hadn't wanted to see them together, he should have driven away or stayed in the goddamn car. That's what he should do now. Go back to the car and drive away, but he couldn't. He had to know what Olivia was doing here.

She pulled a wide Ace bandage from her bag and set it down on the shiny wood floor. Theo crossed the room and knelt on his haunches behind her, resting his fingers easily on her shoulders. She lifted her left hand and tugged her swimsuit strap down, pulling her right arm out, then repeated the process with the other strap. Once both arms were free, she tugged the front of the leotard down.

Ryker's breath stopped.

Olivia sat in the middle of the studio with her glorious breasts bared to Theo and, with the sprawling window, exposed to the world.

His stomach lurched. He didn't want to see Theo kiss her firm, full lips and stroke her lush breasts. She'd agreed to be Ryker's woman. At least for a little while. Witnessing her betrayal would be like an ice pick to the chest, but his eyes were glued to the window. He stared, breath tight in his lungs, waiting, but Theo didn't move. He remained kneeling behind Olivia, chatting and laughing as if the sexiest woman on the planet wasn't sitting half-naked in front of him.

Ryker squinted, not able to fully process what he was seeing. Olivia was holding the edge of the Ace bandage under her arm with her right hand and stretching it across the front of her breasts with her left. She said something, and Theo took the bandage from her, tugged it taut and flat across her back, then passed it around to the front so she could pull it over her breasts again.

What the hell is she doing?

They worked together winding the bandage until her breasts were bound tight to her body. When they finished, Olivia tucked the end of the bandage under the edge of the wrapping, donned a spaghetti strap sports bra over the bandage, then pulled the leotard back into place.

Breath still eluded him. The process had been so natural, it must be part of her regular routine. But how was that possible? How could Olivia even breathe like that? How could Theo do that to her?

They'd turned her gorgeous, full breasts into small humps, making her look too angular and too thin. It was barbaric. Like the ancient Chinese practice of feet binding.

His fingers itched with the desire to march into the studio and rip that horrible wrapping off her. He even took a few steps forward before forcing himself back to his original watching spot. Olivia wouldn't appreciate him charging into the studio. She was too strong and independent. She wasn't the kind of girl who needed to be rescued.

* * *

Inside the studio, Sage pressed both palms against the ballet barre, circling it with her fingers. The smooth, worn wood was warm and welcome. She glanced at herself in the mirror. Black leotard, pink tights, shoulders back, heels together, head high. It had been months since she'd been in a ballet studio. She looked exactly the same, yet so much had changed that she didn't even feel like the same person. Still, being here was like coming home.

Familiar music filled her ears, and Theo came to stand next to her. "Ready?"

She couldn't have been more ready. "Yes."

They both faced the mirror in first position. Theo called out the first few steps of their standard ballet warm-up. "Plié. Roll through. Rise and first. Plié. Roll through. Rise and first. Plié. Roll through. Rise and first."

They continued the warm-up in synchronized silence. The motions were automatic but required concentration. Heels needed to be pressed tightly together, toes perfectly pointed, arms bent at just the right angle, and she was out of practice. The type of dancing she'd been doing at the Black Cat required different types of movement. Ballet was the perfect balance of fluidity and precision. Stripping was sinuous seduction.

The bounce of the mylar floor felt like air compared to the hard sheen of the Black Cat stage, and her soft ballet shoes were a gift from the gods compared to heels. Her muscles burned as they stretched, but it was a good pain. A welcome pain.

She was regaining part of her soul.

The warm-up music faded, and Theo faced her. "Ae you ready to tell me what's going on?'

"What do you mean?"

"Why aren't you back at school? I took a ride up to visit, and Olivia told me you were taking the semester off."

Sage bent down, adjusted the strap of her ballet shoe, and avoided his gaze. "It's been hard. With my mom gone, I can't leave Rosemary alone. I told you she's sick again."

"I know. I get that, but you dropped off the face of the earth. No one's heard from you in months. Your cell number doesn't work. I went to your house looking for you, and the maid said you don't live there anymore. No one knows how to find you. Not even Olivia."

Sweet Olivia. When Sage needed a fake ID, Olivia had duped hers, no questions asked, and she'd kept Sage's secret about where she was living. Sage hated that she'd put Olivia in a position where she'd had to lie to Theo, but she couldn't risk Davis finding her. The fewer people who knew where she was, the better.

Sage finished adjusting her shoe and stood back up, hoping a watered-down version of the truth would placate Theo.

"I didn't mean to make you worry. Like I said, things have been rough since my mom died. It's a long story, but Davis lost it. He kicked us out and cut us off. He won't do anything to help Rosemary, and he's spreading all sorts of nasty rumors about me. So for now, we're just laying low and avoiding him."

"That's crazy. Why would he do that?"

She trusted Theo, but she didn't want to talk about Davis right now. It was amazingly joyful and peaceful dancing with Theo again. The specter of Davis was not welcome here.

"Let's not talk about him. It's so nice being here with you. Talking about him will make me grumpy and ruin our night."

Theo's lips thinned into a straight line. "Fine, but at least tell me if you need help. Are you OK with money? Do you have a job? The studio's still getting off the ground, but I can find a way to help if you need it."

Heat curled up her neck, even though she knew she had nothing to be ashamed of. She was doing what had to be done for Rosemary.

She met Theo's gaze squarely. "I'm dancing at a gentleman's club. It gives me time during the day to take Rosemary to her appointments. The money's really good, and it's easy to fly under the radar there."

"Ugh. Sage, I'm so sorry. It must be so hard for you. Not being able to go back to school, worrying about money and Rosemary at the same time, and dealing with it all without your mom." He squeezed her shoulder. "I'm here for you if you need anything."

Sage's cheeks warmed even further, and tears threatened to spill. It *was* hard. She missed her mom. She missed Theo. She missed her friends, her school, and her nice, easy, simple life. But getting justice for her mom and taking care of Rosemary were the most important things right now, and she was the only one who could do them. There was no white knight waiting to ride to her rescue.

"Shall we mark it once or just dance?" Theo asked.

He was intentionally changing the subject. He was always so good to her. On the phone, Theo had told her he wanted to show his students the lyrical routine he'd choreographed for his senior performance, and she was nervous about it.

Even though she'd been only a sophomore, he'd asked her to be his partner. He'd said she was one of the most talented dancers he'd ever known, but she'd never been able to perform the dance with the emotion Theo expected even though they'd practiced endlessly. Her soul ached to live up to his expectations.

"Let's just dance," she said.

She didn't need to mark the steps. She remembered every motion. She braced her shoulders, ready to try again to make each step perfect, but with the first few notes, terror squeezed her lungs. This time something was different. This time, the haunting notes made her heart pound.

Her body moved instinctually, but she wasn't herself. The dance portrayed a twisted love. A man so obsessed he was abusive and a woman too terrified to escape. Thoughts of Davis slapping her cheek, screaming in her face, squeezing her arms, and threatening her all skittered through her mind. Now she knew the whipping pain of being struck by a strong man, the pressure of strong fingers gripping soft flesh, the despair of betrayal by someone you loved, the desperation of feeling trapped and alone.

As the music built, even darker images invaded. Davis striking her mother. Davis dragging her mother's unconscious body to the bath. Davis holding her mother's head down until the bubbles stopped and the water turned a pale shade of pink.

Davis had taught Sage to be afraid.

She let that fear flow into every step, into every push and pull and grapple for power. She leaped and fought and turned and flung her body like her life was on the line. Her chest ached. Her heart thumped. Panic clutched her spine. She was desperate to escape. To regain control. To live. To be free.

She twisted away from Theo, but he gripped her waist and pulled her back. He pushed her down. She rolled on her back and thrust her arms up as if pushing Theo away as he executed a perfect diving roll over her prone body.

She almost felt the blows as the precisely choreographed battle raged on. She and Theo were connected by bonds of anger, terror, and oppression. Inhuman bonds that had to be broken. Even if death was the divider.

When the music stopped, she crouched in the middle of the floor, sweating, shaking, tears flowing fast and free. Theo's lean, muscled arms slid around her waist and pulled her into a tight embrace. He rubbed a calming hand slowly up and down her back as the sobs wracked her body, making her ribs ache.

"For God's sake, Sage. What happened to you?"

What had happened to her? What could she say? How could she explain the collapse of her entire world, the chaos, the destruction, the terror?

She hadn't even realized how deep the emotions were until she'd begun to dance. Words were inadequate and would only make the tears flow faster. She was already out of control, and she hated it.

"I'm...I'm sorry. I can't believe I'm falling apart like this."

"Please tell me what happened. Who hurt you? You'll feel better if you talk about it."

The denial was on the tip of her tongue. She hated the idea of sharing her pain and fear, but hadn't she already done that? She'd opened her soul on the dance floor. Laid it bare with every movement. There could be no denial. Theo knew. He may not know the details, but he knew. That's why he was holding her like she was broken.

The realization hit hard.

Davis had broken something in her that might never heal.

She'd let herself trust him. After her father's suicide, she didn't think she could love a man like that again, but she'd loved Davis. Trusted him. Thought of him as a father, and he betrayed her. Even worse, he betrayed her sunny, sweet, loving mother.

Someone she loved had murdered her mother.

How could she ever recover from that? How could she ever trust again?

Theo pushed her gently away from his body, studying her face. When Sage tried to look down, he slipped a finger under her chin and pulled it up.

"I don't know what happened, but I know you're hurting. I know you're in some kind of trouble. Please let me help you."

Sage pulled out of his arms and walked toward the large wall of windows facing the street. She pressed her fingers lightly against the glass, giving herself room to recover. The chilled glass grounded her. The desire to confide in Theo was so strong that she had to grit her teeth to keep the words in. She couldn't involve him. It wasn't fair, and it wasn't safe.

The more people who know where she was, the greater the risk of Davis finding her. If Davis found out where she was, he might learn Ryker was helping them and put a stop to it. She couldn't risk leaning on Theo or anyone else for support. Letting her sorrow free on the dance floor was one thing. She couldn't allow herself that kind of weakness anyplace else.

Not if she wanted to save Rosemary.

Chapter Eleven

Ryker knew Olivia couldn't see him. First, basic science made it true. She was in the light of the studio, and he was in the shadows across the street. Second, if she could see him, she'd have stormed outside and confronted him by now.

He'd had tastes of her temper. She wasn't intimidated by him, and she didn't simper and hang on his every word. Sometimes he thought she might even be playing it straight, which was both terrifying and refreshing. Right now, with her body flowing and that haunted look on her face, she was dancing her way straight into his soul.

Theo had cracked a window before they'd begun the dance, so Ryker could hear the strains of the lilting song even from across the street. He'd never seen anything like it. She was fluid perfection. Every step was pure emotion. He thought she was mesmerizing on the stage at the Black Cat. This was a whole new level.

She courted Theo with grazing fingertips as she leaped and spun. Their coming together was so intimate, his instinct was to avert his eyes, but he was too entranced to look away. When the back of Theo's hand connected with her face and Olivia fell to the ground, Ryker stepped toward her, anger heating his chest. Then she curved up from the ground in a motion that defied gravity, and he realized Theo hadn't actually struck her. It was part of the dance.

The dance was an epic battle. A tale of love gone horribly wrong. No mouths moved, but in his mind, he heard cries and shouts. The dance was a dagger cutting free memories of a long-buried past, forcing him to relive a story he'd worked so hard to suppress.

He was back in the rundown apartment of his youth, watching his mother grapple with her boyfriend of the hour, their bodies striped by the slats of the closet door. First, screaming and pushing. Then slaps and fists. He huddled in the dark closet, squeezed between old boots, a broken vacuum, boxes, and smelly coats, with Christian a warm weight in his lap.

Ryker clutched Christian tightly to his chest and held a hand gently over his brother's small mouth, praying Christian would keep quiet. The urge to protect his mother warred with the desire to keep Christian safe. The need to protect his baby brother always won, but guilt that he wasn't strong enough to do both was a hard nut in his chest.

The desire to protect battled with anger at a woman who'd rather buy drugs than feed her children. A woman who let dangerous men into their home and loved them in the face of abuse. He didn't understand how his mother could forgive. How she could accept the kisses and comforting words that always came after, but he was seeing it all over again as Olivia fell into Theo's loving caress.

The dance was so real he stood on frozen steps with a dry mouth and sweaty palms, but as it progressed, he realized this wasn't the exact story of his youth. This story was different. This woman refused to remain a victim. His mother never fought back—this woman did. And in the end, neither she nor her abuser lived to tell about it.

When the music stopped, Olivia rose slowly from the floor as if her body were truly battered. Theo appeared to comfort her, but she slid away, staring out the window, fingers pressed to the glass. Collecting herself.

Ryker lifted a hand to his face. His eyes were wet, just like Olivia's.

He was too far away to see her tears, but there was a tell-tale brush of her fingers before they returned to the window. Her slim fingers seemed to be reaching for him, connecting them, linking their souls in a tragedy he hadn't known they shared. Olivia knew what it was like to be small, battered, betrayed, terrified, and alone. There was no other way she could dance like that.

She knew the pain that haunted his soul.

Then Theo's voice floated from the open window, words too muted to hear, and Olivia turned away, breaking the spell.

The tightness in Ryker's chest eased, and he could move again. He squared his shoulders and pushed the memories back into their cages where they belonged. He'd fought hard to get past them. Fought hard to make a good life for Christian and himself. No good would come from letting the past invade the present.

A light gray sedan slowed as it approached the studio and stopped a few feet past the entrance. Toyota Corolla. Older but not too old. Scratch on the rear panel but otherwise in good shape. Ryker memorized the license plate out of habit, as he had done so many times in his youth when he'd wanted to report a drug dealer's car to the cops. It never seemed to help, but he'd kept doing it just the same.

There were lots of reasons cars stopped in the middle of the street, and not all of them were good. A tickle of tension crept up Ryker's neck, but his spine didn't itch. A black minivan pulled behind the Corolla and put its flashers on. Still no itch, but Ryker eased closer to the street. It had been a long time since he'd had to rely on street sense.

What if his spine radar didn't work anymore? Olivia's safety was too important to risk.

Ryker was halfway across the street when the van door rolled open and two young girls climbed out. Both had dark hair twisted into buns and wore sweatshirts over tights and leotards. As more cars pulled up, each spit out a little dancer before pulling away. Ryker made a quick right and walked briskly in the opposite direction of the studio, the sidewalk cold and firm under his feet. The last thing he needed was a concerned parent calling the cops to report a strange man lurking around.

He walked a few blocks, allowing the crisp night air to clear his head and soothe his nerves, then slowly zigzagged back to his spot on the concrete stairs across from the dance studio. His timing was perfect. All the cars were gone. Soft music escaped the cracked windows and lilted through the air. Little dancers stood in a line at the ballet barre, pointing toes, bending knees, and reaching tiny arms toward the ceiling.

Olivia and Theo walked up and down the room. They tugged shoulders back, straightened arms, and stretched legs. None of the children seemed to mind the corrections. Instead, they smiled and giggled when Olivia made adjustments. She always followed an improvement with a tap on a nose or whisper in an ear.

Ryker rubbed his hands together, blowing on them. He'd been standing outside for more than an hour. It was too cold to stay outdoors much longer. It was decision time. Leave. Wait in the car. Or bite the bullet and go inside.

The pavement was icy, and the street was dark. Light and warmth emanated from the studio. The safe choice, the smart choice, was to wait in the car and follow Olivia later, at a distance, just to make sure she got back to the hotel safely. But every time he'd played it smart with her, they'd wound up arguing, and she was so deep under his skin that he was starting to think he might have to take a step into her world to get her out.

Screw it.

Ryker crossed the street and climbed the stairs to Theodore's Dance Academy.

Inside, the hall was wide, and the ceilings were high with thick dental molding. The five-inch boards of the walnut floor were marred and worn with age and countless steps. The sleek, light floor of the studio he'd seen through the window appeared new. Not this one. This one was decades, maybe even a century old.

Ryker could almost see the men from a bygone era lugging heavy wood and tools, carving, hammering, carefully lining up floorboards edge to edge, sweat beading, backs aching. Just as his back had ached when he worked construction to pay his way through college. That was when he'd decided he'd become a builder. He'd loved watching buildings come to life under his bare hands.

Or at least, he used to.

Ryker looked down at his hands, turning them palms up. He couldn't remember the last time he'd done anything at a construction site other than look, yell, or talk about the budget.

What happened?

The music picked back up and pushed the thought away. He looked for the source of the sounds. A heavy stairway stood to the right, and the studio itself was on the left. It was easy to spot. A large window occupied half the wall, and eager parents crowded around, peeking inside. Ryker lifted his hand in what he hoped was an appropriate greeting. He knew how to conduct himself at a board meeting, a cocktail party, and on the golf course, but normal families were outside his realm of experience.

It was hard to understand something he'd never had.

Ryker positioned himself behind a short, full-figured woman who jabbered endlessly to the brunette beside her about her daughter's perfect pliés. The incessant chatter was annoying but worth it. He had a perfect view into the studio over her head. The class had transitioned to turns, which Olivia demonstrated with the same precise, elegant grace innate in her every move.

How many years had she trained? How many long years of discipline had it taken to make the difficult appear natural and effortless?

Little bodies stumbled and tripped in their effort to duplicate her movements. One little girl slipped and tumbled to the floor. The studio door was cracked open, and he could hear Olivia's encouragement from the hallway.

"No tears, my little pet. There's no reason to cry. You're doing such an amazing job. You should have seen me when I was learning to pirouetté. I fell so often that my dance teacher asked if I was wearing ice skates."

Senpai Joe. Olivia instructed with the same patient, encouraging grace as Senpai Joe. Senpai Joe was Sensei Joe now and owned his own academy. Ryker hadn't been there in more than a year. Instead, like a spoiled, ungrateful shit, he trained at the upscale mixed martial arts center a block from his apartment. Visiting Sensei Joe meant going back to the neighborhood he'd worked so hard to leave behind.

God, what a coward I've become.

He'd let the discomfort of facing the past keep him from doing the right thing. Time hadn't just made him soft. It had hardened him in all the wrong ways, and that was nothing to be proud of.

Loud voices interrupted his thoughts. Parents were rushing into the studio, and children were talking and laughing. Class must be over.

Ryker sucked in a long, settling breath. He should be too old and jaded to be nervous, but his blood pumped a touch too fast, and the sound of his racing heart filled his ears. Then, without planning, without taking a minute to prepare a proper explanation of why he was here, they were face-to-face.

"Ryker? What are you doing here?"

The ability to speak abandoned him. There was something about Olivia that kept him unsteady. He felt like he was standing on a mountain during an avalanche. No matter which way he stepped or what he tried to hold on to, he just kept losing his footing.

She laid gentle fingers on his arm. Her touch was fire even through his jacket. "Are you OK? Is everything alright? Did something happen with Christian?"

Her concern freed the hold on his tongue. "Everything's fine. I was worried about you. I didn't like the look of the Uber driver, so I followed you—I mean, followed him. To make sure you were safe."

"So you've been here watching?"

"Yes. I figured I'd just wait to see if you need a ride home." The excuse sounded weak, even to his own ears.

She smiled. A full-face smile that brightened her eyes and crinkled her nose. "Your brother was right. You are overprotective."

"Is that a bad thing?"

"I think it's kind of sweet."

Olivia slid her hand down his arm and linked her small, slim fingers through his large ones, pulling him into the studio. "Come and meet my friend Theo."

The rush of innocent pleasure from holding her hand was unexpected. He should be cautious. She was a stripper with an agenda, not his high school sweetheart, but they'd come to an uncertain truce. He was going to let go for once and enjoy the feeling.

* * *

Sage led Ryker across the room and made quick introductions.

Theo shook Ryker's hand. "Sage and I went to Julliard together."

Sage's heart flipped and sank.

Why did Theo have to mention Julliard? The Julliard comment wasn't enough to blow her cover, but she still had a hard time steadying her pulse. Ryker was smart. If too much information slipped, he might add it up and figure out her relationship with Davis. The less he knew about her, the better.

"Julliard. I didn't know Olivia went to Julliard, and why do you call her Sage? I thought that was just a stage name."

Her stomach spiraled. She may not survive this night.

Theo arched a brow and opened his mouth to respond, but she cut him off before he could speak. "It's always been my nickname. My mom loved 'Scarborough Fair.' You know, the English ballad? I'm sure you've heard the Simon and Garfunkel version. That's why she called me Sage and my brother Thyme and my...well, anyway, that's where the nickname came from."

Shit.

She was panicking and babbling. She'd said too much.

Parsley, sage, rosemary, and thyme. What if Ryker knew the song? What if he realized Rosemary was her sister?

Rosemary Cashman. Caroline Cashman. If he started putting the pieces together, he'd know her mother was Davis's recently deceased wife and she was Davis's black sheep stepdaughter.

Would Ryker be willing to ruin his business relationship with Davis for her? A stripper he wanted but barely knew? Maybe. He kept surprising her. But she couldn't put Rosemary's life in someone else's hands. Especially a man. They always disappointed.

Lovely, blessed Theo came to her rescue, but with a sharp-tongued sarcasm that assured he'd be demanding explanations later. "Yeah. Everyone calls her Sage. It's funny, some of her friends don't even know that Olivia's her real name."

"Well, regardless of what you call her, you're both amazing. I watched your performance through the window. I've never seen anything like it." Ryker's eyes met hers. "Sage, you move like water. You left me speechless, utterly speechless."

Warmth curled through her stomach. She'd spent two years with the Chloe Dance Company in Paris before heading to Julliard. For some reason, Ryker's simple compliment meant more than the hard-earned praise from her mentors at Chloe and instructors at Julliard.

Ryker continued to stare, his eyes slowly grazing her leotard. The warmth turned to fire, dropping from her belly to her core. Her breasts ached and tingled. Her heart raced. Lightning licked at her thighs.

All simply from his eyes on her body.

It was too much.

Sage slung her arm around Theo's shoulders to break the intense intimacy of the moment. "Theo choreographed the piece. It was his senior project."

"It's very powerful."

"Thank you," Theo said, his brown eyes warm but serious. "That dance is a piece of my life. I grew up in an abusive household. My dad was an alcoholic. We were dirt poor in a shitty neighborhood the cops didn't even feel safe in. I didn't think I'd ever get out."

"How did you survive it?" Ryker asked.

"My mom worked up the courage to leave. She got lucky with county aid, and we got housing in a better place. Then this lady came and started teaching dance at the Y. It became my lifeline. Dance helped heal me."

Theo was a strong, open person. Sometimes people didn't know how to respond to his candid honesty. Sage watched Ryker's eyes transformed from blue flame to ice to soothing empathy.

Ryker reached out and squeezed Theo's muscled shoulder. "I know how you feel. I grew up in a neighborhood just like that, but my mom wasn't like yours. She was a drug addict. She'd do anything or anyone for a hit, and the men she brought home had no patience for kids. I had a baby brother to take care of. It was hard. Really hard."

Ryker's words were few, but the meaning was clear. Sage imagined him younger, weaker, hurt, afraid, trying his best to care for Christian.

She laced her small fingers through Ryker's long, strong ones. "How did you get by?"

He shrugged. "I did what I had to. Hustled, hid money, stole food. Then I got lucky. I learned jujitsu from a big-hearted man who saw something more in me than the stubborn, foul-mouthed street punk I was. Once I could fight, it was easier to keep Christian safe."

"What about your mom?"

She didn't want to ask, but she had to know.

"She died from a drug overdose when I was a teenager. I felt like such a horrible kid, because even though I was sad, I was relieved." Ryker twisted the dark, wooden band on his middle finger as if it were a talisman. "What kind of son is relieved that his mother is dead?"

He tugged his hand from hers, and his face shuttered into the impassive mask Sage had come to know so well.

And then she knew.

That was how he'd survived his childhood. Emotional retreat. And even though he now wore that same empty, cool expression that had annoyed her so many times, her heart melted. Melted because she'd glimpsed the guilt and pain that lived behind the mask.

Sage's stomach rumbled loudly, breaking the tension. Both Theo and Ryker laughed.

"It sounds like you're hungry," Ryker said. "Let's get some dinner. Theo, will you join us?"

Sage hadn't expected the invitation or the sincerity. A week ago, she was certain Ryker was too arrogant to share a meal with a starving dancer, but then she hadn't known Ryker and Theo were connected by the shared suffering of poverty and abuse. All three of them had experienced trauma. It should be disheartening, but instead she felt bonded and comforted.

"I'd love to join you for dinner," Theo said. "There's a great diner not too far from here. Are you parked out front?"

Ryker nodded.

"Great. I'm around the block, in a battered, light blue VW van. It's got a Scooby-Do vibe to it. You can't miss it. I'll pull around, and you can follow me."

Sage's stomach growled again as they headed outside. She was starving. The crazy thing with the squirrels at the Black Cat, the argument in the car, and stress about the wedding and the inevitable sex with Ryker had put a damper on her appetite, but that all seemed worlds away. Right now, she was going to enjoy a meal with an old friend and, possibly, a new one.

Her dance bag slipped from her arm as she pulled the door of Ryker's car open, and the contents spilled across the sidewalk. Sage scrambled after ChapStick, eyeliner, mints, KT Tape, her sewing kit, toe pads, and the host of items that always seemed to collect in her dance bag. Ryker crouched next to her, helping her pick up things, laughing at the random objects he was finding.

"What the hell is this? It looks like a medieval torture device."

She snatched it from his hand. "It's an eyelash curler, silly. I thought you were a sophisticated, worldly man. How do you not know what an eyelash curler is?"

Just as she tucked it back into her bag, a thud and low scream cut the cool, night air.

That sound was wrong, horribly wrong.

Ryker's strong hand gripped her elbow, yanked her to a standing position, and pulled her toward the corner. Somehow her jellied legs remembered how to run. Cold air hurt her lungs, which were warm and tired from dancing. She stumbled, but Ryker tightened his grip, holding her steady.

Sage glanced at his face. His lips and jaw were tight. She had a feeling Ryker knew what the sound meant, and from the look on his face, it couldn't be good.

It wasn't.

Theo lay in the middle of the street, crumpled and bleeding.

Chapter Twelve

The band of sunlight streaming in from the narrow slit between the edge of the window and the curtain crossed Sage's face. She snuggled into the unfamiliar, lush softness surrounding her. Her thrift store mattress and bed set had never been this comfortable. This was such a nice dream, there was no reason to rush to wake up.

Or was there?

Doubt and something else, something unpleasant, niggled the base of her skull.

Am I late for work?

Muffled voices and footsteps reached her ears. She didn't want other people in her dream. She wanted to be alone in the downy embrace of the comforter.

But she wasn't alone.

Heavy arms wrapped around her, and muscled thighs pressed against the back of her legs. Her wayward subconscious had conjured a dream lover. She welcomed the slumber fantasy. Falling for Ryker in the real world would only end in disaster. Letting him slip into her dreams, however, was an entirely different—and incredibly sexy—matter.

Hot breath touched her neck and shoulder. Her stomach curled in response. Her dream lover pushed closer, and his hard length pressed tight against her rear. Heat pooled between her legs, and her breasts grew heavy and wanting.

Lips grazed her ear, and strong fingers squeezed her hip, pulling her even closer so the entire lengths of their bodies touched. His hand sent bolts of electric heat to her core, but that odd feeling still tickled the back of her neck, and the stream of light was too bright even through her closed lids. Sage tried to sit up, but she remained cocooned in the heat of her dream lover's arms. She wiggled again and realization dawned.

This wasn't a dream. The hard body pressed against her back was one hundred percent flesh-and-blood male.

As sleep faded, reality invaded like a knife to the gut. Once the images started, they wouldn't stop. Theo on black macadam, unconscious, his leg bent at an odd angle and blood pouring from his head and nose. The blinding lights of the ambulance and police cars. The rush of doctors and nurses in the emergency room. The terrorized faces of Theo's mother and sister in the waiting room of the hospital. Coming back to the hotel and crying her heart out.

She'd cried herself to sleep in Ryker's arms.

It had been a long night full of pain and panic and guilt. That guilt crept back now.

She'd almost left Theo.

For a moment, as the police cars raced down the street, she'd wanted to flee. Fear had consumed her. Fear that the police wouldn't accept her fake ID. Fear that the police would discover who she was. Fear they'd somehow contact Davis, and she'd lose all the hard work she'd put in making a life where he couldn't find her and Rosemary. Fear that Ryker would discover her true identity and back out of their deal.

She hadn't let the fear control her. She hadn't fled, and the police hadn't even asked her for ID. She and Ryker hadn't witnessed the crime, so no statements or identification were needed. She'd never really been at risk, yet for an instant she'd considered running from one of her best friends.

How could those thoughts have crossed my mind while Theo laid injured on the ground? What kind of friend am I?

The arms enveloping her squeezed tighter. "You're upset. Your entire body's tense. There's no reason to worry. The doctors said Theo will be OK."

She couldn't explain her guilt without revealing her secrets. She had to let Ryker think her unease was concern for Theo. That wasn't really a lie.

"I know, but he has a broken leg. He won't be able to dance for months. What if it doesn't heal properly? What if he never fully recovers?"

"The broken leg will be hard on him, but it could've been much worse. He was lucky to walk away with just the broken leg and a slight concussion. The police said there were no skid marks. The car didn't even slow down."

Sage shivered. "The driver must not have seen him. Maybe they were drunk. I can't believe they didn't stop to help. I don't understand it."

Ryker's arms squeezed even tighter, and she instantly felt soothed and grounded. He was like a human gravity blanket. It was so nice to have someone to comfort her. To have someone else take control. Like he had last night at the accident and the hospital, then at the hotel.

She was tired. It was a bone-weary, months-long tired. Months of nerves and hiding and scrambling to figure out how to live on cash and cell phones registered in Olivia's name. Months of scraping to make ends meet. It had worn her down and made her weak. Made it easy for Ryker to swoop in with his cool, efficient strength and take over.

But leaning on Ryker was a dangerous choice.

Her mom had trusted Davis—and look where that had gotten them.

A muted, repetitive buzzing gave Sage the excuse she needed to extricate herself from Ryker's arms. Her cell phone vibrated on the nightstand. The distance was necessary, but a cold, emptiness slid under her skin as she wriggled out of his tight embrace to answer the phone.

It was Justin. Her finger hovered over the button to answer. She wasn't quite ready to face the world, but Justin was staying with Rosemary for the weekend, so she couldn't ignore the call. Her sister might need her.

"Hey, friend. How's it going? Is everything OK? How's Rosemary?"

"We're good. Everything's fine. Rosemary just got in the shower. We're thinking of going to an early movie, then dinner, but I wanted to check in to see if you needed us to come pick you up before we settled on plans."

Dinner?

"What time is it?"

"Almost three. Were you still sleeping? I didn't mean to wake you. I know you were up late. I was just worried. We haven't heard from you since last night. How's Theo? Are you going back to the hospital? Rosemary and I can come there if you need us. We could pick you up from the hospital and bring you home."

"You know I can't come home. I'm going to the wedding tonight with Ryker. Don't you remember?"

"I can't believe that asshole is making you go to the wedding after what happened with Theo!" Justin yelled.

Sage cringed and walked over to the window, creating as much distance as she could, hoping Ryker wouldn't hear him through the phone.

"It's fine. I don't mind going to the wedding. They're releasing Theo today, and he's going home with his mom and sister. The doctor said he's supposed to rest, so I'm not going over. I'll visit next week when things settle down."

"You're just saying that because you think you have no choice. We can figure out another way to get Rosemary her medicine. You don't have to stay with him."

Justin meant well, but there was no other option. Rosemary needed Remiza, and Ryker was the key. Even if he weren't, the wedding would be a welcome break. With all the stress and chaos of the last few months, a night of dancing, good food, and wine in a place where she could have fun, relax, and ignore all her problems would be heavenly. And even if she didn't want to admit it, she liked him. Their souls had connected.

She *wanted* to go to the wedding with him.

Ryker sat on the edge of the bed in light gray sweatpants and bare feet. His chest was a hard, lean swath of muscled, bronze skin. His biceps and triceps flexed as he gripped the edge of the mattress. He must work out. *A lot.* He had the lightest sprinkling of dark hair on his pecs. The dusting of hair began again a few inches below his belly button, disappearing into the low waistband of the sweatpants. She could count his abs. She'd done her own share of planks and sit-ups. Muscles like that required hard work. They didn't spring up overnight.

The dull, yearning ache of her dreams returned. Her nipples tingled. Desire swirled in her stomach and inner thighs. She tried to distract herself from the physical and think about who Ryker was as a man. He was a study of contradictions. He was arrogant, rude, temperamental, and quick to judge, but he was also a protective, compassionate, fiercely loyal man who'd survived a difficult childhood.

Ryker stood, and heat replaced thought. Her mind may have been conflicted, but her body was emphatic that he was the sexiest man she'd ever seen. The last few drops of moisture fled her mouth. She tried to swallow but ended up coughing.

"Are you alight? What's going on?" Justin's worried voice filled Sage's ear.

"I'm fine. I've just got a tickle in my throat," she said.

"Are you sure? You don't sound like yourself. Rosemary and I can come get you. It's no problem at all."

"I'm fine. Really. Thanks for the offer, but I need to do this. I'm going to stay. I'll call you tomorrow."

Sage set the phone down on the desk and braced herself to face

Ryker. The intimacy of their waking moments was gone, replaced with the nervous strain of two people who'd never shared a bedroom.

He met her gaze. His expression was grim. "I already have Rosemary set up to get Remiza. You don't have to go to this wedding with me, Olivia. You don't have to sleep with me. I know you have this notion that there has to be a fair exchange, but I won't go back on my word. Trust me."

Trust me. Wouldn't that be nice? To trust him. To let him take over. To let him carry her heavy burden on those strong, muscled shoulders. The idea was so very tempting, but she knew better.

What was the saying? Burn me once, shame on you. Burn me twice, shame on me.

Her little family had been burned more than twice. Her father, her uncle, her neighbor, Davis. No matter the weight of the load, she couldn't trust Ryker to carry it. She couldn't leave Rosemary's life to someone else's whim—not when the ability to save her sister was in her control. This was a business deal, and in the business realm, Ryker was a man of his word. If she kept up her end of the deal, he'd keep up his.

And what better time to do it than now, when her body was still hot and yearning for him?

Sage sauntered toward Ryker. To be successful as a stripper, she'd learned how to move slowly and enticingly, but this wasn't an act. She wanted this man to think she was beautiful, to desire her. She tugged her flowy sleep shirt over her head as she approached the bed, revealing her red lace bra. The cool air and lace teased her nipples. The heat that had settled in her belly curled up to her breasts. They ached for Ryker's hands.

His eyelids dropped, and his nostrils flared. As soon as she was within arm's reach, he gripped her hips tightly, pulling her toward him so his head was even with her breasts. Her stomach muscles clenched with anticipation. His mouth slid over the lace of her bra and grazed her already hardened nipple with his teeth. A rush of liquid heat pooled between her thighs. His teeth tightened, and a jolt of electricity coursed from her breast to her core.

He alternated flicking her nipple with his tongue, sucking it into his mouth and tugging it with his teeth. Her breast became the center of her body. She couldn't think of anything except the sensation of his hot mouth on her skin. When he stopped, she cried out at the loss. She opened her eyes to find his hard gaze glued to her chest. He slid his hands from her waist to her bra, pulling the lace of the cups under each of her swollen breasts so they were exposed, propped on the underwire.

Ryker rolled both her nipples between firm fingers. "Your breasts look perfect like that. I like them bare and ready for my mouth."

More liquid heat flowed. She should be embarrassed. Instead, his words were gasoline on the fire swirling between her thighs.

He continued to explore her breasts, kissing, sucking, squeezing, and tugging. The sensations were overwhelming. She gripped his thick hair in her hands as lightning coursed from her breasts to her stomach and then lower. Her muscles trembled.

With his teeth nipping an engorged nipple, Ryker's hands traveled down and behind her, squeezing the backs of her upper thighs. His rough, callused fingers supported her shaking legs, gripping soft flesh mere centimeters from her aching core. Anticipation flared, and her muscles quivered. He pulled her legs up and forward, lifting her like she was weightless, settling her on his lap. Burning, swollen flesh met long, thick steel, and one strong hand tugged her bottom even closer, impossibly close, deliciously close, while his other hand slid up her back and grasped her hair.

"Open your eyes."

The brusque, impatient edge to his voice spoke volumes. She wasn't the only one losing the fight for control. Pride and lust flared. It was her body making his breath quicken. Her body making the iron-willed Ryker Madsen frantic with lust. The idea was exhilarating and insanely erotic. Her swollen core throbbed.

A quick flash of shyness made her hesitate, but she followed his husky command. She opened her eyes and found his normally glacial gaze transformed to warm, Caribbean blue. Hot fingers closed around the back of her neck, and his face blurred as firm but surprisingly gentle lips met hers. His tongue pushed between her lips, then swirled in her mouth, teasing, exploring.

He was an amazing kisser.

The ache in her core grew into a fiery craving desperate to be satisfied. Her body responded wildly, instinctively, rubbing against the length of him. In one quick move, Ryker stood, reversed their positions, and laid her faceup on the bed. He tugged her loose pajama pants off and tossed them onto the floor.

He knelt over her. Massive, strong, and insanely attractive. Nerves and anticipation mixed, then settled as he eased down beside her. His hands were gentle as he ran them down the sides of her face, over her shoulders, breasts, and stomach, halting at the edge of her thong.

He leaned his face close to hers, his mouth hovering a centimeter above her own. "Do you know how many times I've fantasized about having you next to me like this? I can't get you out of my mind. I've dreamed of touching you for weeks."

His index finger drew lazy circles on her stomach. "Your skin. It's so crazy soft. Like velvet. Or kitten fur. I never imagined it would be so soft."

Sage squeezed her thighs together. He'd barely touched her, and she was already swollen, throbbing, and slightly desperate. She was in trouble. Need was controlling her. Eating her whole. This was supposed to be about saving Rosemary, not igniting desires she'd given up on having for any man.

Why this man? Why did her body have to melt under this man's hands when her response to other men had been tepid?

Ryker slid two fingers under the waistband of her thong. The heat of his hand erased every thought except the burning need for those fingers to slide lower. Hot breath tickled her ear as his thumb grazed the smooth skin at the juncture of her legs.

"Tell me you want me to kiss you. Right here. Tell me you've fantasized about my tongue inside you."

How could he know she'd dreamed of his hot, firm tongue slipping between her slick folds? How could she admit such a thing to him?

His hand slid lower, and he slid one finger into her heat, slowly circling the one spot that was now the nerve center of her body. Every touch, every whispered word sent a whip of volcanic heat between her legs, and now those deliberately teasing, slow circles might just drive her mad.

He dropped his head to her breast and tugged her nipple between hard teeth. Her core clenched, but there was nothing to squeeze. She needed him inside her. Any part of him. His finger, his tongue, the erotic steel searing her thigh. She had to have him inside her or she might not survive.

"Please," she begged, her voice so husky and pleading it was barely recognizable to her own ears.

He had to touch her harder, faster. Had to bring the slowly building storm of desperation to completion. Her body bucked up from the bed, gyrating against his hand. Everything was gone. The worry, the stress, the disappointment, the fear. There was nothing else in the world except Ryker's hands and lips on her skin.

It was exhilarating, terrifying, and wholly unexpected.

* * *

Olivia's silken skin under his fingers was exhilarating, terrifying, and unexpected. He'd hoped for this. He'd dreamed about this. He'd been on a singular mission for the past few weeks to bring this moment to fruition, but he still hadn't expected it.

Now that it was happening, his heart hammered. His breath came in short, quick bursts. He couldn't slow it down. His hands were shaking.

Nerves.

He shouldn't be nervous. He knew exactly how to please a woman. Sex was just one more tool in building the machine of success, and like any other tool, you had to know how to use it. He'd practiced, took control, and was always careful. Never stepping in blind or too fast. Because that's how people got hurt, and he couldn't let that happen.

If he got hurt, there wouldn't be anyone to take care of Christian.

He'd constructed his entire life around protecting his brother, and when he was younger, sex had been one more way to do it. Back then, if he made a mistake, failed to exercise one bit of charm or artifice at the right moment, things could go south fast. Jumped in the street or bullet in your back fast. Sex might not stop bullets, but it sure as hell could smooth the way for a piss-poor kid from a shit neighborhood with a baby brother to feed.

The rich women who watched him swing a hammer were more than happy to slip him cash, pass on an investment tip, or put in a good word with the dean of the Wharton School of Business, who just happened to be a guest at their next dinner party. All in exchange for a roll in the proverbial hay with a hired hand from the wrong side of the tracks. He was a walk on the wild side, a rebellious bit of excitement in dull days spent decorating, lunching, shopping, and planning charity events. He was a way to stick it to the rich husbands who gave them unlimited budgets but no attention.

He'd sold himself to get ahead. Because it was the fastest way to get Christian out of the hellhole they grew up in. Not anymore. Not for years. But sex was still one more weapon in the arsenal. One more brick in the shelter he'd built for Christian and himself. And it was a cool, distant, efficient way to give his body the physical release it needed.

Until now.

His armor of emotional detachment was swept away on the wings of Olivia's shuddering breaths. His hands and lips roamed like a New World explorer claiming territory. He couldn't get enough of her lips, breasts, silken skin, and fiery, slick heat. Her skin glowed in the warm afternoon light that snuck around the curtains. Her hair was the dark halo of a fallen angel. He'd never seen a woman more achingly beautiful.

Heartbreakingly beautiful, if he weren't careful.

Olivia's fingernail grazed his inner thigh, tentative and delicate.

Lightning raced straight to his granite-hard cock. His balls tightened. He sucked air into his lungs, trying to slow his pounding heart. If she moved that finger one more inch, he might embarrass himself.

He eased down her body, sliding off the bed. Kneeling on the floor, he gently spread her thighs apart. He didn't know which was trembling more, his hands or her body. Her fingers gripped his wrist, trying to tug him back up on the bed.

"What's wrong?"

Her eyelids dropped, avoiding his gaze. "I feel so exposed."

"Do you want me to stop?"

Her perfectly straight white teeth bit into her plump, pink bottom lip. She seemed shy, almost nervous.

How could a stripper be nervous about sex? Did she think he wanted her to play the virgin?

It didn't matter. Even if it was an act, he knew her arousal was genuine. Her core was centimeters from his tongue. He could see her liquid heat glistening. There was no way she could fake that.

She hadn't answered, so he said, "How about I start, and if you want me to stop, just say so."

With her slight affirmative nod, he gave in to the burning need to taste her. With careful fingers, he opened her sweet, bare folds and flicked his tongue against her most sensitive spot. His cock throbbed as her hips bucked hard against his mouth, her nails digging into one shoulder while her other hand squeezed tight in his hair. He thought he might explode, but with a few more quick flicks of his tongue, it was Olivia who was exploding. He didn't stop. He licked that sweet honey harder and faster, forcing a second and third orgasm while she was still in the throes of the first.

She was wild, pulling his hair, gyrating against his mouth, panting and moaning, making his face wet and slick.

"Inside me, please. I need you inside me," she begged.

Condoms. *Where the hell are the goddamn condoms?*

Desire clouded his thoughts and slowed his mind. Then he remembered. Gym bag. The condoms were in the front pocket of his gym bag. He tripped over his sweatpants as he stumbled to grab the bag. He was normally good at multitasking, but he couldn't get out of his pants, get the bag, and get back to the bed fast enough.

When the condom wrapper wouldn't open, he ripped it with his teeth. Finally, he stood at the edge of the bed, rolling on the condom. Olivia slid her hands over her own skin and cupped her own breasts, and he had to close his eyes. She was so goddamn hot, and he was already too close. Way too close. If he kept watching her, he might come before he even got inside her.

He climbed onto the bed, gently pushing her legs apart so he could kneel between them. The plush mattress sank beneath his knees. He used one hand to brace himself over her and the other to press the tip of his hard length against the entrance to her core. She was molten lava, even through the condom. A primal need to bury himself deep inside her rose within him, but he held back.

"Are you sure you want this?'

He always asked. He needed to be sure. He'd had a friend in high school who hadn't been asked, and he'd never forgotten the look in her eyes. He waited for Olivia to answer. He might spontaneously combust if she said no, but he wouldn't press forward without a yes.

She nodded.

"Absolutely sure?"

"Yes." Olivia nipped his shoulder, and her small hands gripped his thighs, pulling him inside her with surprising strength. Glorious heat surrounded the tip of his dick. He had to fight the pressing urge to bury his full length inside her, to feel that hot core envelop him. She was small and tight, and he wanted this to be good for her. Needed it to be good for her.

"Are you OK?" His voice came out husky and strained.

She giggled against his shoulder, a light, sweet, impatient sound. "I'm fine, silly. Just impatient."

She slipped her hand lower, running a finger across the underside of his balls.

His vision turned black, and he thrust forward, losing himself in her tight, slick heat. He set a slow pace, finding her lips and breasts with his hands and mouth as he thrust, squeezing, biting, sucking, and kissing. His hands were everywhere. Her hands were everywhere, nails scratching. Their breaths mixed, heavy and erratic.

Her silken thighs gripped his hips as she locked her feet behind his back, giving him deeper access. He thrust faster and harder. He couldn't help himself. Each thrust demanded another. Her head whipped from side to side as her muscles grew tighter and tighter. He was out of control, but so was she.

"That's it. That's it. Please, Ryker, please."

The sight of her begging for release was pure sin. His balls tightened, and he increased the already whirlwind pace of their lovemaking, fighting to hold himself in check, fighting to push her over the edge.

He pressed his thumb in her mouth. "Suck it."

And she did. His dick throbbed as his seed gathered for release. He pulled his wet thumb from her mouth and pressed it firmly on her clit. She flew apart, screaming his name, squeezing his ass, biting his shoulder.

Then he was the one flying, exploding in rush after rush of mind-numbing pleasure.

When he'd recovered enough to stand, he tossed the condom in the trash, then hopped back in bed, pulling the fluffy, hotel-white comforter over them. He didn't want to move. His bones were jelly. The soft warmth of Olivia's body tucked against him brought a sweet, grounding peace he hadn't felt since Christian was small.

He could stay in the bed forever...if whoever was pounding on the door would leave them the hell alone.

"Go away," he yelled, startling Olivia who lay dozing in his arms.

"Come on, Ryker. Let me in. It's five o'clock, and the ceremony starts at six. I need to shower and get dressed. You've got all my clothes in there."

Ryker groaned and glanced toward the drawn curtains. The light peeking around the edges was dim. They must have fallen asleep.

He'd rather stay snuggled in bed with Olivia, but he couldn't blow off the wedding. He'd never do that to Alex. It was time to get moving. Still, he couldn't resist brushing her silken lips one last time before climbing out of bed and sliding on the sweatpants he'd discarded on the floor.

He tugged the door open and waved Christian inside. Christian's gaze roamed over Ryker, taking in his bare chest and feet. Christian arched a brow as his attention shifted to the bed where Olivia sat, hair rumpled, clutching the comforter against her chest. Her bare shoulders shone in the soft lamplight. There were dark smudges on her arms. He hadn't noticed them until now. He'd been too wrapped up in their lovemaking.

Christian's expression shifted from teasing smirk to grim concern. He strode across the room and sat on the edge of the bed next to Olivia.

Olivia gripped the blanket tighter. "Ryker?"

Ryker followed his brother's path, but approached the other side of the bed, climbing in and pulling Olivia into his arms, careful to keep her fully covered. He worked to keep the fury from his voice.

"What happened to your arms?"

"My arms?"

Christian pointed. "Those marks. They look like bruises. Did someone hurt you?" He paused and took a long breath, staring gently into Olivia's eyes. "Did my brother do that?"

A knife turned in Ryker's chest. Christian should know he would never hurt a woman, but he'd been wild in the old days. Tough and violent, fighting when it was necessary, breaking the law when he had to. He'd done what he'd had to do, and more often than he would have liked, Christian had seen him do it.

Ryker hated that Christian could doubt him, but his heart still swelled. Christian was offering Olivia his protection, even against his own brother. He'd raised a man who did the right thing, even when it was hard.

Olivia's eyes widened, and her mouth opened into a shocked O. "Oh God, no. No. No. No. Not Ryker."

Christian's body sagged in relief. "I didn't think so, but I had to ask."

Ryker pulled her tighter. "What happened?"

Her body stiffened. "It's nothing. Really."

Ryker tipped her chin up. "It's not nothing. I'm not going to let this go. Tell me."

Olivia twisted the covers in her hands.

"I needed clothes for this trip. I left my old house in a hurry, and I didn't leave on good terms, so I didn't take much with me. I went back for the clothes." Olivia paused. "Let's just say it was not a happy reunion."

"Who did this?'

Olivia flinched.

He could hear the promise of retribution in his own voice. He hadn't meant to use that tone, but rage was acid in his veins. She was his, under his protection, yet someone had grabbed her hard enough to leave bruises. He was going to find out who had done it and make sure it never happened again.

"I'm a grown woman. I can handle my own problems. I don't need you involved in this."

"Who did this?" he pressed again.

"I'm done with this conversation," Olivia said, then grabbed the extra blanket from the bottom of the bed, wrapped it around her, and stormed into the bathroom, leaving way too many flashes of skin in her wake.

Ryker ran a hand through his thick hair and squeezed it at the roots. She'd been running from Davis that night at the party. Could something have happened between them?

"I'm going to find out who did that to her, and I just might kill the man."

"Maybe you should let it go. Let her past be her past. You can be her future."

"Her future?" Ryker sputtered. "What are you talking about? Olivia and I have a casual thing. You know I don't do relationships."

"Oh. Right. A casual thing. Why would I think it was something more? Could it be because you practically threw your body in front of a moving car to protect her? Or maybe because you flew out of here to follow her Uber because you thought the driver looked a little sketchy? Or because you stayed at the hospital with her all night long? Or maybe because you wrap yourself around her as if she's going to break. You've got it bad, bro. You might as well admit it."

His brother's words hit way too close to home. He already knew he had it bad. He just hadn't realized it was so obvious.

"I needed a date for the wedding, and she was available. It's that simple."

"Why can't you just admit that you like her? Why can't you just let yourself be happy?"

"What the hell are you talking about? I'm plenty happy."

Christian's face flushed. "Right. I forgot. You've got everything all figured out, just like you always do. You spend so much time controlling every little thing, that you don't take any time to live. You've got the job, the money, the penthouse apartment, but it's a half-life. It's too safe, too reserved, too distant to be real. You can't ever truly be happy living like that. Open yourself up. Trust somebody. Love somebody. This woman is good for you, Ryker. Let her in."

Let her in. It was tempting.

Her laughter. Her kindness, Her empathy. The way she danced. The way she mixed sweet and steel. The way she'd do anything to save her friend, just like he'd do anything for Christian.

Ryker would never admit it to Christian, but Olivia made him feel more alive than he had in years. Since the first day he'd met her, she'd been slowly working her way under his skin. Maybe his brother was right.

Maybe he should open up and let Olivia in.

Chapter Thirteen

Sage cha-cha'd up the cracked, concrete stairs to her rented rowhouse, lifting her chin so the bright sun could shine on her face. The winter air was cold, crisp, and clear. A light blanket of snow coated the street and sidewalk, muting the city sounds. It was a gorgeous day.

She unlocked the front door and pushed inside, pulling her suitcase in with her. The living room was warm and cozy. Rosemary and Justin sat on the thrift store slip-covered couch, sharing a pizza and playing Scrabble. Sage's heart melted. She could always count on Justin to take care of Rosemary.

Rosemary's lips split into a smile. "Sage! You're home with perfect timing! Justin is insisting that *hoss* is a word. Have you ever heard anything more ridiculous?"

He laughed. "Hoss is definitely a word. You just don't know it because you have crap taste in movies. If you watched old Westerns, you would know there's nothing more American than ridin' a hoss."

Sage flopped on the couch next to Rosemary with an exaggerated eye roll. She slid her left hand over Rosemary's forehead and neck while she typed "hoss" into her Scrabble dictionary app with her right.

Rosemary pushed her hand down. "I'm fine. I don't have a fever."

Justin coughed into his hand, muttering. "Not at the moment."

Sage set her phone on the coffee table, forgetting about the word dispute. "Are you still getting fevers at night? How high are they?"

Rosemary whacked Justin. "You need to mind your own business. And you, little sister, need to relax. I'm going to be fine. Yes, the fevers are back, but they aren't that high and don't last that long. Plus, thanks to you and your new friend, I have my very first Remiza appointment tomorrow. A few doses of that wonder drug, and I'll be good as new."

Warm relief flooded Sage's veins. Ryker had come through. Rosemary was going to get the medicine she so desperately needed. The ever-present coil of tension in her chest loosened. She hadn't let herself admit it, but part of her had doubted him. She'd pushed forward, full speed ahead, because failure wasn't an option, but until this moment, when she'd learned that Ryker had kept his word, she hadn't realized how terrified she'd been that he wouldn't.

She shouldn't be surprised. She'd learned a lot about him at the wedding. Everyone was eager to talk about the elusive Ryker Madsen. Incredibly intelligent. Ruthless but honorable. A man who didn't tolerate fools. Self-made. Would do anything for his brother. Someone you could count on but should never cross.

Reason told her a man like that wouldn't make a promise he didn't intend to keep, but too many disappointments had made her cautious. She was in the habit of keeping herself distant. Safe from betrayal. Safe from pain. She had the few friends at school who had fought their way through her defenses, like Olivia and Theo. She loved them, but she didn't let herself rely on them. Now that her mother was gone, the only people she could really trust were Rosemary and Justin.

Could I even consider adding Ryker to that list?

"How's Theo? How was the wedding? Why did you stay over again last night? Tell me everything!" Rosemary's quick questions brought Sage back to the present.

"Theo's doing much better. Of course, he's upset about his leg, but the doctor said with time and physical therapy he won't have any residual issues. He's worried about the studio. His sister is going to cover classes for a few weeks, and I'm going to see if I can help out a day or two as well."

"Sage, you already have too much on your plate. Between working and taking care of the house and Rosemary, you're already exhausted. Driving more than an hour to teach dance classes is too much," Justin said.

"Justin's right. You're doing way too much. I'm the big sister. I'm supposed to be the one taking care of you. Speaking of that, what's really going on with this whole Ryker Madsen thing? I have a hard time believing he's helping me out of the goodness of his heart. What if he has ulterior motives? I won't have you selling your soul to the devil."

Sage laughed. "He's not the devil."

"You said he has ice in his veins."

"It can seem like he does, but it's just an act. He actually has a really warm heart."

Rosemary cocked her head and lifted her eyebrows. "Oh my goodness! You like him! That's why you stayed the extra night. You're sleeping with him, aren't you? Sage Elizabeth Cashman, you better tell me every single detail right now!"

Sage squared her shoulders and adopted her sternest voice. "You've lost your mind. I don't know where you would ever get an idea like that."

"Oh no you don't! You can't fool me with that high-and-mighty nonsense. You're most definitely sleeping with him!"

Sage's lips bent and curled, and a giggle escaped. She was brimming with joy. It would be nearly impossible to hide that from her sister.

"What is it with sisters? How do they know everything? A girl can't have a bit of privacy when she's got an older sister all up in her business."

Rosemary leaped up from the couch. "Wait, wait, wait. I need popcorn for this. Don't let Justin pry any info out of you until I get back."

Sage watched her sister race into the kitchen. Her limbs felt light, and now that she'd let the secret out, she couldn't stop smiling.

Justin glanced toward the kitchen, then shifted into the seat Rosemary had vacated. He squeezed her hand. A tendril of fear soured her excitement.

"What's wrong? Is it Rosemary? Is there something you need to tell me?"

"No. Rosemary's fine. I just want you to know you can be honest with me. I know you're telling Rosemary a modified version of the truth to protect her. I know you think you're doing what you have to do to save her. I get that. But you don't have to pretend to be happy. You don't even have to do this at all."

His face was pinched with stress. Sage hated seeing him so distressed. "I'm not doing anything I don't want to do."

He released a long breath. "I shouldn't have gone along with this. We've been friends forever. Let me help you. My birthday is in a few weeks."

"Why are we talking about your birthday?"

"The trust. You know how it works. If I'm married when I turn twenty-five, half the corpus of the trust gets distributed out to me. That money's our golden ticket. I'll be able to get Rosemary whatever she needs."

Sage was still confused. "Rosemary said she's starting Remiza tomorrow. What else would she need?"

"I'm saying that once Rosemary gets started on Remiza, we can quietly get married and invent some reason for you to leave town for a few weeks. Maybe a sick relative...I don't know. We'll come up with something. You can avoid Ryker, and Rosemary can keep getting the medicine. Then, after my birthday, I'll have enough money to buy Rosemary the best doctors and medicine in the country, and you won't have to stick with this crazy deal with Ryker."

Sweet, sweet Justin. His offer was so incredibly selfless and kind, especially since he'd been complaining about the trust since the day they'd met. He chafed at how it tied him to his family, and he especially hated "the ball and chain clause." The trust prohibited a prenup, so a quick marriage and divorce wasn't an option. Justin's father used the trust money to control him. Justin always said getting married would be trading one master for another, and he preferred the devil he knew.

They'd talked about the trust so many times over the years. Regardless of whether he got married, he'd get his portion of the trust on his thirtieth birthday. Justin intended to quit the family business the minute he turned thirty, move to LA, play music, and maybe even start his own record label.

Justin had confided all his secret plans during late nights while they laid in lounge chairs next to the pool. Even in winter, they'd snuggle under a blanket, the cool air freezing their noses, and he'd share his hopes and dreams.

Their teenage years had been hard for both of them. She'd been intimidated by the new world her mother's marriage had thrust them into, while Justin wore his wealth like a second skin. Justin guided her through the ins and outs of country clubs, maids, charity balls, private schools, and semi-private jets. He taught her the rules of the strange world where money meant more than love.

In exchange, she'd given Justin the gift of loving him for who he was and letting him be himself. His mother had died when he was young, and his father wasn't an easy man. Sage, Rosemary, and their mother had made Justin part of their family. They listened to his hatred of the strings that bound him, his anger over being trapped by his status as heir apparent to a family fortune that made Davis's money look like small change. His family's expectations were high. They had no patience for a creative kid who preferred music to business.

Her mother's world of yoga, crystal healing, homemade Halloween costumes, following your heart, and living each day to its fullest was like a flame, and Justin was the moth. Their friendship was born of shared fears, shared hopes, and shared dreams.

But it was just that. Friendship.

Somewhere, deep under the iron around her heart, marriage meant something to her. Despite too many disappointments and betrayals, despite building barriers to protect her soul, during the in-between times, right before sleep and right before wakefulness, she still dreamed. Her mind spun pictures of a warm kitchen filled with the aroma of freshly baked Russian tea cookies, playful snowball fights, nights spent making love on a soft rug in front of a blazing fire, and a man who didn't leave and didn't lie. A man who would cherish and protect her. A man she could trust with her heart.

Sage could give Justin lots of reasons why she couldn't accept his offer, but this was the real one. Her heart yearned for the type of love found only in fairy tales. Even though she knew her fantasy would never become a reality, she couldn't bring herself to marry a man she loved like a brother.

She couldn't live a lie.

Bizarre as her arrangement with Ryker was, at least it felt honest.

She laid her hands on either side of Justin's face. "You are such a good friend to me. You always have been. You deserve more. You deserve true happiness. There's a perfect girl waiting for you, and if you marry me, you might not find her."

She injected levity into her voice. "Plus, your father would go nuts. He hates me."

"I don't care what my father thinks. I never have."

Sage slid her hands down to Justin's shoulders and squeezed. "You tell yourself that, but I know you still want to please him. That's why you're not playing full-time with the band. That's why you're getting your MBA and working in the family business. I won't be the cause of friction between you and your dad. It's not necessary."

"It is necessary. What kind of person would I be if I didn't do everything in my power to help my best friend? Plus, I'm worried about you. I've heard Ryker's ruthless. You spending time with him makes me nervous."

"He's actually kind of sweet."

Justin rolled his eyes. "Don't bullshit me."

Sage pressed her fisted hand to her mouth. How did she explain it to him? Justin was aware of her general aversion to men, especially wealthy, arrogant ones. They were generally bullies, and she hated bullies. Maybe if he knew more about Ryker, he'd understand.

"He grew up hard. Really hard."

Justin repeated the eye roll. "I doubt that."

"It's true. His mother was a prostitute and a drug addict. They had no money, sometimes not even for food. He essentially raised his little brother himself. He built his fortune from scratch with nothing but brains and determination. Yes, he can be hard and demanding. Yes, he can come off as an arrogant ass, but it's a façade, a barrier against the people who look down on him because of his background. He's a total marshmallow with his brother, and he's genuinely upset about Theo even though he'd never met him before that night. He was really kind to me this weekend."

Justin opened his mouth, but before he responded, Rosemary skipped back into the family room, carrying a large, orange plastic bowl. "Alright, I've got two bags of micro-pop here, and I added extra butter. I'm ready for all the sexy deets."

Justin, laughing, rose from the couch. "I think I'll pass on the girl talk. I've got to get back to the office."

"How can you leave without getting the skinny on the wedding?" Rosemary pursed her lips, then made a *tsk* noise with her tongue. "Putting work before gossip. Where are your priorities?"

Justin tapped his Apple watch. "I've been here all morning, and you know how my dad is. I don't think I can endure another hour-long lecture about my substandard work ethic, so I better get back before he realizes how long I've been gone."

Sage reached up and squeezed his hand. "I really appreciate you staying with Rosemary this weekend. You always come through for us. Always. It means everything to me."

"It's no big deal. I was free this weekend except for band practice Friday night, so it was easy for me to pop in and out. You and Rosemary are my best friends. You know there's no place I'd rather be."

Sage's stomach warmed. She snuggled into the soft couch and pulled a chenille blanket over her legs. The sun made the small room light and bright. Rosemary was starting Remiza tomorrow, and despite Theo's accident, the weekend with Ryker had gone so much better than expected. For the first time in months, things finally seemed to be going their way.

A chilly breeze ruffled her hair as Justin opened the front door. He stepped outside, paused, and came back in, his arms full of envelopes and advertising circulars.

He dropped the pile onto the coffee table. "When was the last time you brought in your mail?"

"There's no reason to bring it in," Sage answered. "The landlord comes around once a month and collects the rent in cash. I pay the other bills online. You and Olivia are the only ones who know we're living here, so I figure it's all junk."

Justin plucked a letter-sized, dark yellow envelope from the pile, studying it. "This doesn't look like junk."

Sage took the envelope from Justin's hand. Her gaze focused on her name printed in black marker on the front. There was no stamp or address.

Justin was right.

The letter did not look like junk mail.

Her light, bright mood dissipated. Goose bumps prickled her arms. Dread curled up her spine, but she kept her hands steady as she opened the flap. She was probably overreacting. It could just be a note from the landlord.

Her fingers found thick, glossy papers wedged too tightly into the envelope to easily pull out. She flipped the envelope over and shook it. About fifteen 8x10 pictures spilled out. Some landed on the coffee table. Others fell to the floor.

Every picture was of her.

She was on the stage at the club, walking down the street, shopping at the corner store, dancing with Theo, eating plates of pasta with Rosemary on the very couch where she sat right now. There was even a picture of her and Ryker from the wedding, sitting at a table with their foreheads so close they almost touched.

One lone paper bore a message in the same black printing:

I'M COMING FOR YOU.

Sage's breath fled her lungs. The edge of the envelope cut into her skin as it crumpled in her tightly clenched hand.

Someone was trying to scare her.

And it was working.

Rosemary knelt next to the coffee table, setting the bowl of popcorn on the floor. Her fingers shook slightly as they hovered over a picture of her and Sage. Her already pale skin whitened further. The sight of Rosemary's terror cut through Sage's own fear. Her sister shouldn't have to worry about some crazy stalker on top of everything else she was going through.

Sage leaped to her feet, collecting the pictures. The idea of someone spying on her, following her through her daily routine, and peering into her private moments was downright creepy. It also pissed her off. She crammed the photos back into the envelope, crinkling some of them and finally ripping the envelope when she shoved too hard.

When the photos were safely out of sight, Sage slid her cool hand into Rosemary's warm one and pulled her up. "Don't worry about the pictures. Just ignore them."

Rosemary's eyes widened. "Ignore them? *Ignore* them? Someone's been following you, and you didn't even know it. This is crazy. First your tires. Then that dead animal in your locker at work. Next the hit and run with Theo, and now these pictures. You're in danger. You need to call the police."

There was no way Sage was calling the police. One of the cops Davis had in his back pocket would be burning up his phone line in a hot minute. Then Davis would call Ryker, and her carefully constructed plan would implode.

How would Ryker react to my lying to him about my identity? What would he think of me putting his business deal with Davis in jeopardy?

Would he believe all the lies Davis is sure to tell about me? If he does, what will that mean for Rosemary?

"I'm not calling the police! And don't get any bright ideas about calling yourself. I'm not risking Davis finding us or Ryker finding out who I am."

"What do you mean, Ryker finding out who you are?" Rosemary asked, her words slow and stern.

Ugh. Her stupid, stupid mouth.

Sage flopped on the couch and pulled Rosemary down with her. "I lied to him about my identity. I used Olivia's ID when I got the job. Ryker and Davis are working together on a hotel deal. If Ryker learns I'm Davis's stepdaughter, he's bound to ask Davis about me."

"Davis is an ass. You said Ryker's crazy smart, so he has to know that."

"That doesn't mean Ryker won't believe Davis. Davis convinced the chief of police that I was a Molly-loving party girl. If he'd lie like that to the police, imagine what he'd say to Ryker. Davis wants to control us. What if he pressures Ryker to cut off your access to Remiza? We can't risk that, so we can't call the police."

Rosemary pursed her lips. "If we don't go to the police, who's going to protect you from this crazy stalker? How is your life less important than mine?"

"We don't know even know if I have a stalker or if I'm actually in danger. Maybe Davis hired a PI who found where we're living and took the photos. This could be Davis's way of trying to scare us into moving back home. We don't know what's going on with these pictures, but we do know that your cancer's back and Remiza is the only chance you have of getting better. So, you're starting Remiza tomorrow, and we are *not* going to the police."

Rosemary didn't look convinced. Sage grasped her sister's smooth hand and interlocked their pinkies. "I'll be extra careful. Pinkie promise."

Rosemary's slim arms encircled her, and the smell of Rosemary's coconut conditioner filled her nostrils.

"You're playing with fire, Sage. Lying to this man is a bad idea. You know what Mom always said. 'A lie is a weed. If you don't nip it in the bud, it'll take over the whole garden.' Have some faith in him and tell him the truth. You're going to regret it if you don't."

The swirling, sick feeling in Sage's stomach grew stronger. Rosemary was right. She was playing with fire. She and Ryker has shared something intimate this weekend, and not just in a sexual way. They'd each shared a little part of their souls. Lying to Ryker felt wrong, but she couldn't risk telling him the truth.

There was just too much at stake.

Chapter Fourteen

"Ryker, you're not paying attention."

Veronica was right. He wasn't paying attention. He didn't care about the waterfall. He didn't care about the timing of the put option. He didn't care about events of default or remedies. In fact, he didn't care about anything in the partnership agreement.

"Sorry, I'm just not focused today."

Veronica set her pen down and pulled her reading glasses away from her face. "What's going on with you? These are important, complex provisions. Rubber-stamping them is a bad idea. Should we do this another day when you can concentrate?"

"Actually, I don't want to do this at all."

The fact he'd let himself speak those words out loud was evidence of how off his mood was. Something was definitely wrong with him. For some reason, he just couldn't muster the energy to give a shit about the project.

Did Philly really need one more goddamn hotel? What would it accomplish?

He wasn't building to put food on the table or keep a roof overhead. He didn't need the income to buy clothes for Christian or pay his tuition. The hotel would tie him to Davis Anderson for the next two years. Tie him to a man he didn't like or respect. A man who could've been the one to put bruises on a woman's arms. His woman's arms. And that was the crux of it. He couldn't concentrate on the partnership agreement because he kept thinking about Olivia.

Olivia pushed him and questioned him in ways no one other than Christian ever dared to do. She didn't take his word as gospel and called him out when he acted like an ass. She made him look at himself. Really look. That night at Theo's studio brought him closer to his roots than he'd been in years, and he wasn't sure he liked how far he'd traveled.

Veronica's fingers were cool like paper as they settled on top of his hand. "What are you talking about? What do you mean you don't want to do this at all?"

Ryker leaned back into the perfectly ergonomic conference room chair. The chair tipped back, and the tight mesh gave way slightly under his back.

"I met one of Olivia's friends Friday night. He grew up like I did. Well, maybe not as hard, but close enough. He's doing something valuable. He's back in his neighborhood giving kids something special. Giving them a chance. What am I doing? I'm sitting in a steel tower throwing cash around."

"You're kidding me, right? You've spent years funding counseling centers for children of drug addicts. That's why you're the guest of honor at the mayor's banquet. How can you say you're not giving back?"

"It's money, Veronica. It's easy to give money. It's a hell of a lot harder to give of yourself."

That's what Olivia had said when they'd talked at the wedding about the counseling centers. She's called him out. Said he gave money but not his time. That he wanted the counseling centers to be brick-and-mortar testaments to his success, not a reminder of where he'd come from.

When he'd told her he'd considered developing low-income

housing instead of the hotel, she'd said he didn't have the guts to put a low-income housing project in the heart of Center City because it would remind people of his roots. Roots he was ashamed of. Her words had rung too true for comfort. He hadn't just forgotten his roots, he'd intentionally turned his back on them. He'd prioritized prestige over his own moral code and gotten in bed with the devil on this hotel deal.

Veronica's slim, cold fingers pressed down harder. "I don't understand. You're not making sense."

"I'm not doing anything valuable. The hotels, the luxury apartments, even the student housing—those projects don't mean anything. I thought the drug companies would be different, but they're not. At the end of the day, they're all about sales, not patients." Ryker pushed his chair back from the table with satisfying force. "I think that's why I can't bring myself to sell the Black Cat, because the people who work there are real. The fact that I'm more interested in a strip club than a $250 million deal says something. There has to be something more important than profit and cashflow and who's wearing the most expensive suit in the room."

"So, what do you want to build instead? An orphanage?"

"I was thinking about low-income housing."

"In Center City? Are you nuts?" Veronica's near-shriek made Ryker smile.

NIMBY at its finest.

"What is going on with you?" she asked in a lower tone. "We've been working on this hotel deal for months. You told me you needed this deal. You said building this hotel and establishing a relationship with Davis Anderson was—what were the words you used? Oh yes, imperative and essential. Now you're going to scrap the hotel and walk away? I guess getting Christian admitted to the Lincoln Club is no longer imperative and essential?"

The warm glow in Ryker's gut evaporated in a flash. He hadn't even thought about the Lincoln Club.

Where the hell is my brain?

He did need this deal. He didn't want it, didn't care about it, but he needed it. For Christian. It wasn't about the money. He had plenty of that, but despite his wealth, he still wasn't accepted in the elite social circles. He didn't give a shit if those crusty blue bloods snubbed him, but the Lincoln Club would open doors for Christian that no amount of money could, and Davis Anderson was chair of the membership committee. As a member of the Lincoln Club, when Christian graduated and came back to Philly, he wouldn't have to face any of the same obstacles or fight his way to respect the way Ryker had.

"No. I'm not over it. I won't allow those assholes to reject Christian's application. Did you know Charles Witt wouldn't let his daughter go with Christian to the senior dance at Penn because of his background? No one's going to slam a door in my brother's face just because we grew up poor."

"Right. That's the whole reason you agreed to let Davis be your partner on this deal. Davis is old money. If Davis supports Christian's application, the rest of the membership committee will go along with him. When he graduates from the MBA program at Georgetown, he'll have his pick of jobs in the city."

If Christian weren't so hell-bent on not taking a job from Ryker, this wouldn't even be an issue, but his brother had vowed that when he graduated, he was going to make his own way, and Ryker knew he meant it. If Christian wouldn't take money or a job from him, Ryker was sure as hell going to do every goddamn thing he could to make things as easy for his brother as possible.

Ryker squeezed his jaw. "What if we ditch the hotel and let Davis partner on the low- income housing project?"

"Have you met Davis?" Veronica sneered. "He wants his name associated with luxury. He'd be mortified at the idea of supporting Section 8 housing. If you back out on this deal, Davis will be pissed and throw every roadblock he can in Christian's path, and knowing him, he won't be quiet about it."

Ryker's gut burned. "I'm trying to make things easier for Christian, not harder, and he hates when I interfere. If he finds out I'm doing this deal to try to smooth his way into the Lincoln Club, he'll go nuts."

"It doesn't have to be hard. You just have to stay on track. Why are you having such a hard time keeping your eye on the ball?"

He didn't answer.

Veronica's eyes narrowed, and she pressed her lips together tightly. "It's that stripper. Isn't it? What, did she sell you on some sob story about helping poor little girls like her? She wants you to think she's a little saint with a heart of gold, but that's bullshit. She's after your money. I guarantee she'll be the first in line to collect on your new charitable nature."

Hot fury blazed up Ryker's spine. He slammed his hand down on the hardwood table and leaped up. "You've gone too far!"

Veronica sprung up from the chair, like a cobra ready to strike. "Have I? Or is it you who is too far gone? Get your brain out of your dick for a minute and think! What do you know about her? I'll tell you what I know! She magically shows up at your club, and then what? Lights get smashed in the parking lot. Her tires get slashed. Someone hangs a dead animal in her locker, and now she's preaching all sorts of nonsense about giving your money to others. It's too much of a coincidence. Open your eyes! It's all a setup to make you feel sorry for her, to make you feel the need to protect her, and then *bam!* She slides her hands right into your pockets."

"Olivia isn't like that."

"I don't care what Olivia is like. I do, however, care about keeping some trashy schemer from making an ass out of you. She's playing the beautiful damsel in distress, and you've stepped right in as the prince riding to her rescue. Did you even run a background check on her? You have the PI firm run everybody. What did they find on her? Tell me."

Veronica's words were like nails on his own personal chalkboard. Each syllable she spoke cut a bit from the wonder of the weekend with Olivia. He'd been relaxed, at peace, and utterly entranced. They'd stayed an extra night in Lambertville because he wasn't ready to return to reality, but Veronica was forcing it back, hard and fast.

He fought the fierce temptation to tell her to get the hell out of his building and never come back. He fought it because her words had created a slowly creeping inkling of doubt, shifting his fiery anger into spiky unease.

Why didn't I have the standard background check run on Olivia? He'd meant to do it after that first meeting in his office, but she'd been so different than what he'd expected. He'd been mesmerized by her kryptonite combination of sexy, innocent, satin, and steel. The background check had slipped his mind.

After what they'd shared this past weekend, ordering an investigation of Olivia's past felt like a betrayal, but Veronica was right. He wasn't acting like himself. Veronica was warning him about the same thing he'd vowed to never let happen again. Bethany had taught him the danger of letting a woman get under his skin, and Olivia hadn't just gotten under his skin—she was slowly sinking into his soul.

He could almost feel her soft body curved against his. He'd been at work only a few hours and he was already desperate to see her again. He wanted to tell her he was ditching the historic hotel and building low-income housing instead. He'd create a bright, airy building with quality apartments, a computer room, a job advisory clinic, and a childcare center. They could have an all-purpose room where the kids could take art or jujitsu—or maybe dance. Olivia would be willing to donate her time and teach. She'd love that.

That idea shoved his still-floating feet back on the ground.

What the hell is the matter with me? How could he even be suggesting that an exotic dancer teach dance classes to children? That would look fantastic on his tax credit application.

Veronica was irritating as hell, but she was right. The weekend in Lambertville was like the Lotus Casino in the Percy Jackson books. Olivia had sucked him in and made him forget the three basic rules he lived by: Ask questions first. Don't trust anyone. Keep your heart to yourself.

A surreal emptiness filled Ryker's chest and mixed with icy resolve. He settled back down at the conference room table and pointed to the chair opposite him. "Please, sit down."

Veronica tossed her platinum hair, adjusted her jacket, then retook her seat.

"Would you like to discuss the partnership agreement?" she asked formally.

"No. I want to hear what you're thinking. Despite giving you hell just now, I value your opinion. I wouldn't have you working for me if I didn't. You're smart, shrewd, and perceptive, so I'm asking for your honest opinion. Do you really believe Olivia has ulterior motives, or are you just hurt because I took her to the wedding instead of you?"

Veronica didn't speak right away, and when she did, her tone was carefully neutral. "It's hard for me to have an honest opinion because I have so few facts on which to create one. That said, the facts I do have make me nervous. This woman appeared out of the blue, and suddenly, all sorts of odd things started happening at the club. You're driving her home from work, taking her away for the weekend, texting her during meetings, and generally treating her like a girlfriend when—and don't be offended by the truth—she's a random nobody who takes off her clothes for money. You're moony-eyed, talking about canceling an important, lucrative project we've been working on for months. I don't know enough about her to know what her motives are, but my instinct says something's not right."

Veronica paused and once again laid a chilly hand over his. "I think you should be careful and hold off on making any big decisions until you know her better."

Ryker ignored the nausea welling up in his throat. He hadn't gotten where he was today by letting his guard down.

"Call the PI. Order a full investigation and tell them to expedite the report."

For the rest of the day, he couldn't quite shake the sick feeling in his gut. No matter how sensible, having a PI spy on Olivia was a shit thing to do, so he'd intended to wait until the background check came back to see her again. Instead, he went right from the office to the club, lingering in the shadows while she danced. It was like that very first night when she auditioned. He couldn't take his eyes off her.

Annoyance flared as Bryce approached. He wanted privacy while he watched Olivia dance. It was a ridiculous notion since the place was packed, but standing alone in the dark, he could pretend they were the only two people in the club.

Bryce lifted a hand in greeting. "I thought you said you weren't coming in tonight."

"I didn't think I was."

Bryce nodded toward Olivia. "Passion over reason."

"Passion over reason?"

"David Hume. Scottish philosopher. He taught that men are ruled by passion, not reason."

"Give me his number. I'll invite him here for a drink. Maybe he can help me figure out how to be reasonable instead of being ruled by"—Ryker waved his hand down his body—"my passion."

Bryce's laugh was deep and throaty. "You don't know your philosophers, do you? Hume's been dead since 1776, and I don't think he was a strip club kind of guy, but if someone could draw him in, it'd be that girl." Bryce gestured toward the stage. "She attracts the suits. The big spenders."

Ryker studied Olivia. She moved like water, gliding sinuously across the stage. An almost reverent hush had settled over the crowd. Bryce was right. She was definitely good for business. He'd looked at the numbers, and the club was the most profitable when Olivia worked, and there'd been a noticeable increase in corporate customer traffic in the past few weeks. Despite the progress made by the Me Too movement, the strip club visit was still a type of Neanderthal, male bonding experience for lots of men. It wasn't his thing, but he'd been in the business world long enough to know it worked well.

"So how's it make you feel?" Bryce asked.

"How does what feel?"

"That your woman is up there swaying those hips with nothing but a string of lace and pasties on?"

How did it make him feel? It made him want to yank her off the stage, drag her to his apartment, make love to her until she couldn't remember her own goddamn name, and never let her step through the door of the Black Cat again. Of course, he couldn't say that to Bryce.

"What makes you think she's my woman?"

Bryce arched a thick, dark eyebrow. "You're kidding me, right? You really think I'm that dumb?"

"Actually, I think you're way too smart to be working here. You've got as good a head for this business as I do, and I can't imagine most gentlemen's club managers go around quoting eighteenth-century philosophy. What's up with that?"

Bryce's smile turned tight. "I've got to collect the cash from the registers. I'll catch up with you later."

As Bryce walked away, Ryker returned his attention to the stage. Standing in the dark, his back sinking into the soft, fabric-covered wall, he could tune out the crowd and pretend Olivia danced for him alone. Depeche Mode's "I Want You Now" hit a synthesized clang, and Olivia thrust her body into the air from the ground, making a motion that required years of training and epic strength to appear gracefully simple.

She was wasting her talent at the Black Cat.

When the song ended, she slammed her body against a backlit board the mechanic had rigged to spring metal cuffs around her arms and legs. The crowd roared at the sight of Olivia bound to the wall clad in tiny strips of black lace. Every man in the room was thinking S&M, but he saw Andromeda sacrificing herself to save her people.

Goddamnit. She wasn't going to be sacrificing herself to this crowd tonight.

His heart couldn't take it.

Ryker strode toward the stage. Customers separated to make way for him, as if sensing the violent anger quivering under his skin. The bouncer guarding the hall that led backstage nodded respectfully as he passed. Ryker intercepted Olivia as she scurried down the back stairs. Her smile made her eyes bright, and her body glistened with sweat. Her small hand gripped his arm and fire shot straight to his gut.

"Hi! I didn't know you were here. I was scanning the bar, but I didn't see you. I thought maybe you weren't coming."

"I told you I'd be here, didn't I?"

She dropped her hand, and cool emptiness replaced the soothing warmth.

"Why are you so grumpy? Did something happen at work?"

I decided to order a background check to see if you're a scheming gold digger.

"Or did something happen here?"

You're getting ready to stroll into that crowd and slide your sweet body all over strangers for the price of a lap dance?

Ryker squeezed his hair in his hand, the motion calming him slightly. "I'm just tired. I don't want to be here tonight. Will you leave with me?"

"I can't."

"You can't or you won't? Why don't you quit this job and let me take care of you?"

Olivia's lips pressed into a thin, straight line. "I take care of myself, and I pay my own way. I don't take gifts with invisible strings. I told you that when we made our deal."

He hated her cool, reasonable tone, and he hated the reminder of the business nature of their relationship even more. If she wanted to play that way, he'd renegotiate.

He pulled his wallet from his pocket, grabbing a handful of cash and shoving it toward her. "Fine. Let's make another deal. Take it. It's more than you'll make the whole night, probably the entire week. Pretend I'm a customer paying for your time."

"Olivia," one of the other dancers called as she approached from the dressing room. "Are you alright?"

The woman's hard gaze met Ryker's straight on. She was tall and lean with espresso skin that shimmered in the soft hallway light. Her face was cut stone, with sharp cheekbones and a smooth, high forehead. Her close-cropped hair accentuated the drama of her face. Despite wearing only a thigh-length, jade-green satin robe, she looked like a queen.

"Anise, this is Ryker Madsen, the owner of the club," Olivia said.

Ryker shook Anise's hand. He'd seen her around, but they'd never been formally introduced. Her fingers were long and elegant like the rest of her.

"You should be on a runway."

"That's a hard life," Anise said with a touch of a French accent.

"And this isn't?"

Anise ignored his question and stepped between him and Olivia. "Are you alright? Is he bothering you?"

"I'm *fine*," Olivia answered.

Anise raised a skeptical eyebrow, which was annoying as hell. He was trying to protect Olivia, and Anise was acting like he was an obnoxious, handsy customer.

Olivia rolled her sapphire-blue eyes. "Ryker tries to be scary, but he's not. I was trying to tell him that I can't leave early because I promised to watch Simon for you, but he's in domineering tycoon mode, so I can't get a word in."

"Who's Simon?" Ryker asked.

Anise squared her shoulders, making her appear even taller. "He's my son. My girlfriend usually watches him for me while I work. She has a boy about the same age, so we help each other out, but she couldn't take Simon tonight. She has the flu."

His childhood rushed back. Mothers, aunts, and neighbors alternating shifts of childcare. Toddlers playing with blocks on the floor behind checkout counters while their parents worked. Christian crying in his crib, wet, hungry, and neglected.

Ryker's stomach bottomed out. Was Simon at home alone?

"Where is he?"

"There's a private dressing room connected to the main one. He's in there. The girls have been taking turns keeping an eye on him. I know it's against policy to bring him to the club, but he's only five. I couldn't leave him alone, and I didn't want to cause a problem by missing my shift."

Ryker didn't buy Anise's responsible employee schtick. She'd come to work because she needed the money, but she'd brought her son because she was a good mother. He respected her for that. His mother would have just left Christian alone.

Olivia's small hand squeezed his elbow. "I told Anise I'd watch Simon except when I'm scheduled on stage. I'm going to skip the floor work for tonight. I told Bryce he doesn't need to pay me the hourly rate."

"Ugh. I feel horrible. I know you need the money too," Anise said.

Ryker's chest tightened. This was the reality he'd let fade. People working hard to take care of their families. Long days, short nights, and never quite enough to go around, but somehow, there was still laughter, love, loyalty, and compassion. Not in his house, but he'd seen it in his neighbors. They were bound together in the face of adversity and leaned on each other for support.

Those flashes of Senpai Joe that had been invading his thoughts the past few days returned. He was being a selfish, jealous ass. He'd just shoved a fistful of cash at Olivia expecting her to walk away from an honest night's work. She was as disciplined and hard-working as he was and had just as much pride. He was lucky she hadn't slugged him.

How can I expect her to take money from me when I'd rather take a boot to the teeth than accept charity?

"You ladies should both work. I'll watch Simon."

"You?" Anise's elegant composure couldn't hide her shock at the suggestion. "Do you know anything about kids?"

"Ryker practically raised his younger brother," Olivia interjected.

Is that pride in her voice?

"I know how to take care of kids."

"Are you sure?" Anise looked skeptical.

"Yes, I'm sure. Don't worry. I'll order dinner. We can play cards and draw. It'll be fun."

And it was.

Simon was just like Christian. Sweet, innocent, and hungry for attention. Kids like Simon were the reason he should be building low-income housing instead of a hotel.

But if he canned the hotel, Christian would always be the kid from the wrong side of the tracks.

Chapter Fifteen

Sage's feet hurt. Between dancing at the studio Friday night, the heels she'd worn to the wedding, and the six hours she'd just spent in stiletto platforms, she could barely put one foot in front of the other. She'd changed into sweats and moccasins, but her feet were still throbbing. She was tired and hungry and couldn't wait to collapse into bed, but she had to talk to Ryker first.

She was going to set things straight between them. His shoving that cash at her before Anise interrupted them was a stark reminder of the actual status of their relationship. A business deal. They weren't friends. They weren't dating. She wasn't Cinderella, and he wasn't Prince Charming. He was trying to lull her into letting him control her life. When their agreement came to an end, she'd be a regular girl with bills to pay. If she let herself rely on him, she'd only end up hurt, disappointed, and broke.

She pushed the door to the small private dressing room open. Ryker sat on the floor, his long, dress-pant clad legs spread out and crossed at the ankles. His back and head rested against the painted concrete wall. Simon lay sleeping next to him on a bed constructed out of the leather cushions from the couch in the club office. A rolled sweatshirt served as a pillow. Ryker's suit coat was the blanket. Simon's small hand encircled two of Ryker's fingers.

Ryker's eyes flashed open, blue lasers zeroing in on her. He carefully extricated his hand from Simon's grasp and rose from the floor. A scrap of black paper fell from his lap. He bent at the waist to retrieve it, then shoved it in the pocket of his suit pants.

"What's that?" Sage asked.

"Nothing."

Curiosity piqued, she stepped close to him, running her fingernails down his chest to his thighs. As his breath rushed out and his eyes hooded, she slipped her hand in his pocket. Strong, rough fingers gripped her wrist.

"I told you how I grew up. I wouldn't have lasted a minute if I'd fallen for tricks like that."

"Come on," she whispered, afraid of waking Simon. "Just show me. Please."

Ryker pressed his free hand into her lower back, pulling her body against him. His muscles were like sunbaked granite. Warm, hard, and unbending.

His thumb traced slow circles on her wrist, and his other hand slid into the waistband of her cotton sweats. "What will you give me in exchange?"

Hot breath tickled her neck, and the crisp evergreen smell that was so uniquely Ryker made her almost dizzy with lust. Heat pooled in the juncture of her thighs.

This man was dangerous. He turned her on so fast, she could barely think.

She jumped back at the creak of the door and the sound of footsteps, but Ryker stood firm and unapologetic.

"Oh." Anise stepped fully into the tiny room. "I didn't mean to interrupt."

"We were just..." Sage couldn't think of anything to fill the hanging silence. The blood that should be feeding her brain seemed to have been diverted elsewhere.

"I was just about to ask Sage to find you. Are you ready to take Simon home? Do you need a ride?" Ryker's voice was professional and kind.

Why couldn't Sage sound like that? Why was she stammering like a kid caught snooping in the Christmas presents?

Anise cast her a "you're giving me the full story later or else" look, then gently scooped up Simon from the makeshift bed. "I drove, so we're good. I really appreciate you doing this for me. You're different than I thought."

Ryker was different. He hid his heart behind that cold, demanding, professional veneer. It was like he lived behind a shade with his true self occasionally shining through the open narrow space before the window's edge. His capacity for kindness was so great. It was crazy to hide who he was, but she had no right to judge. She did the same thing.

After saying a quick good-bye to Anise, Sage turned back to Ryker. "Now that you've got Anise wondering what's going on between us, you owe me. What's in your pocket?"

He pulled out the crumpled mess of paper, smoothed it out, and slid it over his head. "Homemade eye patch. Simon said my scruff made me look like a pirate. It's amazing what I can do with paper, tape, and a Sharpie."

Oh, he was a dangerous man. She was safe from Ryker Madsen the ruthless real estate magnate. It was this hidden Ryker Madsen who would turn himself into a pirate for a little boy who could make her fall hard and fast.

The problem was, there was no one to catch her.

"It was really nice of you to help Anise."

"Simon's a sweet kid. Madsen Enterprises has an emergency backup childcare program as one of our employee benefits. I'm going to have my HR folks talk to Bryce and get that program extended to the Black Cat employees."

Ryker picked up her coat and leather knapsack from where she'd dropped them on the floor. "It's late. Let me drive you home."

Sage's head ached, and her eyes were gritty. Driving home would suck, but she had to reconstruct the crumbling distance between them.

"I can drive myself."

He stalked closer, towering over her. "Don't be stubborn. You'll fall asleep at the wheel. You can barely stand up. Your eyes are closing just standing here."

"I'm not that tired. I'm just hungry, and my feet are screaming."

Ryker slid his hand behind her neck and pressed his fingers into the rigid muscles at the base of her skull. It felt so good, she almost cried.

"Let me drive you home. We'll stop at Pat's and grab steaks."

It was the promise of "one whiz with" that broke her. No self-respecting Philly girl could resist a cheesesteak, especially one from Pat's. She'd give him the lecture about maintaining a business-like relationship in the car.

Forty-five minutes later, after a few bites of gooey, meaty heaven, Sage decided cheesesteak should be added to the list of medicinal foods. Each nibble restored her energy. They picnicked in Ryker's car in front of her rented rowhouse. The Audi's heat beat her Mazda's by tenfold, and the heated seats were heaven.

This was true luxury.

Unfortunately, Ryker's next statement took a bite out of her relaxation. "I need to talk to you about Davis Anderson."

Spiky fear prickled her spine. Did Ryker know her true identity? Was he baiting her to see how she would respond?

"Davis isn't my favorite topic of conversation." That response certainly straddled the line.

"I sensed that. I don't need or want the details of your romance. Just tell me if he was the one who bruised your arms."

"I told you before. We didn't have a romance. Why are you asking me this?"

Ryker ripped the paper on his sandwich, sending onions flying, but his voice was even. "There are some things I won't tolerate. Violence against women is one of them. I won't do business with a man who hurts women."

"If you think he's that type of man, why would you do business with him at all?"

Ryker's eyes narrowed. "The business world is complicated, and so is the social world. Oftentimes, success hinges on who you know."

"You don't seem the type to need someone like Davis to make you successful."

He chuckled. "No. I don't need Davis's help, but I don't want Christian to have to work and fight as hard as I did. Davis is a scheming slug, but he can help give Christian credibility my new money can't buy. Christian doesn't want to take a job from me. He says it doesn't feel right. I want to set him up with every advantage possible when he finishes his MBA and moves back home. I don't want him to have to struggle or ever feel like he's not good enough. Putting up with Davis for one deal is worth it if it helps Christian in the end, but not if he's the type of man who hits women."

Sage twisted her hands in her lap. Her mother always said the truth was easier than lies. It didn't feel easier now.

Ryker tipped her chin up with gentled tug. "It's OK, Olivia. There's nothing to be embarrassed about. Just tell me the truth."

The truth. Everyone always seemed to have their own version of it. If she let the words out, she couldn't take them back. She'd have to admit to Ryker she'd lied to him about her identity. Lied to him about her own name. If he got past that and confronted Davis, Davis would fill his ears with all the horrible, fabricated stories he'd used to discredit her to the police.

How can I risk that?

"It wasn't him." The lie tasted like sour milk.

Ryker's gaze held her own for what felt like a full minute, as if his eyes could test the truth of her words. She shivered despite the warm air circling her. She needed to change the subject.

"Christian doesn't seem like the type who'd be friends with Davis."

"No. Christian met Davis once and despised him."

"So why do you need to get on Davis's good side?"

"Christian's going to move back here after he gets his MBA. All the big names in Philly belong to the Lincoln Club. Christian applied a couple of years ago, and they rejected his application. I hate the idea of anyone telling my brother he's not good enough. Davis is chair of the membership committee. If I get Christian in that club, it'll open so many doors for him."

"Are you a member?"

"God, no!" Ryker answered. "But that's different. I'm different. I don't give a shit what anyone thinks. Christian's a gentler soul."

At the wedding, Christian had been intelligent, funny, and kind, but he'd also shown some of Ryker's steel.

"If Christian doesn't like Davis, I'm surprised he's on board with your plan."

Ryker grimaced. Even in the dark car, his golden skin seemed to lose a bit of its color. "He'd be royally pissed if he found out I'm interfering. He keeps telling me he can take care of himself."

"He's probably right. Your brother's a really nice guy. Maybe it's time you let him live his own life."

"I don't need the same lecture from you that I get from him."

She laughed. "Sorry."

"It's OK. You're not wrong. I just don't want to hear it. So, tell me something I don't know about you. I feel like we've been talking about me all night."

Ryker let go of her hand, eased back into his seat, and picked up his steak sandwich.

Sage lifted her own pile of steaming steak heaven to her lips and chewed, staring out the window at the two orange cones that now sat perched at the edge of the sidewalk. When they'd pulled up, Ryker had asked politely if the battered traffic cones were hers before moving them and paralleling parking in front of her apartment with irritating expertise.

He was full of striking contrasts. Rich guys generally didn't know about staking your claim on your shoveled out parking spot with cones, a folding chair, or whatever else you could find or understand you risked a screwdriver to the tire if you parked in someone else's spot.

Ryker was as comfortable at Pat's and the Black Cat as he was in a gleaming skyscraper or at a wedding at a luxury inn. Most people didn't live so easily with their feet in both worlds.

Could she trust him with her truth?

Temptation tickled her tongue. It would be so nice to share her burden, even just for a little while, but then she looked past the snowy sidewalk to her apartment. The apartment she'd rented under a false name and had to pay for every month in cash.

It was her past that brought her here. Her father, her uncle, her neighbor, then Davis. Betrayal after betrayal after betrayal.

Painting Ryker with that same brush wasn't fair. He'd already shown he was better than that. Maybe she could tell him the truth after Rosemary finished her course of Remiza. Maybe he'd accept her. Maybe there could be something real between them. But a pile of future maybes wouldn't save Rosemary's life today. Sticking to their agreement would.

Sage had let things get offtrack with Ryker—too open, too personal. It wasn't the sex. It was the intimacy. It was the quiet conversations making her show too much of herself. If she weren't careful, she'd slip and he'd learn her real identity. She couldn't trust his reaction if he found out that she'd lied. That his business partner hated her. It was time to pull back and reset boundaries.

"Maybe it's better if I don't share. I know I've been the one pushing you to open up, but it feels like things are getting complicated. This is supposed to be a business arrangement. The more personal we make it, the harder it's going to be to walk away from each other. It's better if we just stick to the terms of our deal."

Ryker didn't look at her. His body lounged in the slightly reclined seat. He stared out the windshield, watching the wind swirl tiny snowflakes through the air. She counted eleven twitches in the muscle of his jawline before he spoke.

"What about this past weekend? Were you just holding up your end of our business deal?"

It had been the best weekend of her life. Dancing, snuggling, leaning on him for support. Then there was the sex. Her body melted at the memory of his hands and tongue. The sex was better than she ever imagined it could be and way too close to being something more. If she let those feelings loose, she risked being shattered.

"I think we both got what we wanted out of the weekend."

"You're deflecting. Answer the question," Ryker demanded. "Did you want to have sex with me, or were you just doing it to get what you want?"

"Don't ask me that."

He slammed a hand on the steering wheel. "I want the truth. Were you acting? Just playing a part? Was anything that happened this weekend real?"

It was hard to breathe. Sage pressed her knuckles into the space between her breasts, but the icy emptiness wouldn't fade. Words clogged her throat—the words she wanted to say but couldn't. She couldn't tell him how much the weekend had been to her. How much he meant to her. To explain that, she'd have to share her past, her wounds, her very soul. By remaining quiet she was saving Rosemary... and herself. Her heart couldn't survive another loss or betrayal.

Bring it back to a calm, polite business relationship.

She rested her hand on his warm, hard shoulder. "Why are you so angry?"

Hard, blue ice pinned her like a butterfly to a board.

"I'm not angry. I'm annoyed. I don't understand why you're being defensive and evasive. You're right. This is a business deal, but it includes more than sex. As much as I enjoy sleeping with you, we have social events to attend, and that means spending time outside the bedroom. You don't have to bare your goddamn soul, but I do expect casual conversation."

Sage's cheeks burned. She was a fool. She was falling hard, and he wasn't even stumbling. His questions didn't mean he cared. They were standard operating procedure. This was how Ryker did relationships. He'd told her that. She was the convenient companion of the moment.

There'd been no need to reset boundaries. Ryker was a pragmatic businessman, not the chivalrous medieval knight she'd been building in her fantasies.

The pleasant, bone-warming heat of the car now felt stifling. Sage wrapped the second half of her steak sandwich in its crinkly silver foil. Her appetite was gone. Time to get out of Dodge, or more appropriately, the Audi. She tugged the door handle, but nothing happened.

"Would you unlock the car? It's late. I should go inside."

Ryker's firm, hot hand held her thigh fast to the seat.

"Wait," he said.

She didn't want to wait. She wanted brick walls between them and the escape of her bed. Time and distance would settle her and drive home the sense of Ryker's words. Words that were her own arguments from his mouth.

The porch light flickered on, and Rosemary's head peeked out the door.

Ryker turned toward the light.

"Is that Rosemary?" he asked.

Sage fumbled for the unlock button, found it, and scrambled out. Rosemary was now standing on the porch. Her pink flannel pajamas looked cozy but would be no match for the fifteen-degree windchill.

"Rosemary, go back inside! Get out of the cold!" she ordered, climbing the few steps to the porch.

Ryker's footsteps pounded the pavement behind her. Her plans didn't include Ryker and Rosemary meeting, but instead of going back into the house like a normal, sensible sibling, Rosemary stepped toward them, lifting the long wooden handle of a hockey stick in the air.

"Don't come any closer," Rosemary yelled, waving the stick.

Sage stopped dead in her tracks. Ryker didn't. Hard muscle slammed into her back. Her feet flew from the ground, but instead of hitting concrete she thudded down on flesh with an iron arm around her waist.

Rosemary stood over them, still holding the stick. "Are you OK?"

Sage crawled off Ryker, the cold cement freezing her hands and knees. Ryker stood with annoying grace.

"Put that stick down! What are you doing? Are you crazy?" she asked her sister.

Rosemary lowered the stick. "You were sitting in that car for so long. You looked upset. I was worried." She pointed to Ryker. "He was chasing after you. I thought he was the stalker who sent those pictures."

Ryker's brows furrowed and his lips thinned. "What pictures? What stalker?"

Sage shot her sister a forbidding look, but sweet Rosemary was no match for Ryker's demanding glacial stare. She folded in a second.

"Um. It's nothing really. Just some silly pictures that were in the mail. I'm sure I'm overreacting. I've always been a little overprotective when it comes to my—"

"Rosemary!" Sage yelled, cutting her off. "Get inside before you make things worse."

By calling me your sister.

This time, Rosemary dashed back into the house.

Ryker's strong fingers gripped her arm. "Give me the pictures."

"It's really not your concern."

He tugged her closer, his warm breath caressing the side of her cheek. "My patience is at its end. Your safety is absolutely my concern. Give me the pictures."

Ryker wasn't going to give on this, and she was too exhausted to fight. Delay was the only option.

"I'll show them to you tomorrow. It's too late to get into this tonight."

He leaned closer, pressing his still-warm lips gently against her cool ones. "Alright. We'll figure this out tomorrow. Now get inside the house and lock the door behind you."

The lingering sensation of Ryker's lips left her wishing she could stand on the porch all night, but it was freezing, and she was dead on her feet. Plus, she needed her rest.

Tomorrow was the charity ball, and she was praying Davis didn't show up.

Chapter Sixteen

"You look like a princess. A modern, kick-ass princess, but still one hundred percent princess," Rosemary said.

Sage rubbed the smooth material of the emerald-green gown between her fingers. She didn't know if it was silk or satin or some fantastic material she'd never heard of. All she knew was that the dress was gorgeous, comfortable, and fit perfectly. It was as if Andre DeMarco had climbed into her subconscious and plucked out a fantasy dress she hadn't had even known she'd wanted.

Sage twirled in front of the mirror and watched the ankle-length skirt separate at the center and swirl around her bare legs. She loved the way the flowing skirt counterbalanced the sexiness of the high-cut slit and how the halter-style bodice plunged to the cinched waistline.

She sat down on the edge of her bed, where Rosemary was lounging in a bathrobe on a pile of pillows. "I wish you were coming with me."

"And I wish you would tell me what's really going on with you and Ryker."

Rosemary was tenacious. She'd been grilling her all morning.

"There's nothing to tell. He's my boss. He got you Remiza, so I'm returning the favor by going to a few events with him. He needed a date."

"Oh, right. Because a millionaire cross between Adonis and Ares must have a really hard time getting dates. Don't bullshit me. I know when you're lying. Monday you were on cloud nine, but you've been quiet and sullen all day today. You told me you slept with him, so it's not just"—Rosemary made air quotes with her fingers—"going to a few events. If you don't tell me what's going on, I'll march down to the Black Cat and ask him myself."

Rosemary's heart was in the right place, but Sage did not need her interference right now. Everything was under control.

"Please don't push me on this."

"I haven't pushed you on one gosh darn thing since Mom died." Rosemary's voice was high and shaky. "When you accused Davis of killing her, I left home with you without saying a word. You told me to quit my job, a job I loved, so he wouldn't find us, and I did. You told me we were living here. I moved right in. You have Justin come babysit me every time you leave the house, and when you leave, you strip to support us. So don't you dare tell me not to push you! I have every right to push you."

Sage's ribs squeezed her lungs. She battled for air as she spoke. "Everything I've done, I've done for you. To protect you. To keep you safe. All for you."

"*All* for me? Are you sure it was *all* for me?"

Sage leaped off the bed. "Did you think I wanted to leave school? Do you think I like living here? Do you think I like stripping?"

"I think you focus all your energy on me so you don't have to focus on yourself. I think you're controlling my life because you're afraid to live your own. I think you like hiding out because you don't actually have to live."

Tears burned Sage's eyes. They were in danger. All the choices she'd made had been to protect them. How could Rosemary doubt that?

"Davis killed Mom. He threatened us. We had to leave. You believe that, don't you?"

Rosemary climbed off the bed. Her hand was gentle and warm on Sage's wet cheek. "I do believe it. I love you. I hate seeing you cry. I shouldn't have said those things."

"But you think them?"

Rosemary's soft hands tugged her back down to the edge of the bed. "I honestly don't know what I think. I know that something's not right with Davis. He drinks too much and gets violent when he's drunk. He shouldn't have asked me to give him a fake alibi, and he shouldn't have told those lies about you being a drug addict to the police. It's just that, even after everything he's done, I can't believe he killed Mom. Maybe because it hurts too much to think it could be true."

Rosemary's words were a dagger in Sage's heart. Rosemary was all things kind and good and loving, like Beth from *Little Women.* Of course she'd want to give Davis the benefit of the doubt.

"It hurts me too," Sage admitted.

"I know, but you suppress it. You think if you let yourself feel, you'll break. But what's going to break you is taking on everything yourself. I know you're not telling me the whole truth about what's going on with Ryker. I'm tired of you hiding things to protect me. It makes things harder on you and makes me feel guilty and useless."

Sage felt like she was falling even though her feet were firmly planted on the floor. She didn't want to make Rosemary feel that way, but she couldn't risk anything happening to her sister. She needed her too much.

"I've lost everyone I love. I can't risk losing you."

"I know that, but you can't give up your own life to take care of me. It's not good for you, and it's not good for me."

Sage let out a dry laugh. "Last night, I said almost the exact same thing to Ryker about the way he treats his little brother. I told him Christian could take care of himself. Sounds like I need to take a little of my own advice."

Rosemary hugged her. "I love you, little sister. I want us to be in this together. That means you need to stop protecting me and tell me the truth."

Sage rubbed her cheek against the soft fluff of Rosemary's robe while her sister's words rattled around in her head. Rosemary was the one who was sick. It was her life in Ryker's hands. It wasn't fair to keep her in the dark.

"It's wrong for me to keep things from you. Everything's just been so hard since Mom died. It's not fair. Dad. Thyme. Mom. Davis. Your cancer. It's so hard for me, and I can't bear the thought of it being that hard on you. That's why I've been trying to protect you."

"I don't need protection. What I need is the truth."

Sage pushed out a long breath. Rosemary was going to have a hissy fit.

"I made a deal with Ryker so you could get Remiza."

Rosemary pulled back to meet her gaze. "A deal? What kind of deal?"

"I agreed to be his escort for a few events," Sage answered.

Rosemary squeezed her hand. "Again, I'm confused why your personal Greek god needs to exchange favors to get a date."

"That's the thing. He doesn't want a date. He wants a business arrangement. A paid escort with no strings attached. No emotional attachment. No complications. No demands. He wants all the benefits of a relationship without actually having one."

Rosemary lifted a hand to her lips. "Oh no. Tell me this isn't about sex. Tell me you did not agree to sleep with him."

Sage studied the worn carpet, avoiding her sister's gaze, but Rosemary gripped her chin and pulled her face up.

Instead of showing anger and disappointment, Rosemary's face was pinched with concern. "Oh, baby. What have you done?"

"Made an ass of myself, that's what I've done. He didn't insist on the sex—I did. I wanted to make sure he stuck to his end of the bargain. I figured sex with a stranger was an easy price to pay if it meant saving your life. He was so unlikable in the beginning it never crossed my mind that I'd start to get attached." She huffed out a frustrated breath. "The whole thing has become a complicated mess."

"You fell for him, didn't you?"

"Hook, line, and sinker. Now I have to stick it out for another week or so. What if he sees how I feel? What if I can't do it? Now that I care about him, how can I sleep with him knowing he doesn't care about me? How could I be so dumb?"

"You're not dumb. You can't help what you feel, but this is wrong, Sage. We can figure something else out. I don't want you sacrificing yourself for me."

Sage hugged her sister tightly. Getting her secret out didn't change anything with Ryker, but her chest felt looser and lighter.

"It's too late. I can't go back on my word. It's one of the few things I have left."

"Then why don't you tell him the whole truth? Tell him about Mom and Davis. Tell him about those horrible pictures. Most importantly, tell him how you feel. I saw the way he looked at you last night. When you slipped, he threw his body on the ground to protect you. I think he cares about you too. Try having a little faith. Give him a chance. Trust him."

Trust him.

The words were so tempting.

Maybe Rosemary was right. Maybe it was time to take a chance, time to ask for help. After the charity ball, she'd tell him everything. Even if he didn't care for her the same way she cared for him, at least there'd be truth between them. Ryker was a good man. He'd understand why she'd lied. What did she have to lose?

Except everything.

* * *

This could be the best night of his life. Ryker pulled Olivia closer as they danced. He wasn't sure which was softer: the smooth, rich material of her silky gown on his palm or the honey skin of her back under his thumb. His fingers itched to slide lower to grip and knead her luscious ass...but that was probably inappropriate for the guest of honor at a charity fundraiser.

Ryker closed his eyes and breathed deeply, inhaling Olivia's intoxicating lavender-vanilla scent. He felt calm, relaxed, happy. This is what he'd wanted for himself. This moment. This night. He just hadn't known it.

The ballroom was a vestige of days long gone. The intricate woodwork in the ceiling and the marble pillars were original early 1800s. To reproduce them today, a builder would use veneers to keep costs down, but he knew this building. He knew the wood was hand-carved and the pillars were solid, cold stone.

The hurricane sconces and crystal chandeliers cast a candle-like glow over the room, adding to the Old World feel. Evening dresses glistened and jewelry flashed as women danced or chatted. Men in tuxedos appeared gallant and dashing. He felt like a turn-of-the-century oil baron, one of those early Americans who built himself from nothing and reveled in the luxuries he'd earned.

Like them, he'd fought hard for every dollar he made. He just hadn't ever let go and enjoyed his wealth. He hadn't allowed himself to desire something of his own. Working to take care of Christian had consumed him, but Christian was grown, and Ryker had earned enough money to support Christian for three lifetimes. He's earned this one night to relax and enjoy himself, and there was no one he'd rather spend it with than Olivia.

In a week, their deal would end, and he'd have to give her up, so he might as well get as much of her as he could now.

How the hell am I going to let her go?

His arm tightened reflexively. Olivia's warm breath tickled his neck as she joked, "If you squeeze me any harder, you might crack a rib."

Ryker loosened his grip, but she didn't step back. Her lush breasts pressed into his hard chest. He knew she wore no bra. The dress was far too bare to hide one. One slip of his hand under the fabric and he'd be in heaven.

He slid his hand up to the back of her delicate neck, gripping the soft skin firmly as he lowered his head and nipped her soft earlobe between his teeth. Her eyes hooded as a low moan escaped her lips.

She clung into him, her warm body flush against his growing erection.

"When we get home, I'm going to lick every inch of your delicious skin. I can't wait to taste you again." Ryker whispered the words and was rewarded with another moan and the feel of Olivia shuddering against him.

"And I can't wait to feel your tongue on me," she answered.

Electricity raced through him. Images of Olivia's smooth bare skin, of her writhing wet and hot beneath him, filled his mind. There was no way he could wait until they got home to have her, not with the way she looked in that dress.

Ryker glanced at the time. The awards ceremony was scheduled to start in forty-five minutes. Choices were ditch the awards or get creative.

He linked his long, strong fingers with Olivia's delicate ones and strode across the dance floor, the hardwood both firm and springy under his feet. Impatience flared with each person who stopped to offer their congratulations. Every second of polite conversation was one less second with Olivia.

"Where are we going?" she asked when they finally managed to wade through the crowd and into the hallway.

He didn't answer. Instead, he flashed her what he knew was a devilish smile and quickened his pace, following the posted signs for the lobby.

When they reached the front desk and he learned there were no vacant rooms, he asked the obsequious clerk if he could see the manager. While the clerk rushed to comply, he pulled several hundred-dollar bills from his wallet and folded them into his hand.

Olivia pressed close, splitting her legs around his thigh, rubbing her sex against him like a cat. Her eyelids closed halfway, and her lips parted. She was pure, undiluted sensuality. His dick twitched. The reception counter would be the perfect height for her to brace herself while he lifted her dress and...

"Sir. Sir? Did you want to speak to me?" The voice was high-pitched, with a touch of New York. He shifted his body in front of Olivia while he turned toward the voice. That look on her face was for him. Only him.

The manager was a tall, thin, dark-haired man in a mid-level suit. His eyes were sharp, and he took a full step back when his glance met Ryker's.

Ryker made an effort to soften his gaze. "Good evening. I'm Ryker Madsen. I have some urgent business to attend to and need a private space for about the next half hour." He extended his hand to shake and transferred the bills into the manager's hand. "I understand there are no rooms available. Do you have any suggestions?"

The manager rubbed his thumb across the edges of the money in his hand, counting it, then cleared his throat. "Yes. Yes. Mr. Madsen. I apologize, but we are fully booked. However, I'm happy to offer my private office for your use. It's quite comfortable and very private. Hopefully, it will suit your needs."

At this point, Ryker didn't care if the guy gave him a broom closet. All he needed was a room with a door that locked.

With Olivia pulled tightly against him, he followed the manager down a narrow hallway behind the reception desk to a surprisingly cozy office. The room contained a desk, a loveseat, and a credenza that held a printer, manuals, and various office supplies. The room was windowless, and the door had the dead bolt and flip closure standard in most hotel rooms.

"Thank you."

The manager smiled. Ryker was sure the guy knew exactly what he needed the office for, but the man's visage was openly friendly, not crude or judgmental. Ryker made a mental note to grab a business card from the desk before he left. The manager was the kind of honest, get-things-done man he'd like to have on his own payroll.

As the manager exited, Ryker shut and locked the door behind him. The dead bolt clicked like a nail gun in the quiet room, leaving Olivia's quick breaths as the other only sound.

She stood with her back to the desk, resting gently against it, her palms pressed to the dark wood. Her legs were slightly outstretched, and her gown parted along the slit cut up the center of the skirt, baring her lean, muscled legs. The soft light of the desk lamp made the satin of her dress shimmer and gave a lustrous hue to her tawny skin. She was exquisite, and she was his for the taking. The idea stilled his heart and filled his already throbbing dick.

His long legs ate up the distance between them. She lifted a hand to his chest, but he encircled her wrist and pushed it back to its resting position against the desk.

"Don't move," he commanded. "I want to look at you."

Silk brushed the tips of his fingers as he slid his hands up the front of her dress, then circled to the back of her neck. He pushed the hard pearl through the buttonhole, unfastening the halter. The bodice of the dress flipped down to expose her lush, golden breasts to the cool air. Her rosy nipples tightened into hard buds. He stepped back to revel in the sight of her.

"Every man in that ballroom was thinking about you like this, fantasizing about unbuttoning the top of that dress and freeing your breasts, imaging that you loved him."

Olivia shook her head and laughed softly. "That's crazy. You can't possibly think that."

He did think it. He thought it because he felt it. He thought it because he was the one fantasizing about Olivia loving him...because he loved her.

Holy shit. What the hell have I gotten myself into?

Chapter Seventeen

Sage shivered, unsure if it was from the cool air or anticipation. Ryker's eyes were lasers trained on her skin while he stepped out of his shoes, then shed his jacket and tie, laying them gently on the small couch. He didn't avert his eyes once as he unbuttoned his shirt and pulled his white undershirt over his head.

Shyness battled lust. The need to lift her hands to cover her breasts warred with the desire to squeeze her elbows together to thrust them higher. Flaunting her body wasn't her style, but here she was doing it and loving it. Having Ryker's complete focus on this night when everyone wanted his attention was a heady, powerful feeling. The weight of his gaze turned her blood to lava, sending a rush of heat to her core.

He removed the rest of his clothing with excruciating slowness until he stood before her, completely naked, full erection jutting. His tan skin glowed in the low lamplight. His bare, gleaming muscles flexed and rippled as he stepped toward her. It was as if a statue of a Greek god had come to life.

Lord, he's magnificent.

Her thong was already soaking wet, and he hadn't even touched her. She ran her fingers through the wiry sprinkling of hair on his chest. His heart pounded under her small hand. His eyes were hooded, but he gripped her wrist and pressed her hand back down onto the desk. He bent toward her, warm breath tickling her ear.

"I love your hands on me, but let me do this, Olivia. Just relax and let me touch you."

She almost asked him to call her by her given name, but his mouth closed on her bare shoulder and coherent thought was replaced with fire. Sharp teeth scraped and nipped her shoulder, her neck, and the delicate skin above her breasts. Her skin was on fire. Her sex throbbed, empty and wanting.

Ryker stepped back, and the chilly air tingled each spot his mouth had wet. He parted the slit of her dress, tucking the edges at her waist. Calloused hands scraped her thighs and hips, creating delicious sensations as he slid her damp, black thong down her legs and tossed it to the side.

She felt hot and wet and wild. Having her breasts and sex bare while the dress hung like an open cape at her waist made her feel more exposed than she ever had, even when dancing at the club, and more aroused than ever. Ryker knelt in front of her. He blew softly on her exposed flesh, and her knees turned to jelly.

A miniature grandfather clock ticked out the seconds. Her entire world was reduced to his breath on her core, to desperate anticipation.

"Please," she begged.

Ryker's tongue shot out, white heat against her clit. A few quick flicks and she was exploding, her vision going black, her core pulsing, but he didn't pull his mouth away. He licked and sucked relentlessly. She came again and again and again until her legs could barely support her.

"I need you inside me."

The husky, wanton voice didn't even sound like her own. She'd become a creature ruled by her body's demands.

"Turn around," he ordered, even as he was rising and twisting her body with his hands, bending her over the desk.

He pushed the back of her dress up around her waist. His movements were fast and just a bit rough. His breath came in hard, quick breaths. The skin on her ass and the back of her thighs tingled and tightened with goose bumps. Then that hot, long brand of fire filled her in one quick motion.

Satisfaction.

He began to move, and the whirlwind started all over again.

Her body slid across the desk with each thrust, hard wood rubbing against her even harder nipples. Ryker's fingers pressed into the soft flesh at her hips, his pace quickening. It was like he couldn't get close enough or deep enough.

Thrusting. Pushing. Pulling. Climbing.

Thrusting. Pushing. Pulling. Climbing.

Thrusting. Pushing. Pulling. Climbing.

Ecstasy.

He stilled, and she was complete.

"I love you."

Ryker's firm hands pulled her up from the desk and turned her to face him. "What did you say?"

Oh God! Had he read her mind? She'd been thinking, not talking, hadn't she?

"Did you tell me you loved me?" Ryker's face was shuttered. Blue eyes closed and sterile like a frozen lake. She'd seen that expression before. Forced blank. Waiting to react.

Rosemary's words rattled through Sage's mind.

You control my life because you're afraid to live your own.

Try having a little faith.

Give him a chance.

Tell him the truth.

Trust him.

He couldn't judge her too harshly for caring about him, could he?

Sage pushed out a long, settling breath. "I'm sorry. The mind-blowing sex must have actually blown my mind. I'm saying what I should only be thinking. I know you want a no-strings relationship. I didn't say that to tie you to me. It's just that, despite the crazy way things started between us, I care about you. A lot. And the words just slipped out."

The lake thawed, then glistened. The edges of Ryker's straight Viking lips curved into a sexy smile.

"I care about you too. Very much so."

Warmth raced from her heart up to her face and down to her toes. She'd heard about toe-curling kisses, but Ryker had managed to curl her toes and make her blush with three little words.

Very much so. Who would have thought such a simple phrase could make her feel like she was flying, and what would happen when reality crept in, and she came crashing back to Earth?

She squirmed away from him, slipping back into her panties and rearranging her dress. She used the distraction of them both dressing to ask the question that had been popping in and out of her brain all night.

"So what happens next week when our business deal comes to an end?"

Sage purposefully checked her hair and makeup in the mirror from her purse so she didn't have to meet his gaze while he answered. But he lifted her chin with one finger, forcing her to face him.

"Let's forget the deal and start over fresh. Tonight. We can pretend this is our first date." He hesitated, bending his lips in on themselves, a hint of uncertainty in his eyes. "What do you think?"

She thought that sounded like a fairy tale.

"I think I should follow Rosemary's advice more often."

Ryker's Viking arms squeezed her even tighter as his body rumbled with laughter, the gentle vibrations of his joy flowing through her. "What advice did Rosemary give you?"

"She said I should tell you how I feel. That I should give you a chance. That I should trust you. That I should be honest." Sage's gut clenched. She wriggled, loosening his grasp, instantly missing the cherished protection she felt in his arms. "If we're going to try to make something of this, there's something important I need to tell you."

Ryker's face was still light with laughter. He glanced at his watch, then tucked an errant strand of hair behind her ear. "You can tell me anything you want, *after* my speech. They're starting the ceremony in five minutes."

She didn't want to wait, couldn't bear to wait. The truth was a boulder on her chest, making it hard to breathe. He'd opened the office door and was tugging her down the hallway into the lobby, his profile showing a relaxed, easy expression. She wanted to dig in her heels and demand that he stop. She needed to tell him about Davis and Rosemary. She needed to tell him that her name, her real, birth-given name, was Sage. Not Olivia. Every time he called her Olivia was like nails on a chalkboard. He had to know her, really know her, or they'd never have a chance.

The need to scream the truth burned like a forest fire, wild, hungry, and out of control.

But she couldn't tell him now. It wasn't right. It wasn't fair. This was Ryker's night. A night to celebrate him and the good he'd done. The community centers had made an impact on so many lives. He deserved to be recognized. Her story was long and complicated. She needed time and quiet to explain the full truth to him. She couldn't risk making him late for his own award.

"Ryker!" Veronica's voice lashed through the lobby. "I've been looking for you everywhere. We need to talk!"

Veronica's figure matched her voice, smooth and sharp like a whip. Her dress, a straight line of strapless, fitted black, enhanced her lean, keen-edged silhouette. Her eyes blazed, and she brandished a thick folder like a mace. She looked like an avenging dark angel.

Ryker stopped short, tucking Sage under his arm, creating a physical barrier between her and Veronica. Sage's throat clenched at the gesture. He was protecting her. Here, in this public place, he was sending a message that she was under his care. She didn't need it. She could handle herself, but it was exhausting fighting every battle alone. It felt damn good to know Ryker had her back.

Veronica crossed the dark, gleaming lobby tile in long, determined strides. Ryker waited until she was within a couple of feet of them before he spoke. His words were whispered iron.

"Veronica, whatever you need me to review can be presented tomorrow, in my office. Tonight is for pleasure, not business."

Veronica's head swung left then right, as if she'd just noticed the crowded lobby. Her cheeks were flushed. Wisps of hair escaped her severe chignon, and her eyes were bright. She seemed off, unpredictable.

Sage pulled away from Ryker, stepping in front of him.

Veronica eyed her like a roach. "So this is your game? You're going to act like you're protecting Ryker from me? From me? You've got nerve, you little gold-digging slut."

Ryker tugged Sage back and held her against him, the heat of his body radiating through his tux, warming her back.

"What the hell is the matter with you? Olivia is with me. If you insult her, you insult me. Now get out of my way. We need to get to the ballroom."

Sage glanced at Veronica as Ryker led her toward the elevator. Distress had replaced her fiery, angry expression. Veronica looked so upset that for an instant pity filled Sage's chest. Then pity shifted to unease as the sound of Veronica's pounding feet hit her ears.

What is it with elevators? If you're waiting for someone, they arrive in a flash. If you're in a hurry, they take forever.

Sage turned back toward the lobby, resigned to another confrontation. Ryker turned with her. They would face Veronica together.

Veronica thrust the folder at Ryker, her diamond bracelet glittering in the light. This time her face was granite despite the emotion in her voice.

"The PI report came back. She's been lying to you, Ryker. Playing you for a fool. You told me you respected me for doing my job. Well, I'm doing it. I'm saving you from making the biggest mistake of your life."

He'd had her investigated. As soon as he read that report, he would know she'd lied to him.

Sage's stomach lurched, but she pushed down the sour feeling. Once she explained, he'd understand. He had to. She just needed the chance to tell her side of the story.

She wanted to take Ryker's hand, but he was already flipping through the folder, his lips as straight as a ruler.

"If you care about me, you'll close that and take me someplace where we can talk. In private."

Ryker didn't even look up. He flipped pages, his eyes darting back and forth across the pages. He took a step back, physically distancing himself from her. Nausea burned her throat.

"You're Davis's daughter?" Ryker's voice was flat. His glacial eyes burned her soul.

"She's his stepdaughter," Veronica interjected. "He kicked her out of the house for doing drugs. He wanted her to get clean, so he cut her off. Left her high and dry. No money. No fancy house. No designer clothes. What's a spoiled rich girl to do?" Veronica's voice dripped with sarcasm. "She finds a way to get the richest man in the city under her thumb. She's conning you, Ryker, and you can't get your brain out of your pants long enough to see it."

Sage's heart was a pounding drum, filling her ears. She felt hot. Dizzy. Sick. Ten minutes ago, they'd been making passionate love. Now Ryker was looking at her like she was a stranger. No, not a stranger. He was too fair to look at a stranger with such contempt. That look was for an enemy.

She knew how Ryker felt about drugs. She'd never done them. Ever. But how could she fight the lies? Davis was too rich, too devious, too powerful. Ryker would never believe her over Davis, but she had to try.

"It's not like that. It's not true."

"You're not Davis's daughter? He didn't kick you out? You're not a con artist? You're not a drug addict? Exactly which part isn't true? Let's hear it."

People were staring.

He'd just accused her of being a con artist and a drug addict in the middle of the hotel lobby.

He didn't think that. He couldn't think that. He cared about her. He'd said so. He was just upset. He loved Christian the way she loved Rosemary. Once she had a chance to explain everything, he'd understand.

"Ryker, please, just give me a minute. Let's find somewhere quiet to talk so I can tell you the truth."

She reached for his arm, but he yanked it away.

His eyes were cut ice, sharp and empty. "Give you a minute? So you can trap me in a new web of lies? You may have sucked me in once with that young Fantine act, but I'm not fool enough to let you do it again. I'm done with you and your lies. I never want to see you again."

Ryker turned on his heel and strode down the hall, leaving her abandoned and betrayed.

Pain sliced her chest, deep and sharp. Her fists clenched, instinctively protecting her heart, but it was too late. He had already thrust the blade. Searing, fiery agony slashed through her. She looked down, expecting blood, but of course there was none. The wound wasn't physical, and it wasn't unfamiliar. She knew that pain. Knew it better than she wanted to. She'd promised herself she'd never feel it again.

Nothing cut deeper than betrayal by someone you loved.

How had she let this happen?

She'd let herself fall. She'd let herself trust. She'd let herself hope. She knew better. Knew better than to trust anyone other than her mother and Rosemary.

Oh God. *Rosemary!* What had she done?

"Wait!" The slash of her voice silenced every conversation. She'd be the subject of gossip for months, but she didn't care. Nothing mattered except Rosemary.

Ryker stopped, his broad shoulders firm and square in his perfectly tailored tuxedo.

"What about Rosemary? What about Remiza?"

He didn't turn around, and he didn't answer. He resumed his path down the hallway, like she hadn't spoken. Like she didn't exist.

And if she didn't exist to him, neither would Rosemary.

Ryker was ruthless. Everyone said so. If he was too angry to even turn around and look at her, how could she be sure he wouldn't go back on his word and cut off Rosemary's access to the drug?

This couldn't be happening. Her plan to save her sister had backfired. Horrifically.

She couldn't lose Rosemary.

She couldn't live without her.

She could not let Rosemary die.

Blood rushed to her head. Her heart beat too hard and way too fast. Her throat was closing. She clutched her neck, rubbing frantically, but it didn't help. She sucked air into her mouth, but her lungs wouldn't expand. Her legs were jelly. The voices in the lobby were distant and distorted. Her vision wavered.

She was going to faint. Here in the lobby, surrounded by strangers. But utterly alone.

A strong arm slid around her waist, supporting her, bearing almost all her weight, leading her to a couch against the wall.

"It's OK. I've got you. Sit down. Catch your breath."

Sage let her head fall back against the plush cushions, grateful to be off her feet. She kept her eyes closed and concentrated on slowing her breathing, on fighting her panic.

It would be alright. She'd figure something out. She always did.

Step one. Don't let Ryker see what he's done to you. Get yourself together and get the hell out of this hotel before he leaves the ballroom.

She never wanted to see him again, but she did see him. When she opened her eyes, she found herself staring into Ryker's deep blue eyes. No. These eyes were warmer and a slightly lighter blue. Similar to Ryker's but not the same.

Christian.

Christian sat next to her. He rubbed her cold fingers in his warm, dry, strong hands, soothing her. "Are you feeling better?"

"Well, I can't faint if I'm sitting. So that's a plus."

He laughed. "You still have your sense of humor, so it can't be that bad."

Sage grunted. "I'm not sure I agree with your definition of *bad*."

"I know my brother's not easy. He's stubborn, ornery, and thinks he knows better than everyone else, but he really is a good person. There's nothing he wouldn't do for someone he cares about."

"If you're suggesting he cares about me, you're wrong. He hates me."

"That's impossible," Christian said. "I saw how he was with you at the wedding. He's probably just angry. I saw you two arguing. What's going on?"

She released a long sigh. She was exhausted. The burden of the past few weeks sat too heavy on her shoulders. Davis's treachery. Rosemary's sickness. The crazy nonsense with her locker and the pictures. Theo getting hurt. Giving her heart to Ryker and having it crushed to pieces.

"It's a long story."

"I've got all night."

"Don't you want to see your brother get his award?"

Christian shook his head. "I don't need to see him get an award to know how much he does for those kids. Remember, I was the first kid he fought for. I also know my brother can be a bullheaded ass. You're good for him, and I think he's too stupid or scared to see it. Getting this sorted out between the two of you is more important than me seeing someone hand him a plaque."

"I don't think it can be sorted out, and I need to get home to my sister." The truth felt good on her tongue.

"I didn't know you had a sister. You love her, don't you?"

What an odd question for Christian to ask. Of course she loved her sister. That's how she'd gotten into this whole damn mess.

"Yes. More than anything."

"Well, I love Ryker just as much. I know my brother. You may not see it, but he's devasted. Whatever's going on between you both is killing him. So tell me what happened. Even if you don't get back together, if I know what happened, it'll help me get him through it. Plus, you'll feel better if you talk about it. It always feels better to share your troubles with someone who cares."

Sage couldn't resist the plea in Christian's eyes and the promise of warm acceptance in his voice. The horrible night sat on her chest like a weight, and now, with the PI report in Ryker's hands, she had nothing to hide. She told him. Every word of her truth from the beginning.

She told him about Thyme and her dad, her uncle, her neighbor, and every person who had betrayed them. She told him about her mom, how she loved and missed her, and how she thought Davis had killed her. She told him about Rosemary and her cancer and the drug that was Rosemary's last and only hope. She told him how Ryker was the key to saving Rosemary's life, and how she'd sold herself to save her sister but somehow had fallen in love along the way. She told him how the pain that had flickered across Ryker's face had cut as deep as him walking away.

She told him everything, and it was easy.

Because she'd pretended she was talking to Ryker.

Chapter Eighteen

Ryker's speech was a blur. Words floated into a sea of light and indistinct faces. He wasn't sure he'd even made sense, but the crowd clapped, so he must have managed to string together some coherent sentences.

The folder was burning a hole in his hand. He hadn't put it down. Not while he was giving his speech. Not while he shook hands and smiled for the camera. Not while he sat at the table, pasting polite interest on his face during the award presentations and comments of his fellow honorees, the chair next to him conspicuously empty. Taunting him.

He was desperate to open the folder. Desperate to understand what he'd missed, to figure out how Olivia had broken through his carefully cultivated defenses, to understand how she'd deceived him. He needed to understand to make sure it never happened again, but he was also desperate to learn about her past, to know who she truly was.

What the hell was wrong with him?

Her story didn't matter. The truth of her didn't matter. The only thing that mattered was that he'd been a fool. Again.

What was the saying? Burn me once, shame on you. Burn me twice, shame on me.

It was his shame. He'd broken his own rules, and the hole Olivia had detonated in his heart was the price he was paying for it. He was a dumbass. No. He was a weak, pathetic dumbass. Because he knew he'd spend all night reading and rereading that damn PI report.

Even with her betrayal, he still couldn't get her out of his mind.

The small talk was endless. Even after the ceremony, he couldn't escape. Every goddamn person in the room wanted to shake his hand and talk about the neighborhood centers. Normally, they were one of his favorite conversation topics, but not tonight. He was agitated and unsettled. It was hard to stand still. The urge to leave was overwhelming.

Then someone asked where his date was.

He lied.

He said Olivia had come down with a migraine and had to leave.

What else could he say? That he'd told the only woman he'd ever really loved that he never wanted to see her again? That he'd discovered the love of his life was a fraudster who was only after his money?

As time passed, niggling thoughts invaded, making it hard to concentrate. Hard to respond with the expected social niceties.

His mouth formed words, but his mind wandered.

If Olivia was after his money, why had she encouraged him to turn the hotel into a low- income project when he'd told her he'd barely break even? Why had she refused his money every time he'd offered it? And if she was just after money, why him?

With her looks, she could get anything she wanted from any man she wanted. There were plenty of men at the club who'd gladly shower her with money and gifts.

So why did she eschew them all and choose to work for tips and live in that dive apartment? If Olivia was a liar, why hadn't he seen it?

He'd had suspicions with Bethany. When the dust had settled and the embarrassment had faded, he'd realized he'd known something wasn't right all along. Recognized that he'd seen signs but chose to ignore them. Made excuses. There'd been something in Bethany's eyes. Or, more accurately, something that hadn't been in them. Her joy, her laughter, her love. It had always danced on the surface, never touching her eyes.

Seeing Bethany with her real lover had been heartbreaking and eye-opening. The way she'd looked at her lover made it clear that every emotion she'd ever shown Ryker was a charade. She may have been a gold-digging schemer, but her genuine love for that other man was undeniable. When he realized that, he'd never been angrier...and had never felt more unlovable.

And it had happened again.

A thought came unbidden. He'd seen Olivia's soul. How could that be a lie? He pushed the errant notion away. He'd figure that out later. He'd seen the truth, written in black and white.

She wasn't Olivia Dupree. She was Sage Cashman. Davis Anderson's wayward stepdaughter. He had to start thinking of her that way.

The woman he thought he loved was an image.

Olivia didn't exist.

A glimpse of emerald entered his peripheral vision.

He left the conversation mid-sentence and sprinted halfway across the room before he caught himself.

The woman was too tall. Her hair and skin too light. The dress the wrong shade of green.

Sage hadn't come back.

Disappointment rolled through him. He shouldn't want her to come back. But he did. Her look of anguished, horrified disillusion was branded in his mind. Despite what she'd done to him, he shouldn't have left her like that. He didn't even know if she had money for a cab.

He was a better man than that. He was also a complete and utter fool. He knew he would go to her tonight. He couldn't stand the idea of leaving her with that look on her face. Couldn't stand not knowing if she'd gotten home safely, when he was the one who'd promised to protect her.

The fist came out of nowhere.

Strong knuckles connected with flesh and bone, rocking his head back and to the left. Pain, the kind that made lights flash behind his eyes followed a second behind the shock of the blow, and his reaction followed only a half-second later.

He may have been years off the streets, but he was in the dojo almost daily. Instinct and training curved his body and sent his straightened hand flying toward his assailant's neck, but in the slice of time before impact, a second instinct, deeper and more primal, made him hesitate.

He'd made a vow years ago that no one would ever hit his little brother again. No one. He'd never hit Christian. Even if the punk had lost his mind and sucker-punched him in the middle of his own awards ceremony, which, Ryker thought, rubbing his jaw, it seemed liked he'd just done.

Ryker grabbed his brother's thick, muscled arm, dragging him through the gaping, whispering crowd. Ryker's eyes shot daggers at anyone who tried to follow them or intervene, stopping them in their tracks. This was between him and his baby brother.

After they made it to the hallway, he gave Christian a hard shove. "What the hell was that about?"

Christian shoved back, eyes flashing. "That was for being an asshole!"

"What the hell are you talking about?"

"I'm talking about treating Sage like dirt. That woman is the best thing that ever happened to you, and you let your goddamn ego get in the way of what's supposed to be a fairly intelligent brain. You're a fool, Ryker."

His brows pinched together. "This isn't your business. And what the hell are you doing here, anyway? You're supposed to be back in D.C. You have class."

"Believe it or not, big brother, not everything is about me. I'm a grown man. I can take care of myself and make my own decisions. Good decisions. Not the shit decisions you've been making."

Ryker ran his fingers through his hair. Christian was only trying to help, but he didn't know what Sage had done.

"You're right. I have been making shit decisions, and one of those was falling for Sage's sweet warrior act. She's a liar, Christian. A con artist. I let that woman make a fool of me, and I don't know what the hell she said to you, but it looks like she's still got you snowed."

Christian stepped so close Ryker could feel his brother's hot breath on his face. Ryker would down any man who dared to invade his space like that, but Christian knew he was safe.

"Snowed? Is that what you call it? Didn't you lie to protect me, Ryker? You lied, you cheated, you stole. You threatened people. Intimidated them. Got in fights. Jesus Christ, you carried a gun. You used your brains and your strength to protect me because that was what you had. She used her wits and her looks. How can you judge her for the doing the same goddamn thing you did?"

"I told her to be honest with me."

"Oh, well, I guess that's it then. High and mighty Ryker says tell the truth, so that's what she should have done. That's bullshit and you know it. How could you expect her to risk her life, let alone her sister's, on your honor when she didn't even know you? And now, because she isn't one hundred percent what you expected, because she did what you were practically setting her up to do, because you took a shot to your precious ego, you're sentencing her sister to death? What the hell is wrong with you, Ryker? I feel like I don't even know you!"

Christian was panting. People had gathered at the entrance to the ballroom, staring down the hall at them, but those things were on the edges of Ryker's focus.

Instead, his mind was absorbed in recalling everything Sage had said about her sister. He remembered the raw emotion in her voice when she'd spoken about her. He remembered thinking Sage loved her the same way he loved Christian. He wracked his brain for details.

Where did she live? What was her name? Could he have been so selfish that he hadn't asked? Or had Sage kept details about her sister from him intentionally? And if so, why?

Confusion swirled, mixing with that sense of foreboding that had been slowly building since their argument.

"What the hell are you talking about?" Ryker asked, his voice a mix of worry and demand.

Christian took a half-step back, rubbing his jaw, his gaze fixed on his older brother's face.

Ryker was out of patience. That slow-building fire of agitated concern was now an inferno. Christian was going to tell him what the hell was going on.

Right now.

He grabbed his brother's shirt collar, cool, fine cotton crumpling in the heat of his hand.

"I've never met Sage's sister, so what the hell could I possibly have to do with her dying? Start talking. I've had a hell of a night, and you're walking a fine line. I'm done with secrets, half-truths, and vague innuendo."

Christian's long, broad fingers closed around Ryker's wrist, tugging that hand away from his neck. His brother's grip was strong and firm. A man's hand.

Christian was all grown up.

Ryker released his brother's shirt and ran a shaking hand through his hair. The anger leeched from Christian's face, and his arm wrapped around Ryker's shoulder, the heavy weight providing an anchoring calm.

"You didn't know. Of course. I should have known. Come sit down." Christian's voice was an uneasy whisper as he nudged Ryker into a nearby chair, then sat as well.

Ryker blew out a slow breath, bracing himself for the type of news that would make Christian think he needed to sit. And when Christian told him, he was glad he'd sat.

It was worse than he'd ever imagined.

Ryker leaned back in the chair, letting it all sink in. Rosemary was

Sage's sister. She had cancer. For the third time. Remiza was her only hope. It wasn't some friend who was sick. It was her beloved sister. The only immediate family Sage had left in the world. When Sage yelled after him in the lobby, asking about the drug, he thought it was a last-ditch ploy for sympathy. She'd been begging for her sister's life... and he hadn't even turned around.

Oh, and to add fuel to the inferno, Sage and Rosemary were in hiding from their lowlife stepfather who just happened to be his business partner. Sage thought Davis had killed her mother and was threatening her and Rosemary because they'd shared their suspicions with the police. It was like some bizarre true-crime story, but the PI report had backed it all up. Now that he'd studied it cover to cover.

Earlier, he'd jumped to conclusions without reading the whole thing.

Stupid. So goddamn stupid!

Bateman never left a stone unturned. That was why Ryker used him. Bateman had tracked the detective assigned to Caroline Cashman's case to a bar, bought him a slew of beers, and gotten the real story on Caroline's death. It was still under investigation, in large part due to her daughter's persistence. The detective was suspicious of Davis but hadn't been able to link him to his wife's drowning. The detective didn't believe Davis's lies about Sage doing drugs, but his captain had, so he'd had to ease up on the investigation. Without Sage's tenacity, the captain would have already made him close the case.

Bateman had also spoken to Rosa, Davis's housekeeper. Now Ryker knew where Sage had gotten the clothes for the wedding. Knew where the bruises on her arms had come from. She'd gone back to that house so she'd have something nice to wear. She'd risked her life for a pile of clothes to make good on her deal with him.

She stripped to make money because Davis had left her with nothing. Cut them both off to pressure them to rescind their allegations against him.

She'd made her deal with him because she thought it would save her sister's life.

Sage had done what she had to do. If he'd been in her shoes, he would have done the same goddamn thing.

Having read the folder cover to cover—twice—Ryker hated himself. He wanted to reassure Sage that Rosemary would get Remiza as long as she needed it. He never would've cut her off. No matter how angry he was.

But Sage wasn't answering her phone.

What had been a spark of worry was now a raging inferno, searing and out of control.

He sent his fifth text in five minutes, then leaped from the chair. "I can't sit here waiting for her to answer. I'm going to her house."

Christian's hand closed over his arm. "Wait. Who is that?"

His brother had risen and was staring down the hall. A woman in jeans and a black jacket was running toward them. Her mouth was moving, but music still poured out of the ballroom, covering her words. There was something familiar in her gait and flying honey-blonde hair, something in the shape of her face that reminded him of Sage.

"Rosemary!" He called her name, and his legs propelled him forward the instant recognition hit. In seconds, he'd closed the distance between them with Christian at his side. "Where's Sage? I've been calling her cell, but I can't get her."

Tears poured down Rosemary's flushed cheeks, leaving dark rivulets of mascara. "She came back to the house to change and get the car. She was so upset. She wouldn't tell me what happened. I've never seen her like that. She looked... destroyed."

Ryker's lungs seemed incapable of pushing air.

He'd done that to her.

"Where did she go?" Ryker forced the words out.

"I called Justin," Rosemary continued as if he hadn't spoken. "He went after her. He told me to stay home, but I couldn't. He was at a club, getting ready to play a gig. In New Jersey, I think. I'm afraid he won't get there in time."

Ryker closed his hands gently around Rosemary's shoulders. Her fluffy jacket couldn't mask her thinness, and her pretty face had a ghost-gray pallor, the kind you saw in hospital patients. If Christian were sick, he would have done anything to save him. Absolutely anything. Just like Sage had done for Rosemary.

He'd let Sage down once tonight. It wasn't going to happen again.

He squeezed Rosemary's shoulders lightly but firmly, steadying her. "Rosemary, look at me. Where did she go?"

"She went to see Davis."

Chapter Nineteen

Sage braced her shoulders and turned the icy knob of the kitchen door. It was unlocked. That made things easy. She stepped inside, banging the door behind her, announcing her arrival. She was here to try to reason with Davis, so there was no need to sneak around this time.

Even though the kitchen was dark, the lingering capers and garlic aroma of Rosa's puttanesca sauce filled her nose, igniting memories. Her mother at the stove, stealing bites of whatever Rosa was cooking, and Rosa chiding her good-naturedly. Sitting with Rosemary at the kitchen table after school, doing homework and dipping chocolate chip cookies in milk. Playing hide-and-seek with Justin and Rosemary. It had taken them weeks of lost games to find her perfect hiding spot, wedged under the bottom shelf of the pantry. She was the only one small enough to fit in the tiny space. If she hadn't broken out in giggles, they never would have found her.

Sage took the flood of memories as a sign. For years she'd dismissed her mother and Rosemary's earthy spiritualism, but in this cool, dark kitchen, she felt surrounded by the warmth of her mother's love, and it calmed the battering ram of her heart. Fortified, Sage stepped from the kitchen into the hall. The house was quiet. Pulling along the drive, she'd seen that every light in the front of the house blazed, but she heard nothing but the sharp squeak of her damp sneakers on the hardwood floor.

"Davis? Davis?"

He had to be here. His car was in the driveway, and the scent of fresh cigar smoke floated in the air. If he was in the family room, he should have heard her car approach and seen the headlights.

Was he deliberately ignoring her? Lying in wait, ready to pounce? *Was that what he did to Mom?*

Sage ducked back into the kitchen and plucked Rosa's rolling pin from the cannister on the kitchen island. The heft of the marble reassured her. She'd come to talk, but if he wanted a fight, she'd go down swinging.

She proceeded back down the hallway. The eerie silence sank into her skin, creating goose bumps. This wasn't the greatest plan, but it was the only option left to her. Trading silence for Rosemary's treatment. Davis could pressure Ryker to make sure Rosemary kept getting Remiza. Mom wouldn't judge her. Bargaining with Davis was the only way to save Rosemary's life. Once Rosemary was healthy, she'd push the investigation.

There was no statute of limitations on murder.

Driving over, she'd been sure the encounter with Davis would go smoothly. She'd be offering what he'd spent months trying to achieve, but now the oppressive quiet made her feel like the heroine in a horror movie who headed down the basement steps while everyone in the theater screamed "No!"

Sage shook her head.

Davis couldn't hurt her. Not in his own house. Not when he was already under suspicion for murder. It was too risky.

Or so she hoped.

She took a deep breath and turned left, stepping into the family room. The room hadn't changed. It was still what folks expected to see in an upscale furniture showroom. The rich Brazilian walnut hardwood floor gleamed. Matching coffee-colored leather couches faced each other, separated by a Craftsman-style coffee table over a lush, cream-colored rug. The earth tone pillows on the couch perfectly matched the colors in the oversized patterned armchair that sat perpendicular to the couches. The coffee table held a glass vase of fresh flowers and the same large, illustrated *Philadelphia Architecture* book that had been there the past eight years. Had anyone, other than herself, ever opened it?

Davis sat on one of the leather sofas, looking distinguished in a gleaming white dress shirt, charcoal-gray trousers, and shiny black loafers. His body was so still he seemed part of the decorator's perfectly choreographed scene. He was reading a book.

He had to have heard her approach, but he didn't look up.

"Davis, I need to talk to you." She'd tried to sound calm and business-like, but her words were loud and sharp in the quiet house.

He set the book down. When he lifted his gaze, his eyes were dark and hard, like pebbles in a rushing stream.

"There was no need to hide from me, Sage. We could have settled this long ago. It would have been much easier."

"You killed my mother. You threatened me and Rosemary. You tried to strangle me. I think hiding was a pretty good choice."

He frowned. "You never could hold your tongue. You were never amiable like your mother."

"My mother was a miracle. Her spirit blessed everything she touched and made it good and light and beautiful. You destroyed that. You took that away from me forever!"

"I know you don't believe me, but I did not kill Caroline. I could never hurt her like that. I loved her." Davis closed his eyes for a minute, then let out a long sigh. "This is old ground. Why are you here? You hate me. You must need something very badly to have come."

"I need your help. Help to get Rosemary her cancer treatment."

He jerked his head back. "What are you talking about?"

Sage fought to quell the torrent of anger and frustration. She didn't have the time or energy for Davis's games, but she couldn't risk making him too angry.

"Please, just stop. You know exactly what I'm talking about. You chased us down the hall at Dr. Gerrard's office. You know Rosemary's cancer's back. You know she didn't get into the Remiza drug trial. I'm sure you were thrilled, thinking it would force us back here to beg for your help. Force us to pretend we're a happy family to throw off the police. Well, you won. I'm here."

His face was a kaleidoscope of emotions. Anger, frustration, sorrow, grief, and then, finally, what appeared to be genuine confusion.

"How did we get here? How did I let this happen?" Davis muttered, then stood, shaking his head as if trying to focus.

He stepped forward. She stepped backward, putting the second couch and coffee table between them. He stretched his palm out toward her.

"Wait, please. Hear me out."

Sage stilled.

"I didn't know Rosemary's cancer was back. I vaguely remember you saying something at the party about her being sick, but I was so drunk that everything from that night is blur. And you're right. I didn't appreciate your mother. I took her for granted. Gambled. Drank too much. I still do, but I'm working on it." He heaved out a breath. "When I drank, I made bad decisions. I was unfaithful. I know how much that hurt her. I'll never forgive myself for that, but I did not kill her. You have to believe me."

Sage pressed her hands onto the back of the couch to stop them from shaking. She knew he was guilty. Knew it.

So how could he sound so convincing?

"You threatened me and my sister! You wanted Rosemary to lie to the police and say she saw you at the club around the time Mom"—she thrust her fingers up into air quotes—"fell. That's not the behavior of an innocent man!"

"I never should have acted that way. I was drunk...and scared." Davis gripped the back of his neck. "Not all of my business deals are on the up-and-up. Actually, most of them aren't. I wasn't worried about the police thinking I killed Caroline, because I know it's not true, but those crazy claims of yours got their attention. I couldn't risk the police looking too closely at my finances. I was afraid of what they'd find. That's why I wanted you to retract your statement."

Bile touched the back of her throat. Davis sounded sincere. If he was telling the truth, everything she'd been through the last few months was unnecessary.

A thought snaked into her mind.

"You're lying. I know you bribed the receptionist at Dr. Gerrard's so you could find us. I'm sure she was more than happy to tell you Rosemary was rejected for the Remiza trial."

"I didn't. I swear. Justin knew I wanted to talk to you and your sister and told me Rosemary had an appointment. I assumed it was one of her regular checkups. I had no idea her cancer was back. No idea at all."

"Justin? Justin would never tell you anything about us."

A soft cluck of a tongue sent Sage whirling. Justin stood in the doorway, pristinely handsome in a dark blue suit, white shirt, and solid sapphire-blue tie. The expensive material shone just a touch in the room's soft light. He lounged in the doorframe, his left shoulder against the thick, decorative molding. His raised right hand held a gun.

Sage lifted her gaze, trying to read the intent in the lightly tanned, model-perfect face she'd known for almost ten years. It seemed like the face of a stranger. The hard emptiness of his blue eyes wavered when she met his stare.

Justin flicked the gun. "Don't worry, this isn't for you. Be a good girl and run to the garage and find some rope or duct tape or something. I wasn't expecting to have to come here tonight, so I'm not prepared."

He waved the gun toward the couch. "Sit down, Davis."

Sage's legs were frozen, but her heart and mind were like runaway horses, racing erratically. Nothing made sense.

"What are you doing here? Why do you have a gun?"

"I'm here to protect you, of course. Like I always do. Rosemary called and told me you were coming to see him. Him! I can't believe you went running to him!" Justin's voice rose, and she could see his lean chest expand under his slim-cut dress shirt. "He's worse than the other one. You know better, Sage. You can't trust him. You know what he did to your mom."

Suddenly, she felt like she didn't know anything. She loved Justin, but he was scaring her. The gun was scaring her. She needed time to talk to Davis.

"Put the gun away. What if it accidentally goes off? And what is this crazy talk about rope and duct tape? Why don't you go get a snack in the kitchen while I talk to Davis? He won't dare hurt me. Too many people know I'm here."

"No. We need to leave. Come with me."

"I can't. I need to talk to Davis about Rosemary."

Sage sensed movement behind her. Davis had risen from the couch.

"Why didn't you tell me Rosemary's cancer was back?" Davis's question hung heavy in the air.

Sage stood perpendicular to the two men, shifting her gaze between them, assessing.

She stepped away from Justin toward the wall at her back. "Justin? What's going on here?"

Justin glared at Davis, his face red and scrunched like a painted Aztec mask. "Do you think I would've let them come back to you? You've always been the problem. Always. You're lying, cheating scum. You're not good enough for them! You never were. You don't deserve them!"

Sage's hands were shaking again. Her feet were unsteady, as if she stood in mud. She couldn't understand, didn't want to read into Justin's words and comprehend the truth of his deception.

"If Davis is so horrible, why would you tell him how to find Rosemary and me at Dr. Gerrard's?"

"Don't you see? I had to make you think he was chasing you, that he would hurt you. That was the only way to keep you away from him. I did everything I could to keep you away from both Davis and

Ryker, but you were so stubborn. So stubborn. You always have been."

Unease pricked the back of her neck. "What do you mean you did everything you could? What did you do, Justin? What did you do?"

Justin's shoulders squared, and his lips thinned. "I was just trying to scare you enough so you and Rosemary would leave town with me. I thought the slashed tires and the animal in your locker would be enough, but you still went to that damn wedding with him. And even after Theo's accident you stayed. I was so sure you would call me to come help you, but you stayed with that asshole instead."

Her knees almost buckled. "You were behind everything. My tires, my locker, those horrible pictures. You're the one who hit Theo, aren't you?"

Guilt washed across Justin's face.

"I just meant to tap him. To scare you so you'd come home. We're a family, Sage. We always were. All I ever wanted was for us all to be together like when we were younger. Remember? Davis would go on those long trips, and I would stay here. The four of us made such a perfect family, but I always had to go home when he came back. Davis was always driving us apart."

Justin strode across the room, pointing the gun toward Davis. His eyes were wild, and spit flew from his mouth as he spoke. "This is all his fault. Caroline and Rosemary loved living in this house. You were going to come back after Julliard. We could have all lived here together. I told Caroline that. I told her about those other women so she would divorce him, so we could all be together. She already knew. She already knew, and she wouldn't leave him. How could we be together if she wouldn't leave him?"

Sage pressed her fingers to her temples. Justin wasn't making sense.

"I don't understand. We've grown up. Why would we all live here together?"

"This is my only real home. The only place I ever felt loved. You know how horrible my family is. Rosemary and your mother were more family to me than my own blood. And you, Sage, you are my life." Tears now flowed down Justin's face. "If she'd just left Davis, we could have lived together like a real family. She chose him over me! Over me! I didn't mean to push her. I never meant to hurt her."

Sage felt like the room was whirling in circles like an old-school board game spinner, and when the rotating stopped, there was nothing but icy realization.

"You killed my mother."

* * *

Ryker stilled. The yelling had masked the sound of his progress down the hallway, so he'd watched the scene unfold for the last few minutes. Sage's words were a grenade, creating a pall of expectant silence.

After a moment, she repeated them, but this time with more inquiry than accusation. "You killed my mother?"

Justin's breathing was like thunder in the room. "It was an accident. We were arguing. I couldn't believe she could stay with him, that she would choose to stay with him. Choose him over us. I lost my temper. I pushed her. It wasn't hard. I know it wasn't hard, but she fell and hit her head. It was an accident. A horrible, terrible accident."

"Why didn't you call 911? Maybe they could have saved her."

"I panicked. All I could think about was losing you and Rosemary. You're the only family I have. I couldn't risk losing you. We're destined to be together. Don't you know that?"

Sage didn't respond. Justin's checks reddened, and his voice grew hard. "You should have married me and waited for the trust money like I told you to. We could have avoided all of this, but instead you had to go spread your legs for Ryker Madsen of all people, and when he betrayed you, you came running back to this asshole." Justin gestured toward Davis. "Family sticks with family, Sage. I'm going to take care of you and Rosemary from now on. We just have to deal with Davis first. He knows too much."

Jesus Christ! Justin's off his rocker!

This was not the time for her to blurt out what she was really thinking, and Sage sucked at keeping her opinion to herself.

Keep calm. Play along. Don't rattle him.

Ryker peered into the room from the hallway, still as a statue, thinking. He needed a plan but had no good options. He'd rushed into the house intent on keeping Sage safe from Davis. Like an idiot, he'd left his tux jacket in the car, his cell phone in the pocket.

Creeping back down the hall was out. The floors creaked, and his dress shoes were hard-soled. And the situation had gotten too volatile to take the time to go back for the phone. Even if he managed to get back to the car without Justin noticing, anything could happen in the few minutes he'd be gone. He couldn't risk it.

Ryker shifted slightly, trying to put himself into Sage's line of sight, but her gaze was fixed on Justin.

"What are you going to do?" she asked.

Ryker winced at her frigid tone, but Justin didn't seem to notice it.

"We'll take some valuables and make it look like a break-in."

"You can't possibly be implying that you're going to kill him."

"What choice do we have?"

Sage's tone was low and soothing when she answered, as if she were talking to a skittish animal. "Everyone always has a choice. This has already gone too far. Way too far. Please put the gun down. We can call the police, and you can turn yourself in. I'll stay with you and support you. I think you're mentally ill. You need help."

Justin shifted the gun away from Davis, pointing it at Sage. "Mentally ill? Turn myself in? How are we going to be together if I'm in prison? I want to marry you. Start a family. How the hell are we going to do that if I turn myself in?"

Sage's eyes blazed, and Ryker's stomach dropped.

"You expect me to marry you? Marry you and have a family with you? You murdered my mother!"

Without warning, Davis ducked and charged Justin, grabbing his arm. The gun fired, shattering a vase on the mantel over the fireplace.

Sage screamed.

How many movies had Ryker seen where tragedy unfolded in horrifically slow motion? Now it was happening to him, but this was real life. Sage's life. Two men were grappling with a loaded gun. The shattered vase had been only a few inches to her left.

Ryker rushed into the room as the gun discharged again, followed instantly by the sickening sound of a bullet hitting flesh. Davis slid to the floor, hands pressed to his stomach. With Davis down, there would be no barrier between Justin and Sage. He had to distract Justin long enough to let her escape.

"Run!" Ryker ordered as he leaped through the air.

His body made full contact with Justin's, and they hit the floor hard, nearly landing on top of Davis. Ryker scrambled to grab Justin's hands, trying to pry the gun from his fingers. He was bigger and stronger, but Justin was no slouch, and their hands were slick from Davis's blood. Ryker's fingers slipped and slid over warm skin and cold metal.

Sage flashed in his peripheral vision. She wasn't running.

Damn her.

He needed her gone. Safe. Away from the gun and the violence and Justin's insanity.

"Get the hell out of here!" he yelled in her direction, taking his eyes off Justin for a second. Hard knuckles crunched his nose. Pain swam behind his eyes. Blood gushed, hot and wet down his face. He leaned toward the hand that was still fighting for the gun, letting the blood from his nose drip and further slicken their fingers.

Pushing, pulling, grappling.

Justin's fingers were clenched too tightly.

If Ryker didn't get that gun, Sage would never be safe.

He went for the wrist, bending Justin's hand inward, then punched his arm hard, hoping he'd let the gun drop.

The gun screamed. Sage screamed. Justin screamed, but Ryker continued to fight.

They rolled, punching, kicking, sliding.

Sage was still in the room. He could sense her.

Stubborn. So goddamn stubborn.

The gun went off again.

Branding heat sliced his chest.

A shadow fell over him, then something hard and heavy struck his head.

Everything faded to black.

Chapter Twenty

Beep. Beep. Beep.

Beep. Beep. Beep.

What was making that noise? It was annoying as hell. Ryker tried to reach in the direction of the sound but managed only to slide his fingers across a cool, scratchy sheet.

He wasn't in his own bed. This bed was too hard. The blankets were too rough and thin, and the sounds were off. It wasn't just that infuriating beeping. Muffled voices ebbed and flowed, and a constant electronic buzz hummed.

Where the hell am I?

Memory eluded him.

His throat hurt. His head hurt. His chest really hurt. Like he'd been branded. And his eyes were glued shut.

Beep. Beep. Beep. Beep.

The sound was faster now. Much faster. He heard a quick intake of breath, followed by rustling clothing and quick footsteps. A large, warm hand pressed gently onto his shoulder. A wash of eucalyptus and spice passed over him.

"Christian." The word was a painful croak through his bruised, dry lips.

The hand squeezed softly. "Ryker, thank God you're awake. I'm so sorry. This is all my fault."

Christian's voice was thick, almost teary. His brother sounded anguished. Temper nipped at Ryker's groggy mind. His brother needed him.

Ryker forced his eyes open.

The light was dim and fluorescent. Definitely not home.

The beeping quickened still faster. It matched the pace of his heart. Tubes coiled from his arms. Monitors flashing numbers and lines stood feet from his head.

A hospital. He was in the hospital.

His gaze settled on his brother. Christian's skin was pale, and his eyes were red.

"What happened?"

"You were shot. They had to operate. You lost a lot of blood."

Ryker shook his head slightly. The pain from even those small movements was so intense his vision dimmed, but he fought to remain conscious. He had to know what was bothering Christian.

"No. Not me. You. What happened to you? You look awful."

"You almost died, you idiot! That's what happened, and it's my fault. If I hadn't harassed you into going after Sage, this never would have happened."

Memory rushed like a flash flood, racing and swirling, followed by searing panic. He leaned forward, trying to sit. Pain made his vision blur.

The beeps fired like machine-gun shots.

"Ryker, relax. You're going to hurt yourself."

Again, Ryker fought the black haze invading his mind.

"Is she...is she OK?"

"Who? Sage? Yes. She's fine. Safe. Unharmed."

The beeps slowed. Minutes passed.

A nurse came in chattering about pain medicine and fiddled with his IV. Cool liquid pushed through the vein in his arm, and the pain receded.

Christian's strong, warm hands rubbed along his bare arm. Ryker wasn't sure if his brother was trying to reassure him or himself, but it didn't matter. It was good to have him close, but he hated the miserable expression on his brother's face.

"Not your fault."

"What?" Christian asked, leaning in closer.

Ryker cleared his throat. It was easier to talk now that the pain meds had kicked in. "This is not your fault. It's my fault. I drove her to Davis. If I had been a better man, Sage wouldn't have been there in the first place. Do you know what happened? The last thing I remember is wrestling with Justin."

"Justin shot you. The bullet nicked your right lung, but the doctors say you were lucky. Sage whacked him on the head with a rolling pin, and from what the cops said, it sounds like she hit you when she got him." Justin shook his head and frowned. "I feel so bad for her. She's been through hell. Her best friend killed her mom. Her sister's got cancer, and her stepdad is an alcoholic, self-centered crook."

"Is he OK? Justin shot him."

"He'll be alright. He's a few rooms down. Not to speak ill of the injured, but what would possess you to do business with an asshole like that anyway?"

Embarrassment flared. What he had at one time thought was important now seemed ridiculously silly and petty, but keeping the truth from Christian was one of the things that had gotten Ryker in this mess in the first place. He was done with lies and backroom schemes. Christian would be pissed, but he was a grown man and deserved the truth. It had just taken Ryker awhile to realize it.

"Davis is on the board of the Lincoln Club. Since you said you wouldn't let me help you get a job, I wanted you to be able to join. I thought it would open doors for you. I hated it when they rejected your application."

"You're kidding me, right? That was two years ago, and I only applied because Thad kept hounding me about it. I can take care of my own life. I don't need Davis Anderson's help to get ahead, and believe it or not, I don't need your help either."

Yep. Christian was royally pissed.

"I know. You're right. I was an idiot. I'm sorry."

Christian opened his mouth, shut it, opened it again, and shut it again. After a minute of looking like a fish out of water, he said, "Did you actually just admit that I'm right?"

"Yes, little brother, you're right. You're right now, and you were right the other day when you said I was trying to control your life so I didn't have to take any risks in mine. I was so bent on making sure no one hurt me, so focused on making sure my emotions didn't impact my judgment, I ended up driving away the only woman I've ever truly loved." Ryker scrunched his hair in his hand, wincing from the pain from moving his arm. "I had a good thing with Sage, and I made a goddamn mess of it."

"That you did, my brother. She stopped in here earlier to check on you. I think she wanted to make sure you're going to be alright. But I don't think she's coming back."

Of course she wasn't. He couldn't blame her. He'd been a haughty, obnoxious prick. He hadn't trusted her, hadn't given her chance, hadn't tried to see her point of view, but had judged her for doing the exact same thing for her sister that he would have done for Christian.

Problem was, he wasn't sure he could get by without her. He couldn't go back to the dry, emotionless life he'd been living. She'd broken through the barriers around his heart and reignited the passion in his soul. She'd brought him back to life, and he wasn't sure he could survive living without her.

"I can't believe you thought I wanted to be a member of that stodgy old elitist club."

"I thought it was important to you. That you knew it would help you find a good job at a reputable developer, although I still think you should just come work for me."

Christian closed his eyes for a few seconds, then released a heavy sigh. "There's something I need to tell you."

Ryker wasn't sure he could take another surprise, but he was done with trying to control his brother.

"Go for it."

"I'm working for the FBI."

"*What?*"

"The FBI. I'm working for them. In the cybersecurity unit."

"What about Georgetown and working in real estate?"

"I never enrolled. It's not what I want." Christian dropped his gaze to the linoleum floor. "I just didn't know how to tell you. I was afraid you'd be disappointed."

Christian had pursued his own passion and landed the job of his dreams. How could Ryker be disappointed about that? Of course, the idea of his baby brother working for the FBI in any capacity was scary as hell, but he couldn't have been prouder.

"So you're not mad at me?" Christian asked.

"How could I be? You're probably the best guy they've got."

Christian smirked. "I am pretty damn good."

Ryker felt his lips curve in a small smile. Christian was truly happy. His own life might be a pile of steaming shit right now, but he was thrilled for his brother.

The direction of his thoughts must have shown on his face because Christian squeezed his hand reassuringly.

"If you want to be with Sage, don't give up on her. You can do anything you put your mind to. I've seen it happen. Against all odds. You saved me. Protected me. Fought and worked so goddamn hard so that I could be safe and have every opportunity to succeed. If you put that ferocity of love and effort into Sage, there's no way she can resist you."

No way she could resist him?

Ryker doubted he could ever get her to speak to him.

He'd screwed up everything. Royally. Christian's confession highlighted just how skewed his own priorities had been. He'd gone into business with a man he distrusted and didn't respect, a man who had threatened Sage and her sister, to add Christian's name to a list of snobs at an old boys' club. A list Christian never wanted to be on in the first place.

Sage had put her faith and trust in him, and when the going got tough, he'd abandoned her.

How could she ever respect him? How could she ever forgive him?

Ryker closed his eyes, with a gaping hole in his chest that had nothing to do with his bullet wound.

* * *

Sage hated hospitals. Hated everything about them. The too-white walls and too-bright lights. The over-starched, fake-perky, gossipy staff. The stomach-wrenching stench of cafeteria food, antiseptic, and death. Muscle memory made her stomach clench.

Rosemary has spent too many days in places like this.

Sage's sneakers squeaked on the hard linoleum. She hadn't dressed up, just thrown on jeans and a sweatshirt. Ponytail. No makeup. She needed comfort after the trauma of last night.

Room 726, 728, 730. This was it.

She closed her eyes and rubbed her icy hands down the front of her jeans, wiping off imagined sweat. She was here because it was the right thing to do. The mannerly thing. She had to thank the man who'd saved her life, even if he'd also broken her heart.

The door to the room was open. She wished it were closed. Much easier to knock than just walk boldly into the equivalent of someone's bedroom with that awkward hospital visitor hello. Like things weren't already awkward enough.

Ryker lay on the bed with his eyes closed. His tan skin had a slight pallor, and bruises marred his left check. His lip was cut, and his right eye was dark and swollen. He may not even be able to open it when he woke.

Maybe she could leave a note or send him a gift basket. It would be the coward's way out, but she was tired of being brave. Actually, she was just plain tired. Physically. Mentally. Emotionally. Psychologically. Justin's betrayal was the last straw, crumbling her toothpick house of strength. She needed to rest, rebuild, and start over. She'd follow Rosemary's advice and try to open her heart a little. Try to live for herself.

She just had a gaping hole in her chest that needed to heal a bit first.

Justin's actions had sapped her strength, but Ryker had broken her heart. She shivered at the memory of the bitter disdain in his gaze when he'd learned her true identity. Better to take the coward's way out than have him look at her like that again.

She turned back toward the door, her sneaker squeaking loudly.

"Wait."

Shit. He'd woken up.

His voice was throaty and a little faint, but she was too close to pretend she hadn't heard. She squared her shoulders, blew out a soft breath, and turned back around to face him. Even battered and bruised, he still looked like a Viking. Her Viking. Her stomach clenched again, but this time it wasn't nerves. It was her traitorous body's reaction to seeing Ryker.

"Hi," she offered lamely.

"Hi," he said. Then silence.

Yawning silence that she felt compelled to fill. "I came to thank you. You saved my life. Despite our...differences. I'm incredibly grateful. So thank you."

She'd been studying the shine of the bed rail as she spoke, but now she lifted her gaze to his face. She expected that soul-crushing ice that she hated so much in his eyes, but instead met summer-lake-in-sunshine blue, and her battered heart ached. Ryker had saved her. Even though he despised her, he'd taken a bullet for her. He looked strong and wounded and beautiful. The edges of the hole in her heart started to burn.

Time to get to the punch line and make a run for it before she made an even bigger fool of herself.

"Christian told me you'll make sure Rosemary gets Remiza for as long as she needs it. Both Rosemary and I truly appreciate what you're doing for her."

"Yeah, I'm such a great guy for not letting your sister die." Ryker's tone was sharp and odd, almost self-deprecating.

What was she supposed to say to that?

She lifted a wrist to check a watch that wasn't there, then continued the upward motion, as if she'd meant to tuck a stray hair behind her ear. "I should go."

"No! Stay!" His voice gentled and took on a pleading note. "I mean, please stay. At least for a minute. There's something I want to say." He lifted a hand slowly, seeming surprised it was an effort, and gestured toward the visitor's chair. "Please, sit."

Sage shook her head. She'd said her piece. She didn't want to settle in. "I'll stand."

Ryker stared down at his empty, upturned hands and shook his head slowly from side to side. "I'm sorry."

"For what?"

"For everything. For how I treated you from the first minute I laid eyes on you and every minute after. You bewitched me, and I hated that I felt out of control. I trusted a woman once, thought I was in love, and she betrayed me. It hurt so goddamn much that I swore I'd never let it happen again. Swore I wouldn't let anyone get close enough to hurt me."

Ryker paused and cleared his scratchy throat.

"I fell in love with you, Sage. Desperately in love with you, but I was too weak to admit it. Not to you and not to myself. You trusted me, and I turned my back on you. I was a coward."

She turned toward the door. His words were killing her. She didn't want to let him see her cry.

"Please, wait. Just hear me out."

How could she refuse? He'd saved her life. She faced him again, praying she could hold back the tears threatening to spill.

"I never would have cut off Rosemary's access to Remiza no matter what you did to me. Never." He coughed and gingerly lifted a small plastic cup of water from the side table and took a sip. "I failed you. I let you down, and I know you probably won't believe me when I say this, but I love you. I am happier with you than I've ever been. Happier than I ever imagined I could be. Happier than I deserve. I can't imagine going back to a life without you. Can you forgive me? Can you give me another chance? Can we start over?"

Start over. For a split second, her heart sang. This was the man who'd come to save her. Who'd protected her, made her laugh, engaged her mind, and enflamed her body. The desire to fling herself down next to him, kiss his bruised skin, and forget the past flashed—then faded.

Start over. That's what he'd said last night in the manager's office. Mere minutes before he'd crushed her heart and turned his back on her. Literally. The edges of the hole burned hotter. Too hot. Too painful. Too much to risk. No matter what Rosemary said.

"I'm sorry too. I'm sorry I lied to you, sorry I had to deceive you. But I wouldn't change it. I did what I had to do, and I need to keep doing it. We had our chance, and it's passed. It just wasn't meant to be. We're both too damaged, and we've hurt each other too much. We can't come back from that. I appreciate what you've done for me and Rosemary, but it's time for both of us to move forward. Separately."

She kept her voice calm and even. No tears in her eyes. No chink in the armor. No sign of weakness.

She lifted her hand in a slow wave and left the room.

She could fall apart when she got to the car.

"Wait!"

His voice followed her into the hall, but she kept walking. If she turned back, she didn't trust herself to walk away from him again. She increased her pace, but a crash, thud, and smash of shattered glass stopped her in her tracks.

"Ryker!" She rushed back into the room before her mind processed her body's reaction.

He was on the floor, kneeling in shattered gray plastic and glass. The top-heavy monitoring machine had toppled to the ground and lay in pieces. Tubes hung from Ryker's left arm. The too-short, Listerine-green hospital gown exposed his muscular thighs and calves. His strong legs were shaking, and he gripped the IV pole, trying to pull himself to a standing position.

She dropped to the ground, glass biting into her knees through her denim jeans. She thrust her arm around his waist, sliding her shoulder under his arm, trying to help him stand. Even kneeling, his weight was heavy on her shoulders, betraying how weak he truly was.

"I'm OK," he huffed.

"Then why are we both about to fall over?"

A nurse rushed into the room and surveyed the scene disapprovingly.

"What's going on in here?" Her hard tone contrasted with the smiling cats on her scrub top.

"He needed to use the bathroom. He stumbled and fell and knocked the machine over. It was an accident."

Ryker cocked his head toward her, a questioning look on his face. Was he wondering why she'd been so quick to jump to his defense? If he wasn't, she certainly was.

"Well, come on then," the nurse said, easily inserting herself under Ryker's other shoulder, pulling him up, and guiding him away from the broken glass and into the bathroom with swift, competent motions.

"Wait for me, please," Ryker said just before the nurse closed the bathroom door.

Sage looked toward the exit. This was her chance to escape before Ryker was back and she was lost, drowning in the warmth of his Caribbean-blue eyes. Her mind screamed for her to flee for her own self-preservation, but her heart was in control, compelling her to remain. At that moment, he was the moon, and she was the tide, unwilling to fight the gravitational pull of true love, despite her brain warning there was no guarantee of a fairy-tale ending.

He'd let her down once. Could she survive if he broke her heart again?

The bathroom door opened with a loud thud. Ryker's massive body was supported by the stalwart nurse. His thin hospital gown was slipping on one side, exposing his heavily bandaged chest and shoulder. The center of the bandage was morbid pink.

Her stomach dropped, and her hand flew to her mouth. The sight of the blood was too much.

Images flashed in her mind. Ryker defending her to Veronica in his apartment. Ryker's arm holding her back as the car whizzed past in the parking lot of the Lambertville Inn. Ryker's body under hers, breaking her fall when she slipped on the ice on her front porch. Ryker grappling with Justin, rolling in Davis's leaking blood. The barrel of the gun turning toward him. The deafening shot.

His first instinct had always been to protect her. He'd almost died for her. He'd just climbed out of a hospital bed mere hours after surgery and had crawled on his knees to get to her. He might have walked away from her in anger at the hotel, but Christian told her Ryker had wanted to find her even before he'd learned she was in danger. He'd been willing to hear her out.

The nurse eased Ryker into a heavy, faux-leather armchair next to the bed. "Don't move. I'm going to get maintenance to clean this up and bring in new bed linens. I'm afraid glass might have gotten on the bed."

The nurse ambled away, leaving them palpably and uncomfortably alone.

"You came back," Ryker said, his warm-sky eyes beckoning. "Does that mean there's hope for me?"

Hope? There was so much to say about hope. Could two people with a start like they'd had ever hope to work things out? If they didn't, could she ever hope to get over him? Then there was the fact that she was hopelessly in love with him. So much to say about hope, but she said only the one truth burning strongest in her soul.

"I'm afraid to hope. What if it doesn't work out?"

He pushed up from the chair, tugging and twisting the smooth brown band on his pinkie, pulling it off. He held the ring up in front of her.

"I told you Christian gave me this ring for my birthday, right? Did I tell you what he said when he gave it to me?"

Sage swallowed hard. She wasn't sure she could form words without crying, but she knew what the ring meant to Ryker. She couldn't remain silent.

"He told you he put all his love inside it. You said it's the most valuable thing you own."

Ryker nodded. "When he gave me this ring, he told me he was going to give me the one thing I needed most. Unconditional love. It was his promise to love me always and forever. He inscribed those words inside: Unconditional love. Always and forever."

Ryker's strong hand enveloped her own, separating her middle finger from the rest. He slipped the hard, cool circle onto her finger.

"This is my promise to you now. My vow of unconditional love and unconditional support. Always and forever. I know I screwed up. I told you to trust me and then I didn't trust you. I was so wrapped up in protecting my heart, I didn't realize I was hurting yours. I'm an idiot, but I'm an idiot who's desperately in love with you. I want a life with you, Sage. I want to take care of you. I want to know your secrets and your sadness and your joy. I want to laugh with you and hold you when you need to cry. I love you. Please give me a chance to prove myself to you."

Hot tears ran down her face. She bit her lip, tasting salt. She'd been an idiot too. She hadn't trusted him either. They were both flawed, damaged, and afraid, but he'd taken a leap by putting that ring on her finger. He'd fought for her, protected her, and was promising to love and support her. In all her secret fantasies, she'd never imagined her hero weak, bruised, sallow-skinned, and wearing a hideous green hospital gown, but Ryker had the strength, bravery, and loyalty of a knight.

Caution be damned. She was going to grab this man and hold on tight.

She stepped closer, sliding a shaking arm around his waist, pressing tightly into his side, careful to avoid his injured shoulder and chest.

She craned her head back to meet his gaze. "I made mistakes too. I lied to you. I gave you reasons not to trust me. I was afraid, and not just that Rosemary wouldn't get the medicine she needed. I was afraid to trust you, to put my heart on the line. I'm not going to let the fear of getting hurt control me any longer. I love you. I want us to start over. I want us to have a life together with unconditional love. Always and forever."

Those strong hands she loved so much encircled the base of her neck. His head moved toward hers in slow motion. She couldn't take her eyes off his firm, full lips. He was going to kiss her, and she was going to savor every second of it.

And she did.

* * *

Thank you for reading! Did you enjoy? Please add your review because nothing helps an author more and encourages readers to take a chance on a book than a review.

And don't miss more in the Spice Up the Night series with book two coming soon!

Until then read RESCUE ME, by City Owl Author, Lauren Connolly. Turn the page for a sneak peek!

Also be sure to sign up for the City Owl Press newsletter to receive notice of all book releases!

Sneak Peek of Rescue Me

By Lauren Connolly

One of these houses is mine. I'm just not exactly sure *which* one.

A sigh pushes out, weighty and exhausted, from deep in my chest. The sun set hours ago, back when I was still on the highway. Trying to read the tiny print on each of these mailboxes isn't easy after staring out the windshield for the past two days. My eyes practically crackle, begging me to close them.

Sleep. Just go to sleep.

"That one! I...I think."

I pull up alongside the curb, letting the heavy engine rumble on as I flip through photos on my phone. Martin sent me a picture two weeks ago, a selfie of him with a large tan house behind him that looks like the one I've stopped in front of. Unfortunately, the homes on either side of it are mirror reflections.

Normally, Martin's preference for uniformity doesn't bother be. Tonight, though, I wish he had picked a weird bungalow with daisies painted on the siding and a turquoise front door. Just so I know, without a hint of a doubt, that I am parking in front of *my* house.

And I am definitely parking because I need to pick one of these clone homes before I drive myself mad puttering around this neighborhood all night.

As I shut down the engine, the whole car settles as if she's ready to sleep for the night.

"Enjoy your rest, Penelope," I mutter to the steering wheel.

I need a bed bad. A pounding started in my temples way before I even crossed the Louisiana/Mississippi border. The headache comes courtesy of long hours in the car paired with my hair being pulled up into a high, messy bun. I'd let the heavy mass down if I wasn't terrified of its condition. Two days' worth of greasiness has built up. I doubt removing my hairband would even do anything. The hair would likely continue sitting on top of my head, permanently reshaped.

My priorities have changed: before a bed, I need a shower. The vision of scrubbing a thick lather of shampoo into my scalp plays in my brain like a porno. I can imagine the transformation of the knotted mess into its normal smooth cascade.

"Butter on bread," my mom always says when she affectionately tugs on a strand.

Not sure I approve of being compared to a boring slice of white bread, but I take comfort in the fact that she's simply referring to my complexion and hair color rather than my personality.

When I push the car door open, the heavy New Orleans air embraces me. It is almost as warm and wet as an actual shower but nowhere near as refreshing. The humidity sits on my skin, weighing me down as I trudge up the front walk of a house that I hope is mine.

The easy solution would've been to just call Martin on Friday night when I decided to change my travel plans. That way my fiancé would be waiting out on the porch, ready to wave me down.

Instead, I chose the surprise method. I'd like to convince myself that this is a romantic gesture.

I just couldn't stay away from you for two more weeks!

In reality, my silence arises from shame. Whenever I let my thumb hover over his number, I couldn't even imagine how the conversation would go.

"Hey, honey! Guess what? I lost my job!" I whisper under my breath and pause with my foot on the bottom step leading up to the elevated porch.

Well, I guess I *could* say that.

Now that I'm here, potentially a few steps away from Martin, the words don't seem so inadequate. Depressing? Yeah sure. But I can clearly envision his face, how his blond brows will dip in the middle as he scowls. Not *at* me but *with* me. I can taste the glass of red wine he'll pour me as he rages over the unfair treatment.

That's when I realize why the need for surprise. I don't actually want to *talk* about how I got fired from my dream job. All I want is to see my anger reflected in the face of my partner. To feel connected to him in a way I haven't in a while.

With the moving plans, and Martin preparing to start his residency down here, and me trying to finish up all my large projects before going remote, we've barely talked. I can't even remember the last time I looked him in the eyes during a conversation. We usually just shout to each other from opposite rooms.

And sex? Well...it's been some time.

As I knock on the mystery door I hope is mine, I make a resolution. Whether I find Martin in this clone house or the one next door or the next street over, when I finally locate my fiancé, the first thing I'm going to do is stare deep into his eyes. I'll hold his gaze until our connection is firmly reestablished. Then—after a shower—I'm going to jump his bones.

Light spills into the dark night from around the edges of the curtains. At least that means whoever lives here, hopefully Martin, is still awake. After the polite taps of my knock ring out, the steady pad of footsteps sound behind the door. I brace myself, ready to stare my fiancé down.

Only, Martin doesn't open the door.

A small slim woman dressed in a robe stands before me. She is adorably petite. I could practically fit her in my pocket. Her bare feet peek out from under the floor-length robe, and her long brown hair lays in a damp mass over her shoulders.

Envy spikes hard through me. Clearly, this woman has just taken a shower. My greasy strands weep in envy.

Also, her appearance makes it clear my navigation skills have failed me. I am no closer to my own glorious shower, having no idea which one of these houses Martin bought for the two of us to live in.

"Sorry. I thought this might be my house. Do you know a blond man? About so tall?" I hold my hand a few inches above my head like the sleep drunk idiot I am.

I'm ready to continue describing my fiancé out of pure desperation when I notice the woman's face. With a stranger knocking on her door at midnight, I would expect confusion or annoyance. But if I had to guess, her slack-jawed, wide-eyed stare is closer to horror.

Apparently, my need for a shower is even direr than I knew.

"I told you I'd get it..." The familiar rusty voice drifts from behind the stranger as my fiancé trots down a set of stairs visible just over her shoulder.

The showered girl shuffles back, so I have a clear view of Martin, clad in only a pair of gym shorts, his hair just as gloriously damp from a recent cleaning as the woman in front of me.

Our eyes meet. His top half stops, but his bottom half doesn't get the memo. Instead, one of his bare feet slips on the wooden step, and he lands hard on his ass, shocked gaze never leaving mine.

So, this *is* the right house.

It's just everything else in the world that is wrong.

Whatever way I might want to interpret this situation is made impossible when I flick my eyes back to the stranger, who I now realize is wearing *my* green, cotton robe. Red splotches scorch along the tops of her cheekbones, and guilty tears pool on her lashes.

Something dark and sickening rolls in my stomach, but I flash freeze it. After one last look at the boy I've loved since my senior year of high school, I turn to the girl he chose to hurt me for.

"You can keep the robe." Reaching out, I clasp the doorknob. "And the man." I wrench the door closed on the most devastating scene of my life and sprint back to my sleeping car.

Penelope revs to life, more dependable than any man could ever be.

I shift into first gear and tear down the street, not caring who I wake up. With the roar of my sweet girl's engine, I can't hear Martin shouting.

But I can see him. In my rearview mirror, he sprints down the street after me. I skid around a corner and lose sight of him.

And he loses me.

I drive in an emotional fog, unable to dislodge the frozen ball of grief in my chest. The devastation sticks to the inside of my skull, blocking my ability to think.

It's only when I almost run a red light that I realize I shouldn't be driving.

Pulling into the next parking lot, I somehow end up in the drive-through lane of a fast-food joint. Functioning on autopilot, I roll down my window when I reach the speaker.

"What do you want?" The woman asks with the complete disinterest that can only be achieved by someone employed for the night shift at a drive-through.

The question hits me hard. Acting as a chisel, it splits the ice in my chest apart.

Grief flows free.

"What do I want?" I laugh, high-pitched and manic. "Oh, I don't know. How about a job? Or a home? Maybe my dignity?"

And now I'm crying.

"Um...we serve chicken."

I've gone insane. Martin's betrayal has turned me into a raving loon who drives around New Orleans in the middle of the night scaring fast-food workers.

This isn't me. I'm not this *type of weird.*

"Oh. Right. Of course." Swiping away the tears blurring my vision and pulling in a few choking breaths, I attempt to read the glowing menu. "I guess a family meal then."

"Eight, twelve, or sixteen pieces?"

The cracked ice in my chest has given way to a massive aching hole.

"Better make it sixteen."

"You want it with sides?"

I'm not going to be able to manage many more of these questions without the crazy laughing/crying returning.

"Yeah, whatever sides are popular. And biscuits, please. I'm gonna need a whole lot of biscuits." A sob makes the last word come out choked.

She rattles off the total, and I pull around to the window to pay. A short woman wearing a goofy chicken hat gives me a kinder smile than I was expecting after my breakdown.

"I slipped an extra biscuit in there," she whispers while passing me the armload of fried comfort.

"Thank you," I mutter, keeping my eyes to myself and hoping I never run into this lovely woman again.

For a moment, I park and consider consuming the entire order myself.

The idea is tempting.

But I still need a shower and a bed.

Penelope's engine purrs like a comforting embrace, as I pull back out on the road. The headlights point toward my childhood home.

My parents are about to get a late-night visitor, bearing fried chicken and a broken heart.

* * *

Don't miss more of the Spice Up Your Night series, coming soon, and find more from Elisabeth Caldwell at elisabethcaldwell.com

Until then, discover RESCUE ME, by City Owl Author, Lauren Connolly!

* * *

When the universe screws you over, adopt a dog.

Paige Herbert doesn't know how she lost control of her life. Friday morning, she had her future planned. Sunday night, she's jobless and staring at her half-naked fiancé and a woman wearing her green robe.

Taking refuge in her childhood home, Paige decides this time around her life partner will have four legs instead of two. But her newly rescued pit bull is in bad need of obedience training...and the perfect guy for the job has Paige forgetting the past.

Dash Lamont doesn't want to go back to jail. Out on parole and working at an animal shelter, he's focused on living life by the rules. And number one on the list: avoid temptation.
And then, in walks Paige.

The woman parks in the middle of Dash's well-ordered life, demanding his attention with her offbeat conversation, sinful curves, and dream of a refurbished classic Chevy. Despite his decision to keep his distance, he somehow finds himself agreeing to her plea for help.

As the two spend more time together, awkward attempts at flirting, late-night dancing to jazz music, and a chance taken at a Halloween party lure the hesitant pair down a sensual road.

But when sins of the past work against the newly budding romance, Dash will need to decide whether to take his chance on love or stay in his safe lane, watching as Paige drives off without him.

* * *

Please sign up for the City Owl Press newsletter for chances to win special subscriber-only contests and giveaways as well as receiving information on upcoming releases and special excerpts.

All reviews are **welcome** and **appreciated**. Please consider leaving one on your favorite social media and book buying sites.

For books in the world of romance and speculative fiction that embody Innovation, Creativity, and Affordability, check out City Owl Press at www.cityowlpress.com.

Acknowledgments

To my husband - I have no words to express the deep gratitude I feel. You tirelessly supported me on this journey, refusing to give up on me, even when I was ready to give up on myself. Thank you for encouraging me to write and giving me the time to do it. I love you!

Aubrey, Becky and Connor – You are the best! You always make me feel like I can accomplish anything. You also make me laugh ALOT and remind me not to take anything too seriously. I love you guys!

Mom – What can I say other than THANK YOU and I LOVE YOU!

Heather – Thank you for living this dream with me. You are always there for me – whether it is 8 a.m. or 1 a.m. You proofread, brainstorm, plot untangle, prop me up when I am falling apart, and bring me the best damn tea I've ever sipped. You are an amazing friend. I am lucky to have you.

NJRW – New Jersey Romance Writers is an incredible organization. Every one of you is a talented writer, but, more importantly, a warm, welcoming, supporting colleague. You gave me the building blocks I needed to write a novel and so much more. Thank you (with special thanks to Shari and Lori)!

About the Author

Elisabeth Caldwell is an award-winning author of romantic suspense, paranormal and contemporary romance novels. She grew up a Philly (and suburban Philly) girl with thick glasses and her nose buried in a book. When she was 12, she fell into the yellowed pages of one of her grandmother's Mary Stewart novels and has been obsessed with romance ever since. She sees fairies in the trees, mermaids in the ocean, ghosts peeking through shuttered windows, and a story behind every couple that walks by holding hands.

Elisabeth lives in Bucks County, PA with her three vibrant children, a husband who is her soulmate, and one very sweet, albino corn snake. She is a jogger, tea-lover and avid recycler. She practices law by day, writes romance by night and daydreams every chance she can get.

elisabethcaldwell.com

About the Publisher

City Owl Press is a cutting edge indie publishing company, bringing the world of romance and speculative fiction to discerning readers.

Escape Your World. Get Lost in Ours!

www.cityowlpress.com

facebook.com/YourCityOwlPress
twitter.com/cityowlpress
instagram.com/cityowlbooks
pinterest.com/cityowlpress

Made in the USA
Middletown, DE
11 April 2023